Tangled Ambition

SOPHIE ANDREWS

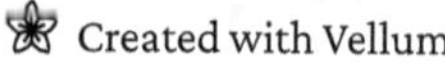 Created with Vellum

Content Note

Tangled Ambition is a slow burn enemies to friends to lovers workplace romance between two headstrong lawyers, but it's also quite angsty. There are multiple discussions of grief, domestic violence, stealthing, and opioid addiction/overdose, and includes an on the page medical abortion, which is a common and safe healthcare procedure that involves ingesting pills.

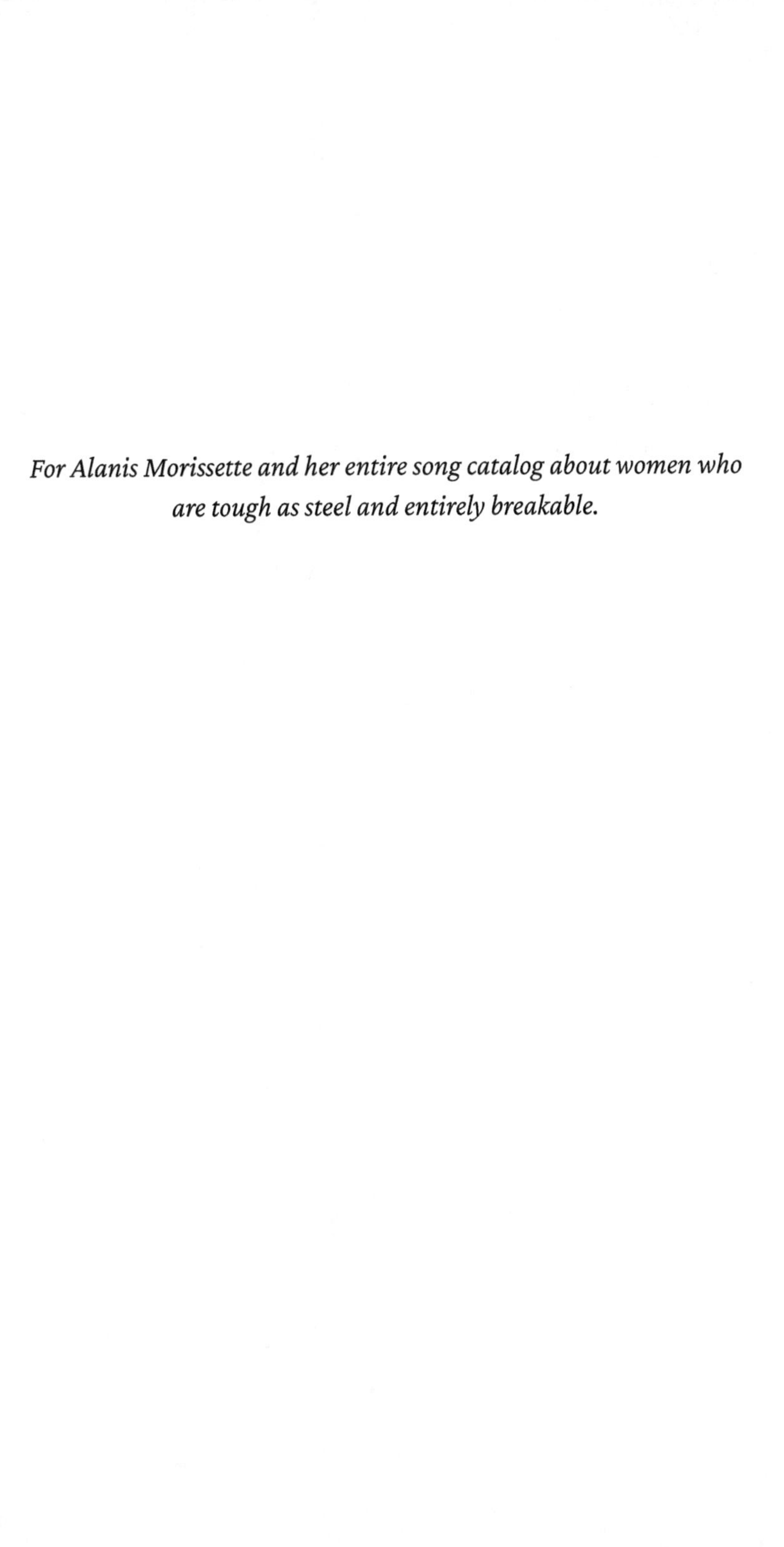

For Alanis Morissette and her entire song catalog about women who are tough as steel and entirely breakable.

CHAPTER ONE

Dean

Multicolored lights twinkled above the bar, reflecting off the cheap tinsel garland along the walls, while a giant eyesore of a Christmas tree stood in the far corner, the floor underneath laden with fake gifts. It was as if an elf puked up all of its Christmas cheer after indulging in one too many eggnogs.

Incidentally, I hated eggnog.

I brought my beer to my lips for another sip, reminding myself to go slow. To try to enjoy the annual holiday party. It was the most wonderful time of the year. According to Andy Williams crooning through the hidden speakers.

Every year, Novak & Novak rented out a restaurant in Philadelphia, the place where it all began and center point for the different offices, for everyone to get together. Which, I guess, was nice. It gave me an opportunity to talk to Barbara Novak, if I could only get her alone. She was the matriarch of the law firm, who was still standing, even at eighty-five years old. While she didn't work anymore, she still had a hand in the business because she was sharp as a tack. And she was, after all, one half of the original Novak & Novak.

The story went, Barbara and William met in law school and were archenemies, but later fell in love and married. Once they passed the bar, Barbara had a hard time finding a firm willing to take on a young, female lawyer, so she and her husband opened their own, slowly but surely building a reputation in employment law matters. Though Novak & Novak now focused on multiple issues—including workers' compensation claims, contract severances and disputes, and noncompete agreement litigation—Barbara's goal had always been to fight for women's rights in the workplace. She earned her status as a pit bull with a trial in the 1980s, by representing a woman who had been fired unjustly when she'd gotten pregnant. It was a huge win for her client and half the population of the United States. After that, Novak & Novak expanded offices outside of the original location in Philly to West Chester, Pennsylvania, Wilmington, Delaware, and Cherry Hill, New Jersey.

While there were multiple offices, the firm at large ran like a tight-knit family. That had always been Barbara and William's policy. Family first, business second. Which was why I was here. Pretending I enjoyed these glad tidings.

"What's up, Charlie Brown?" Seth bumped my shoulder. "You look like someone pissed on your Christmas tree." He grinned, like the douchebag he was.

Seth had been hired full time at Novak & Novak after interning a few years and passing the bar. So far, he had managed to be more of a pain in the ass than a helpful junior associate. Although, I did take a lot of his money at our monthly poker nights. So, there was that.

"Trying to gauge how much longer I have to stay here," I said into my beer.

Seth checked his watch. "It's not even eight yet." When I stayed quiet, he gestured to the bar with his drink. "I'm getting another one. Want?"

I shook my head, still nursing my beer.

"Don't have too much fun without me," he said, and I

turned away so he didn't see me roll my eyes. I tolerated Seth because there weren't many other people in the office to be friends with.

Novak & Novak was a midsized firm, and each branch was run by a partner, with a handful of associates under them. It was both easy and incredibly difficult to work there. Easy because it was so small, a person could move up the ladder quickly, but difficult because they had to prove themselves to be an expert in the field of employment law. I'd been at Novak & Novak since I'd first interned there, and while I was only twenty-nine, I had my sights set on one day being a managing partner.

So, when I noticed Barbara alone for what seemed like the first time all night, I beelined toward her.

Only to spot Shauna headed my way. Shauna, the paralegal from the Philly office, whom I'd hooked up with last year after the Christmas party. Shauna, whom I'd never called back.

"Fuck me," I grumbled, pivoting a tight left out of Shauna's line of vision and away from Barbara.

A familiar low rumble, as if Satan's pet cat had laughed, sounded next to me. "Whatever happened to 'Hello, how was your day?'"

My grip on my beer tensed as I turned to face the bane of my existence, Taylor Novak. With a single eyebrow raised and her thin lips pulled into a taut line of what I assumed was supposed to be a semblance of a smirk, she pinned me with her dark eyes. Even highlighted as she was by all the glittery decorations behind her, I thought her especially proficient in still being able to appear so dark, as if she'd just stepped foot onto our level of earth from her sulfur and charcoal home.

I tipped my head, cupping my hand around my ear. "What is that I hear? The organs of hell calling you home?"

She stirred the toothpick with two olives along the rim of

her martini glass. "No, that's the sound of your backbone cracking under the weight of all your insecurities."

I blew out an annoyed puff of air. "I know you're obsessed with me, but the projection is a little too much, don't you think?"

"*Me* obsessed with *you*?" Her gaze raked over me from head to toe. "Now who's the one projecting?"

I allowed myself a long look over her too. As usual, she was in all black. Like her soul. Her short dark-brown hair was pin straight, cut in a blunt line at her chin like someone hacked it with a sword. Maybe so they didn't have to get close to her.

Painful goose bumps raced up my arms, standing this close to her. As if my body innately knew a deadly predator was on the loose. But I didn't let it show when I met her gaze. That was the key. Establish dominance by looking her in the eye. Never be the first to blink away.

"I see you're full of Christmas cheer," I said, taking a slow sip of my beer.

Her long eyelashes fluttered like she wanted to blink, but her competitiveness would never allow it, and the whites of her eyes grew a bit bigger. "Well, I didn't want to outshine you. I know how you crave being the center of attention."

For almost the last two years of my life, this was what it'd been. Verbal sparring in an attempt to make the other one flinch first. Curt emails exchanged—or rather, she sent them, and I ignored them—about our work. Hers always dripping with condescension. As if her last name on the signage made her my boss. It didn't. It was hours of trying and failing to avoid each other, which was impossible since our office wasn't very big. There was no way I could escape the click of her high heels that put her at the same height as me. She loved that. The ability to stare directly into my eyes. Oftentimes, her gaze rose to my head as she rolled her shoulders back, as if being taller than me would make her better at her job.

But I came in at a respectable 5'11" and a half. *A half.* While her heels had to be at least three inches, she wasn't even close to my height without shoes on.

At least, that was what I told myself.

Sometimes, if I was having a particularly hard day, which was every day lately, I'd imagine her falling and breaking an ankle from those spiky heels of hers. I might've felt bad about that particular fantasy if she hadn't often threatened to throw hot coffee at my face if I didn't stop slurping it. Ever since she'd made her first threat, I had continued to slurp to piss her off.

Now, she stood next to me, shoulder to shoulder, like a pillar of obsidian stone. She'd lost her standard black blazer a while ago, and the few undone buttons at the top of her shiny black blouse hinted at pale skin below her collarbone, the delicate gold chain around her neck occasionally revealing itself when she shifted. If I were more interested in getting to know her, I'd lean into her space, wrap my hand around her tiny, belted waist, and ask what the charm was, but I was raised Catholic. I knew all about Eve and the Garden of Eden.

Taylor Novak was the snake that convinced her to eat the apple.

"No date tonight?" I asked, tucking my hand into my pocket, idly wondering how long Satan allowed her to be in our realm.

She clucked her tongue, deliberately stretching her neck to peer over at the bar, where two men worked. One clean-cut Hispanic guy, the other a white guy with tattoos and greasy-looking hair tucked behind his ears. I squinted to get a better look at the one on his neck. It appeared to be an octopus.

Octopus-tattoo guy lifted his gaze in our direction, and I

felt the subtle shift of Taylor next to me. I slanted my eyes toward her. "You're kidding."

With her focus still over my shoulder, she sipped her martini.

"Him?" I asked. "*Seriously?*"

"What?" she snipped.

"That guy? He looks like he doesn't shower."

"But did you see the way he makes a drink?" she said in return, and I hated to admit I turned over my shoulder to observe him. Sure, it was impressive how he barely looked as he poured the ingredients without spilling a drop, but *that* was her standard?

"He's a bartender."

She narrowed her brows at me, which was really saying something since they were two permanent slashes, always angry about something. "You say it like it's a pejorative. Yes, he's a bartender, which means he's good with his hands."

I snorted.

"Jealous?"

"Of the man who's fallen under the unfortunate jurisdiction of your attention? No, I'm not jealous." Taking the chance, I leaned in closer to her as her eyelashes fanned when she blinked.

I had won.

For only a moment. Because then her dark stare was on me again.

I ignored the goose bumps and said, "I prefer women who don't suck the blood from their partners at the end of the night."

Her focus dropped to my mouth, only a few inches from her own, before she stuck an olive between her lips, which was the first giveaway of her reptilian origins. They were thin and perpetually red. Like she'd just finished her meal.

I watched as she chewed slowly then swallowed, the long column of her throat working.

When I raised my gaze up to her eyes, she smiled. Devil woman.

"I'm sure you prefer girls who do all the work." She shouldered away from me. "Lazy, as always."

Opening my mouth to tell her she couldn't handle all my *work*, I barely stopped myself and snapped my jaw shut. Not only was it inappropriate for me to make insinuations about sexual activity between us, it was totally out of the question. No matter how many times she'd told me to suck her dick.

And I certainly never imagined her sucking *my* dick.

She'd no doubt bite it off.

My eyes involuntarily tracked her as she stalked to the bar, though I didn't know why. She was straight up and down. There was nothing to look at.

Except how she leaned against the bar, her lips tipping up at the greasy octopus bartender.

I spun away, polished off my beer, fixed my tie, and made my way over to Barbara Novak.

She smiled at me, extending her arm, and I let her tow me in for a hug. "Dean, I haven't seen you in so long."

When she let go of me, I stood and stuck my hands in my pockets, returning her smile. Mrs. Novak had always been kind to me, and while I'd never had the privilege of meeting Mr. Novak, I was sure I would have enjoyed knowing him just as much.

"You're working too hard," she told me, and I huffed, refusing to tell her the truth, that it was her granddaughter's fault. Ever since Taylor had transferred to the West Chester office, I'd been billing more hours and hustling for more clients in an attempt to demonstrate I deserved to be next in line on the chain. Not her. I had been there a lot longer than she had. If you didn't count how she had toddled around the Philly office as a little kid, according to a few pictures I'd seen on the walls there.

Instead of acknowledging any of that, I shrugged. "You're one to talk."

Mrs. Novak waved off my words. She had worked well into her seventies. Although she had severely cut back on her workload, she still showed up every day at the office and was the one who had hired me for my first summer internship.

"I noticed you talking to Taylor," she said, her cool and pale hand taking hold of my own as she stood. She had always been tall and slender, according to those same photos with Taylor, but now her shoulders were more stooped, her skin thin and papery, hair completely gray.

"We do that sometimes."

She pinched my arm, and I gave in to a laugh, wrapping her arm around mine. She pointed to the area next to the Christmas tree, where her son, Kevin, stood talking with two other men from another office, and I slowly escorted her there. "When you're not arguing."

Mrs. Novak was well aware of our mutual dislike of each other, and I conceded the point with a nod. "I don't know if you know this, but she can be quite stubborn."

Barbara let out a familiar wistful sigh. One that always accompanied a mention of her dearly departed husband. "Inherited that from her grandfather."

After a moment, during where I ignored Taylor sliding something across the bar to octopus guy, I looked down at Mrs. Novak. "I heard rumors of restructuring."

"Rumors, hmm?"

I waited patiently for her to answer.

"Well then, I think you might be interested in staying at

the party a little longer, instead of running off with some woman like you usually do."

I felt my neck heat, unable to keep a straight face under her intent, matronly stare. "I'd never dream of leaving such a fun party like this."

Her answer was a sardonic laugh and slight push to my arm as I let her go when we reached her destination. "I see everything, Dean Hargrove. Don't forget that."

Then she winked and turned, politely breaking into the conversation with the men.

My smile dropped as I spied Taylor across the room from me, still talking to the bartender, about what I couldn't possibly imagine, and checked the time with a sigh. I still had hours to go.

CHAPTER TWO

Taylor

Mariah Carey belted out "All I Want for Christmas Is You" as my focus snagged on Shauna. She had terrible taste. If her literal ugly Christmas sweater wasn't an indication, then certainly her choice in men was. Dean bent his head down as she giggled about something, and my jaw clenched. He wasn't that funny.

I didn't know why everyone loved him so much.

He was full of himself, refused to take advice, and waited until the last minute to do anything. Plus, he also always —*always*—made some comment about my desk, as if he had nothing better to do than complain about the state of it. Which wasn't even that messy.

"What's that sneer for?"

I whirled around to find Kennedy next to me, her cheeks red from the cold, her long hair windblown.

"I'm not sneering, and what are you doing here?"

"Right. It's your regular face," she said with a grin as she stuffed her gloves into her pocket and removed her coat.

"You're such an asshole," I said, hiding my growing smile with a sip of my martini. "And answer the question, what are you doing here?"

"What? I can't come see my family?"

I eyed her and that overly innocent tone. "How'd you get here?"

"Drove. Well," she backtracked, "my friend drove my car. She was on her way to Jersey, so she dropped me here, and then she was going to Uber the rest of the way."

I waited patiently for the other half of the answer, my hand on my hip, and Kennedy shrank the tiniest bit under my scrutiny until she gave in.

"Can I stay at your place for a bit?"

"Kenny..."

She huffed. "What? Don't get all..." She pulled a face. "I broke up with Jordan."

"When?"

"Last week," she said and stole my drink, downing the whole thing.

"Last week?" I barely refrained from raising my voice. "What have you been doing since then?"

She shrugged. "Couch surfing."

"You're too old to be couch surfing," I told her, snagging my empty glass back to set on the bar.

After I gave a nod to Ace, he made me a refill. Kennedy followed my line of sight. "Ooh."

"Nope." I shook my head.

"You calling dibs?"

I released a low breath. "You don't call dibs on people either."

"Whatever." She plucked at the sleeves of her tight velvet dress then folded her arms across her ample chest. While I took after the Novak side of our family, my little sister took after our mother and the Bellisarios. I was tall and straight. She was short, curvy, and the complete opposite of me. Younger by six years and flighty like our mother, constantly floating from one thing or another, one guy to the next.

"What happened?" I asked, accepting my new drink with a small smile to Ace.

Kennedy tossed her long hair behind her shoulder with a quiet, "Needed some time apart, that's all."

I didn't like the way she wouldn't meet my eyes, and I elbowed her. "You all right?"

Her gaze flitted to me and then away. "Yeah. I just need a place to stay."

"You don't even have to ask," I said, leaning into her, and Kennedy briefly rested her head on my shoulder.

"Thanks, Titi."

I gave in to a snort at the childhood nickname and nudged her off my shoulder. "Come on, let's go see Nan."

When I nodded at Ace, he winked in return, and I ignored the flutter in my belly. He was tall, skinny, and unpolished. Exactly my type. There was something about guys who worked in the food industry; they knew how to fuck and didn't bother worrying about emotions. Usually too busy complaining about their next shift and lack of cigarettes.

Kennedy linked her arm with mine as we made our way across the floor. Uncle Kevin spotted us first, his eyes lighting up at the sight of my sister. "Kenny! Where have you been?"

"Poconos," she replied, though it was muffled by his suit jacket. He passed her off to our grandmother, who kissed both of her cheeks.

"You look wonderful, as always," Nan said, stroking her fingers over Kennedy's face, and my sister held on to her wrist.

"So do you."

"My hair could use a little..." Nan toggled her head, and Kennedy nodded happily.

"A little zhuzhing? I can take care of that."

"Thank you, honey. That would be great." Then she tugged me to her side, slipping her thin arm around my waist. "My two girls. I love when I have you both in the same spot."

"Great party, as usual," Kennedy said, waving her hand in the air.

"You know your uncle. Any excuse for a party."

Uncle Kevin raised his drink in our direction then stepped over to my side. "How's it going at the office?"

"Good," I said, and he pursed his lips, studying in that way he had. As if checking to see I was healthy and whole. After I had passed the bar, I'd started at the Philly office, where he was managing partner, but I felt like he was constantly looking over my shoulder, treating me like a porcelain doll. I needed to get away, so I transferred to West Chester.

"Did you talk to your aunt?" he asked, pointing to where his wife, my aunt Bea, stood with my cousins, chatting and laughing about something, and I nodded.

"Yeah. She invited me for Christmas at your house."

"You're going to join us, right?"

With my sister and grandmother talking quietly, I shook my head. "Since Kennedy's back, we'll probably hang out."

"You sure?"

I nodded again.

"If you change your mind, it's an open invitation."

"Thank you," I said, and he turned away with a squeeze to my shoulder as Kennedy and Nan were in the middle of a conversation about getting her a Netflix account.

"It's so easy to use," Kennedy said. "There's this historical romance I think you'd really like about a woman who travels back in time in Scotland, and, oh my god, Nan, you should see this guy."

Nan smiled and took Kennedy's hand in her own. "That does sound nice, but I don't think I'll need it."

"Well, you could always just use Taylor's account," my sister suggested, and I thumped her on the arm. Although, I shrugged at my grandmother.

"You can if you want."

"You two are so sweet," she said, "but, as I said, that isn't something I need."

"No one *needs* eight seasons of *Great British Bake Off*," Kennedy said with a laugh. "It's self-care."

"Speaking of self-care," Nan said with a pointed eyebrow raise in my direction. "Dean Hargrove."

"Those two things have nothing to do with each other," I squeaked, feeling my face flush as my sister's interested gaze toggled between me and our grandmother.

"I know you think he's your enemy. But he isn't. He's your coworker and quite a brilliant lawyer."

"He's an ass," I said, and when she lifted her brow dubiously, I went on, "He's conceited, he's rude, he's—"

"I've never experienced him to be either of those things," Nan interjected primly.

"Because he's too busy trying to crawl up your—"

"Taylor." Nan stopped me with a warning in her eyes.

"Your back pocket," I said, backtracking while Kennedy snickered.

Nan shrugged. "He's always been very sweet to me, and there's nothing wrong with having a drive to succeed. You're the same way."

"Yeah." I extended my hand to the whole of the party. "Of course I am. I come from a family of lawyers."

"So then, what's the problem between you two?"

I didn't have an answer besides that we had never gotten along. We'd met at Temple Law School, where we had been in the same mandatory yet moot 1L course. Unfortunately, we were paired up to create a PowerPoint presentation on different provisions of a regulation. The first strike was when he showed up late after we agreed on a time to meet. Strike two was when he told me to "relax." Strike three was mansplaining the assignment to me.

He clearly thought he was God's gift, and we'd gotten into a bit of a tiff. When we'd finally parted ways with eye rolls and snarls, I had told him to email me his section when he finished so I could put it together. But, of course, it was last minute. Literally. He'd sent it to me ten minutes before we had to hand it in to our professor.

Since then, we had been at each other's throat whenever we crossed paths, which, thankfully, wasn't all that often. I knew he had interned at Novak & Novak for two summers, but I hadn't realized he'd been hired full time. Imagine my surprise when I'd walked into the West Chester office and saw him and his stupid crooked smile.

Now, I answered my grandmother's question with a question. "Why are you so protective of him?"

She breathed deeply and crossed her arms, cupping her elbows in her hands. "I am no more protective of him than anyone else who works at the firm." When I stared blankly at her, she gave in to a small sigh. "This time of year is hard for him."

"Why?"

"His best friend passed away right before Christmas."

I blanched. "When?"

"I guess..." Nan rolled her eyes up in thought. "When you two were still in school."

"That was a while ago," I said, not that grief had an end date. I knew that all too well. But I didn't understand why my grandmother, who had experienced so much loss, seemed to bend over backward for this guy.

"He took it hard. You know," she said, as if I really did

know, "he had planned on living in Philadelphia, but he was just so distraught."

My attention unwillingly coasted around the room until I found Dean, where he was speaking to Robert, a senior associate in Wilmington, and his wife, Crystal, a paralegal in the same office. He was in profile, and I watched his jaw, covered in a neat beard, work as he talked. He kept one hand in his slim-cut dark pants while he gestured in the air with the other. Occasionally, he combed his fingers through his dark-blond hair that I hated myself for knowing appeared brown when it was wet. He shouldn't have looked so good in that burgundy shirt and black tie, but he did. And I hated myself even more for thinking so.

"Okay," I said, forcing my gaze back to my grandmother, "what does that have to do with anything?"

"I should think you'd be a little more empathetic."

"I feel bad for him, but that doesn't change the fact that we don't get along. And probably never will."

She inhaled audibly, shaking her head at me. "That's a shame. Because we're going to need you two."

"Need *us*? For what?"

With a slight smile, she stepped away from me and waved her arms in the air. "Excuse me! Hello!"

Someone whistled, quieting the small crowd, and everyone turned toward my grandmother still waving her arms.

"Hello. Hi, I'm so glad to see everyone here." A few claps rang out, and she smiled in their direction. "William and I always loved this time of year, but we especially loved being able to gather everyone together like this." Nan pressed her hands to her chest. "You can't know the appreciation I feel for all of you. To know Novak & Novak started in a tiny office with only the two of us, to now having offices in three different states with dozens of partners, associates, and assistants. I thank you all from the bottom of my heart for your dedication and hard work."

Everyone clapped, and I stretched my neck to see almost everyone in the crowd smiling at my grandmother. The same woman who was raised by a single mom and worked her way through college and law school, opened her own firm, and raised two children. She was so incredible. My hero.

"I think of you all as family." Nan extended her hand out toward me and to Uncle Kevin on the other side of her. "*We* all think of you as family. And I love to see it expanding." She waved to a man who appeared to be a few years older than me. I didn't know his name, but I was sure he worked at the Cherry Hill office and was holding a baby.

Nan straightened and folded her hands together in front of her torso. "This coming year will be an exciting one. A lot of change, but I know it will be for the better. I'd like to bring Mr. Reed Johnson up here."

I clapped, letting a smile loose as Reed made his way up front. He was a junior partner at our office and a great guy. He hugged my grandmother, exchanging a few quiet words with her before looking to my uncle. They hugged too, and even before Uncle Kevin raised his glass, I had already guessed what he was about to announce.

"I'd like to introduce everyone here to our newest managing partner of a brand-new branch, opening in Aberdeen, Maryland."

Cheers rang out, and while I was happy for Reed, for the firm to be expanding to another location, my mind reeled with the possibilities of what that meant for me.

And why my grandmother would have said she needed *us*, me and Dean.

Dean and I were on the same level, senior associates, and if Reed was moving, that meant the only other person above us was Dominic Payne, the managing partner. I knew his daughter was a few months away from having a baby and how much he was looking forward to retirement. I saw it. The road to me being managing partner of our office. It was paved in gold and not too far off.

I smiled to myself.

Until *he* caught my gaze. Those sly blue eyes glowing under the garish Christmas lights of this place.

Dean Hargrove, he was my roadblock.

But from the way his lip curled into that mocking smile, I knew he was thinking the same about me.

He wouldn't take this from me, and I raised my brow. With a subtle nod, he accepted my challenge.

CHAPTER THREE

Taylor

After the congratulatory chatter settled and those with better things to do left, the party pretty much died down. That was when I found my grandmother, tucking her arms inside her coat.

"Quite an announcement to make," I said, helping her with it.

Once she had all the buttons closed, a sad smile graced her face. A face I was often told looked like mine. "When Samuel passed away, your grandfather and I wanted to close the doors. We didn't think we could do it anymore."

A familiar tension in my jaw returned. It always did whenever my father was mentioned. I rubbed my index finger under my ear in an attempt to rid myself of the ache as my grandmother went on.

"The plan had always been for him to take over the office, so we felt like..." She lifted one shoulder. "What was the point?" Then she turned over her shoulder to where my uncle Kevin stood next to Kennedy and my cousins, all laughing about something. "Every time I thought it would be impossible to go on, I got up the next morning and brushed my teeth and got dressed and went to work."

She met my eyes again, reaching for my hand, and I traced my thumb over her knuckles as she smiled. "I always found comfort in work. It gave me purpose, and I think you feel the same."

I nodded.

"So, I'm hoping you'll continue to work hard, continue to be a driving force not only for the firm but for the family." She lifted my chin. "You are a rock. You know that?"

The sharp sting of pain moved from my jaw to my throat, and I swallowed past it. That had always been my role, the one who didn't break down. The one everyone could count on to make the right decisions. I had been steady when my father had gotten sick. I'd looked out for my sister, who was only eight at the time, and I'd taken care of my mother when she was too distraught to take care of herself. I had always done what I had to. I wasn't about to stop now.

"But every rock needs a soft spot to land," Nan said and patted my cheek. "I had my William. Who do you have?"

I blew out a breath. "I don't need anyone. I'm fine."

"That's what I thought too," my grandmother said kindly, looping her arm around mine, "until I realized I was wrong."

I ignored the tiny hairs standing on end on my arms and the pressure I felt on my back, like someone was watching me, as I deposited her to my uncle, who would drive her back to her apartment in the independent living facility on his way home. We all said goodbye. Kennedy and I offered hugs and kisses and promises to call on Christmas.

Our family had always spent the holiday together while my father was alive, but after he died, my mother had moved Kennedy and me to be closer to her family. Once we were old enough, Mom flew the coop, so my sister and I always did...whatever.

Holidays kind of lost their shine a while ago.

I loved my family, loved spending time with my grandmother, but sometimes it was easier to stay home in my pajamas and drink mimosas. Which was exactly what I'd planned on doing.

"Love you guys," my uncle called over his shoulder as he hustled Nan and Aunt Bea out the door.

"Love you too," Kennedy said, and after they were out of sight, I towed my sister to the bar.

"So, you going to tell me what actually happened?"

"With what?" she asked, playing coy, her red-painted nails tearing a cocktail napkin into strips.

"Jordan."

She leaned an elbow on the bar. "I love him but—"

"You love him?" I cut in. "Ken, you were with him for what? Like, two weeks?"

"Three months," she corrected. "And yeah, it's possible to love someone in three months. In two weeks, even. Don't look at me like that."

"She can't help it. Apparently no one warned her that if she frowned too much, her face would stay that way."

I turned to Dean and bared my teeth to him. "My sister and I were having a private conversation, so…"

He tipped his head, his gaze assessing me in a way I didn't like—as if he had nothing better to do, which his lazy ass probably didn't—before shifting over my shoulder to my sister. "I don't believe we've ever had the pleasure of meeting." He smiled all cool and good-naturedly. "I'm Dean."

My sister met his outstretched hand around me, like I wasn't even there, and I huffed.

"I'm Kennedy," she said in her usual beguiling voice. She was too sweet, that was her problem, and Dean had already stepped around me with a grin I'd become familiar with. He was about to flirt with her.

"No." I pressed my hand to the middle of his chest. "Uh-uh."

Kennedy's brows narrowed at me. "Why not?"

Dean tipped his chin in my direction. "Yeah. Why not?"

I flicked my fingers between them. "This is not happening. No way." I noticed Dean's attention settle below my sister's face, and I snapped my fingers in front of his eyes. "Eyes up, asshole."

He sniffed a laugh, totally unfazed, while Kennedy leaned even more forward, her cleavage on display.

"I don't mind."

"I do," I bit out between clenched teeth. Then I whipped my head around to Dean. "We're at a work function. Can you try for at least smidgen of professionalism?"

He scrubbed his fingers over his beard, his nails audibly scratching over the short bristles, before he slowly looked behind him to the dwindling crowd then back at me. "I don't know if you know this, but it's okay to relax at a party."

"I don't know if *you* know this, but never in the history of ever has telling a person to relax worked."

He rocked back on his heels, his hands in his pockets like he had no cares in the world. "That's right. It's one of your trigger words, huh?"

"You're my trigger," I said and wrapped my fingers around the bar, willing my blood pressure to settle.

"Well, this is quite interesting," Kennedy murmured.

"Shut up," I grumbled while Dean stepped behind me to sidle up next to Kennedy, and there was no hope for my blood pressure.

"We're closing the bar in a few minutes. Anything else I can get you tonight?" Ace asked me with a smile.

Dean gestured to my sister, and she ordered a ginger ale, while Dean held his hand up. "Nothing for me."

Ace nodded and moved away to pour her soda while Dean placed his palm on the bar, appearing way too comfortable next to my sister for my liking.

"Why don't you go find Shauna?" I suggested.

He licked his lips before pursing them as if struggling to control a smile. "It almost sounds like you're jealous." Then he elbowed my sister like they were old friends. "Right? Sounds jealous."

The traitor's eyes lit up in amusement, and I flipped them both my middle finger. "You're the one who can't keep it in his pants for one goddamn work party."

His shoulders lifted, almost imperceptibly, but I saw how his muscles coiled ever so slightly, my words hitting their mark. "I didn't realize you were keeping track." He swept his hand out in front of him. "But by all means, let's hear all the evidence you've accumulated."

I wasn't about to show him my hand, go off on the times I've seen different women's names displayed on texts or missed phone calls when he'd carelessly left his cell out, or the conversations I'd overheard him have with Seth.

"I don't care what you do as long as it's not with my sister."

"Chill, Titi. We're just talking," Kennedy said.

"Yeah, Titi," he repeated, outright grinning like an idiot at me before dipping his face down toward my sister, who preened under his attention.

Ace slid my sister's drink in front of her, and Kennedy lifted the straw to her plump red lips. I held back an irritated sound as Dean leaned in, exchanging words I couldn't hear. Of course he liked her. Everyone liked my sister.

And I ignored the slither of something awful along my spine. Something I wouldn't acknowledge or name.

"Anything for you, Taylor?" Ace asked, his fingers absently combing through his hair and over his octopus tattoo. He had a small tattoo on his index finger, though I couldn't tell what it was. The idea of getting up close and personal to study it had me *relaxing* a bit.

"Yeah." I leaned in closer to him. "You're almost finished here, right?"

Ace glanced to his watch. "A few minutes to close up."

"You live close by?"

Out of the corner of my eye, I noticed Dean straighten, his gaze hard on the side of my face.

"NoLib," Ace said, and how did I guess? Northern Liberties was the trendy, hipster-y neighborhood not far from where we were in Center City. "My place is small, but I'd love to show it to you."

"I'd like that." Then I turned to my sister, pointedly ignoring Dean. "If I stay, how are you going to get home?"

"I'll drive," she said, and I lifted my brow.

"Are you sure?"

She nodded. My sister hadn't gotten her license until she was nineteen because of her epilepsy, and she still didn't like to do it.

"I'll be fine," she assured me with a smile, and while I wanted her to be more confident behind the wheel, I also didn't want to force her to do something she wasn't ready for. When I refused to move, she slid me an icy glare. She hated that I "babied" her, but I didn't know how else to be with her. She was my *baby* sister.

Dean butted in. "I can drive you home if you need a ride."

I wasn't sure if he was offering to be nice—which, what?—or if he was doing it to get under my skin, but either way, I didn't like the possibilities of what him driving her home could turn into.

I ignored him and removed my apartment key from the ring to hand to her. "Text me when you get home."

West Chester was only about an hour from Philly, but it was after nine o'clock, and the idea of my sister driving at night always made me nervous. Because I knew *she* was nervous.

At this point, I didn't know if proving this point with Ace was even worth it anymore.

But then the sweet summer child said, "I rode my bike here," and I swore I heard Dean snort.

He was such a dick, and I wasn't going to let his arrogant ass ruin this for me.

I curled my fingers around my phone and faced Ace. "That's fine. I can drive."

He nodded and held up his hand. "Gimme five minutes."

"I'll be waiting outside," I said and spun away to retrieve my coat before slipping an arm around Kennedy's shoulders. "I'll be home in a few hours."

"Don't rush on my account."

"I'm not." I refused to meet Dean's gaze as I buttoned up my long black pea coat and slung my purse over my shoulders. "See you later."

"Have fun," Kennedy said, and Dean's mirthless chuckle trailed me out of the door.

"Make good choices, Novak!"

"Suck my dick, Hargrove!"

CHAPTER FOUR

Dean

It was the week between Christmas and New Year's when all time ceased to exist, and the only things to eat and drink in the house were cheese and orange juice. The office had officially closed for the week, but I'd taken a few files to work on while I was home, although I hadn't been able to make myself even open my laptop.

But that was the best thing about Novak & Novak. They respected the nine-to-five workday, and we weren't required to attain 2,000 billable hours. Everyone worked together and supported each other with cases, so we didn't have to break our backs every day.

Or, at least, that was how it used to be for me.

Until Taylor Novak. And her godforsaken confusion about what it meant to be on vacation.

I was having a nice chat with my sister and best friend in my living room when my phone pinged. I picked it up with a grumble. "It's fucking Boxing Day."

My twin sister, Laney, snorted. "Since when do you celebrate Boxing Day?"

Ethan, one of my best friends since high school, shook his head. "I'm not even sure what that is."

"It's a public holiday in the UK and Australia." She nestled into his side when he slung an arm around her. "But not really used for its original purpose and is more or less like our Memorial Day, sales on mattresses and stuff."

"How do you know? No, wait. No." Ethan pushed his glasses up his nose. "Never mind."

I assumed my sister knew because of her ex-boyfriend, who was solely referred to as the Australian prick, if at all. Two years ago, he'd cheated on Laney, which had been the impetus for her moving back home from California. Incidentally, it had worked out well for Ethan since it gave him a second chance at a relationship with her, even though I'd had no idea about any of it until I'd found them together in bed.

And I was almost blinded.

All thanks to that Australian prick.

"So cute how you're still so jealous," Laney cooed, and I grimaced. I still wasn't used to their being together even though they were getting married in March.

Ethan took hold of her left hand, toying with her engagement ring, then kissed her palm.

I ignored them and their glowing happiness and read Taylor's "reminder" with the first line. *As per my last email...*

"Fuck your last email," I snapped.

Ethan laughed. "Hey, whoa, language."

I let out a grunt and stabbed at my phone, typing out a reply, which I wished was, *It's a holiday. Stop working and get a life.* But what I went with instead was, *As per my last email, I will have the contracts to you Monday by close of the business day.*

"Why do you look so squinty lately?" my sister asked.

I tossed my phone next to me on the couch and pointed to it. "Because of that." Then backtracked. "*Her.*"

Ethan spread his arms wide on the back of the love seat. "Didn't we have this conversation already?"

"Yeah, Dean," Laney said, "you gotta chill out with all the girls. Didn't you ever listen to the lyrics of 'Waterfalls'?"

Yes, we'd had the conversation about me sleeping with a lot of women before, but no, this had *nothing* to do with that. I propped my feet up on the ottoman and let my head fall back to the couch cushion. "*You* gotta chill out with all your slut-shaming."

"I'm not slut-shaming," she said. "I'm worried about you."

I picked up my head to eye her. "First of all, I know how to use a condom, and second of all, I haven't had sex in months."

She clapped her hands over her ears. "Ah!"

"You're the one who's insisting on talking about it."

"Is that why you're so squinty all the time?" Ethan asked. "Because you haven't gotten laid lately?"

I slapped my hand on the arm of the couch. "Dude! Don't take her side."

"But it's true. You've been..." He winced apologetically. "Tense."

Well...that was true. Whether it was from not having sex in a while or Taylor, I didn't know. For a long time, my outlet for stress was coming home from work and fixing up my house, but now that I'd completed the renovations from top to bottom, there was nothing left for me to hammer or paint. And as much as I didn't want to admit it, Ethan and Laney lecturing me about hooking up with so many girls on the weekends did strike a chord in me. Just not for the reason they thought.

For years, I'd had to watch my best friends find their "person," and Ethan had been the last one to be single.

There was a group of us from high school. Gabe was up in Boston, and although he wasn't married, he'd been with the same guy since college. They lived in some big brownstone with two dogs. Hank married his college girlfriend and was a dad to a little boy. Now, Ethan and my sister were engaged. A few months ago, they'd sat me down to ask me to be in the wedding, while also alluding to the fact that they thought I was trying to cover up some "bigger feelings" by sleeping around.

And yeah, they were absolutely right. I wasn't lying to myself. I knew I was broken. Ever since Patrick, the missing member of our crew, died, I hadn't been the same. I carried the guilt of his death around with me every goddamn day.

I wasn't there for him when I should have been, and the only way for me to cope with the guilt was by filling my days up however I could. With work, with my house, with women.

But without any house reno to be completed and my apparent inability to close the deal anymore, I was left to find another way to vent. And lately, it'd been Taylor. She was good target practice.

"I told you guys about her before," I said. "My coworker Taylor."

"*Oh.*" My sister's brow furrowed. "I thought she was a man from the way you talked about her."

Ethan nodded. "Yeah, always calling her a dick and asshole."

I shrugged. "'Cause she is."

Laney tossed one of her looks to Ethan, like they were having a whole conversation with only their eyes. God, I hated that.

I rubbed at the knot between my neck and shoulder. "What?"

Laney focused on me, and then *we* were having a conversation with only our eyes. Stupid twin thing. She was reprimanding me with her narrowed stare, but I aimed my finger at her. "Don't give me shit about calling her names. She may be a woman, but she *is* an asshole. And she has called me the same or worse. She can handle it."

"Yeah, but—"

"Put your soapbox away."

"I'm not on a soapbox. I only find it interesting that she gets under your skin so bad, that's all." Laney shrugged as if she weren't goading me.

And I fell for it. "Because she's overconfident, condescending, and thinks she's my boss when she's not."

"People could say the same about you," Laney said. "That you're overconfident and condescending."

I huffed. "I am not."

My sister wagged her head side to side, letting out a little "Well…"

"I'm not." I lifted my hand toward Ethan. "Right?"

"You are confident, but that's a good thing," he said neutrally.

Laney shook her head. "Which can come off as cocky sometimes."

"That's swagger," I corrected.

"And you condescend to me all the time."

"You're my sister," I said, because we still teased each other. All siblings did.

"Yeah, but you think you can comment on whatever I do, like you know everything about everything."

"Because I do." I grinned, and she rolled her eyes.

"Did you ever think, maybe you don't like the qualities in her because they're the same qualities you have?"

I folded my arms and leaned back against the couch. "Nope."

"Okay," she said mockingly.

Ethan studied me through his glasses, and I had a feeling I wasn't going to like whatever came out of his mouth next. "You have the hots for her?"

I barked out a laugh. "No, I definitely do *not* have the hots for her."

Laney jumped on the train. "Is she pretty?"

I turned away from them, picturing Taylor Novak in my mind. Was she pretty? Sure, if you liked the right angles of a geometry problem. "She's like that ice queen from Narnia," I said. "A chill follows her wherever she goes. Plants wither under her feet. I wouldn't put it past her to bribe children with candy to go to war with animals."

Ethan tucked his face against Laney's shoulder as he chuckled, while my sister threw a pillow at me, though she couldn't contain her growing grin. "That's awful."

"It's true." I set the pillow under my elbow.

"Well, I'd like to meet her."

"No. There would never be a reason to."

Laney lifted her finger in the air with an idea. "You need a date to the wedding."

"I do not."

"Yes, you do."

Ethan leaned forward as if to break us up and wrapped his hand around Laney's knee. "Honey, he doesn't have to bring someone."

"Yes, he does. I included a plus-one for him in our final number to the caterer."

"Ah Christ, Delaney," I bit out. "Why?"

"Because I don't want you to be the only one there without someone," she said, and my breath seeped out of me like a pinhole in a balloon. I tried not to let my sister or best friend see how much that reminder affected me.

But I didn't have the mental or emotional capacity to find and *keep* someone. The last time I had, my best friend since first grade died.

I wasn't going to do that again, become so wrapped up in a

girl that I ignored everything and everyone else in my life. There would be no plus-one for me. Ever.

"Hey man, you don't need to bring someone," Ethan said. "Don't sweat it. If you do, cool, but if not, then it's just an extra seat."

"But you should—"

"Lane." Ethan stopped with her a quiet but firm tone, and I was grateful to him. I didn't want to have to explain myself to either of them. When my sister didn't argue, Ethan stood up, towing her with him. "We should get going. I still have to pack."

They were flying to Washington state tomorrow to meet up with Laney's best friends for some annual New Year's tradition.

And I absolutely was not envious.

Since Hank had his kid, he wasn't going to be going out, so that meant Seth was my only choice. Though, with how I hadn't gotten laid in months, I supposed it was time to do something about that, and Seth was nothing if not willing to troll bars. And I was sure women in short skirts would need to be warmed up in the cold weather.

That was how I would spend my New Year's.

I hugged each of them and locked the front door after they left then dropped back down to the couch, raising the volume on *Star Wars* before reaching for my phone. I didn't have to wait until the ball dropped to find some ass. I could text any one of the numbers in my phone, and yet as I scrolled through Abby, Ali, Ashleigh, Ashley, Becca, Brianna, Caitlin brunette, Caitlin blonde, Carina, Carly...my stomach turned.

If I ever actually counted up how many phone numbers I had acquired, how many partners I'd had sex with and never spoke to again, I think I would hate myself.

Then again, that was the point. I worked and fucked so

hard because I didn't want to remember how much I already hated myself.

I closed out my contact list and opened up my email app to find yet another from the Ice Queen herself.

Since I assume you're not working this week, I'll actually be able to get a lot done at the office without your music blaring. See you next year.

T. Novak

Senior Associate, Novak & Novak

"Fuck you," I muttered, typing out my reply.

I'll be in tomorrow. Led Zeppelin on full volume. Just for you.

Dean Hargrove

Senior Associate, Novak & Novak

CHAPTER FIVE

Taylor

"Are you sure you don't want to come with me?"

I glanced up from my coloring book of curse words to find Kennedy wrapped in a towel with her wet hair pulled off her face by a thick headband.

"I'm sure."

"But it's New Year's Eve."

I pointed to my sushi rolls and glass of wine with my fine point aquamarine marker. "I know."

"Come on. It'll be fun." She'd finagled an invitation to dinner and drinks with some vague acquaintances she knew.

"I have absolutely no desire to hang out with a bunch of twentysomethings who post TikToks all night long."

"Don't be so snooty. They're my friends. And you're not even thirty yet, don't pretend like you're some crotchety old lady."

"I am," I said, switching my marker for a petal-pink to start on the E in *asshole*. "And I like it."

She plopped down next to me with a makeup kit and squirted moisturizer onto her fingers before blending it into her face. "I thought you might be going out with Axe again."

"Ace," I corrected. "And no."

She hummed curiously and lifted the lid on the kit, tilting her face side to side in the reflection of the small mirror. "Why not? He was really hot."

"Yeah, but…"

Kennedy paused in dotting foundation along her forehead to turn to me, waiting, and when I only shrugged, she circled her makeup brush in the air. "But what?"

Capping my marker, I leaned back against the couch with my wineglass. Sex had always been an outlet for me whenever I was feeling extra stressed and needed something to take the edge off.

Which was exactly what had happened.

Until it wasn't.

Until I'd kept hearing a voice in the back of my head, one that I *hated*. Until I'd combed my fingers through Ace's hair, and the voice taunted, *"Him? Seriously?"* I'd closed my eyes, and all I saw was his blue gaze watching me, a bristly jaw, and a stupid crooked smile, like he knew exactly what he was doing to me.

Ruining everything.

"It was a one-time thing, that's it," I said eventually.

"That's too bad," she said, absently blending the makeup under her jawline.

I hid my huff in a sip of wine. "Not everyone falls in love in the first five minutes of meeting someone."

"What about Dean?"

"What?" I nearly spat out my Sauvignon Blanc. "I'm not in love with Dean!"

She eyed me suspiciously. "I was asking what his deal is."

I grimaced, ignoring the stinging in my throat from swallowing the wrong way. "Why?"

She shrugged. "He's cute and nice."

"Nice? He's not nice."

"He was very nice to me," she said, wiggling her fingers over her makeup, deciding what to put on next.

"That's because he wanted to fuck you."

She glanced at me, bronzer in her hands. "I didn't get that vibe at all." She swiped the golden-brown hue along her temples, nose, and chin. "I mean, he was really flirtatious but still a gentleman. Helped me with my coat and everything."

"He's a douche," I mumbled, refusing to see any positives about my work enemy.

"I think he's hot. Had a sort of *Suits* thing about him, you know?"

"No, I don't know."

Kennedy exchanged the bronzer for an eyebrow pencil. "You don't think he's hot at all?"

"No." I lifted the TV remote, flipping through Netflix. "He has a douchey face, with the hair and eyes and bone structure. Like the douchebag guy in every '90s teen rom-com. That's him."

She laughed. "You're kind of right, but he's still hot. Oh. No, wait! Go back. *Married at First Sight*, put that on."

I settled back against the couch with my sushi, watching dumb couples get married after meeting for the first time at the altar. Something my sister would do. In fact, she had auditioned for some dating show but didn't make it.

Thank god.

Between her tendency to jump into things without thinking and her epilepsy, I might have been a tad overprotective. But somebody had to be.

Which was why I was glad nothing had happened between her and Dean. And not at all because I felt something funny in my chest, like a knot releasing.

After the episode finished and Kennedy was dressed, she

sat next to me again, her phone pointed so the both of us were on the screen as our mother answered a FaceTime call.

"There're my honey bunnies! How are you two?"

"Great," my sister said as I offered a monotone, "Fine."

"Look how gorgeous you are, Kenny. You got big plans for tonight?"

"Going out with some friends."

Mom's smile was bright in the Nevada sunset. "What about you, Titi?"

"Hanging out at home."

"Aw, why?" she asked as if she didn't give birth to me. As if she hadn't known me for thirty years.

"Not my bag," I said, and she waved her hand, a familiar gesture that sent pieces of her long hair flying.

I recalled, how in the days after my father's death, she could barely get out of bed, and those long tresses, which she had always prided, became limp and snarled together. I remembered how I had to help her shower and wash her hair. How I combed out all the tangles, tucked her back into bed, and then went to the kitchen to make Kennedy dinner.

"Don't you want to keep your sister company?" Mom asked when she really meant, "Don't you want to look after your sister?"

Because that was what I'd always done.

"Mom," Kennedy whined. "I'm twenty-three, not thirteen."

"Well, I like my babies to look out for each other."

"We do," my sister said cheerfully as I sipped my wine. "What are you doing tonight?"

Our mother turned her phone so we could see her boyfriend, Darren Dukakis, a professional poker player who went by the name "Duke" and was not much older than me. I didn't begrudge my mother happiness, but I did begrudge her stealing my youth so she could now live hers out.

"Hey," Duke said with a toothy grin.

"He's got a tournament tonight," Mom explained.

"Hope you win," Kennedy called.

"Thanks!"

Mom shifted her phone so only she was on the screen once again. "I just wanted to call and say I love you both so much and happy New Year!"

"Thanks," I said, and Kennedy blew a kiss at the phone.

"Love you too!" My sister hung up and propped her hands on her hips. "You could be a little nicer to her."

I sighed and set down my wine, reaching for my coloring book again. I paged through it for a new word: BITCH. I opened up a dark purple marker and started in on it.

"I don't see what you have against her," she went on, stuffing items into a small purse.

"I don't have anything against her." I relished the long, easy purple strokes I made.

"You don't sound like it."

I spared her one narrowed glance. "What am I supposed to sound like?"

"I don't know. As if you like her, at least." She slipped into high heels and stood right in front of me. "How do I look?"

Her dress was short, sparkly, and tight on her plus-size frame, her cleavage spilling out. "Like a disco ball."

She kicked her heel up adorably behind her. "Perfect." With her attention on her cell phone while she typed, she said, "Don't have too much fun without me."

"You don't either." Which was really a warning. Don't forget to take your pills. Don't drink anything you didn't see made. Don't get lost. Don't do anything stupid.

She air-kissed me. "See you later!"

With the quiet snick of the door, I released a breath.

My sister was *a lot*. A lot of energy, a lot to love, but a lot of my anxiety too. Kennedy hadn't seen what I had with our mother. I had protected her from our mother's deep depression and darkest days. All my sister had experienced was the fun-loving, almost manic mother who was born after digging out of the hole of her grief. Kennedy didn't understand the resentment I held toward our mom, probably because I never let anyone see it. Never even mentioned it out loud. I merely tucked it away, like I did everything else.

So, I let Kennedy go on, thinking whatever she wanted of our mother, while I quietly attempted to swim through my lingering waves of grief, anger, and stress, otherwise known as my father, mother, and sister, respectively.

I finished my glass of wine and my coloring page, and without anything else to do, I scrolled through Instagram, happening on to a photo of Seth and Dean posted a few minutes ago. Seth had his arms crossed, I supposed in a vain effort to appear...cool? As if anyone would really fall for his smug face. Next to him, Dean was smiling wide with ridiculous New Year's glasses on. I had to hand it to him; he pulled them off. With the button-down open at the collar, the messy, sandy hair, and that goddamn bristly jaw, he looked like the stupid glittery glasses belonged on his face. Like his photo would be in some brochure for party decorations.

What I couldn't stand, besides everything about him, was the girl he had his arm around. She was pretty and smiling and blond and tanned and had her face against his, both of them laughing.

I wasn't surprised.

Yet that knot was cinched in my chest again.

And I really hated that.

CHAPTER SIX

Dean

A week into the new year, after everyone had settled back into work, I was called into Dominic's office, alongside Taylor. Both of us knew what this was about, and I diligently avoided her gaze, thinking of Reed, next door in his office, a few boxes half packed up, a sign of his impending departure.

"How were your holidays?" Dominic asked, leaning back in his chair, his suit coat draped over the back. He was a tall Black man with his hair cut short, a shadow of gray at his temples, his hands relaxed across his stomach.

Taylor and I answered at the same time.

"Good."

"Got a lot of work done."

My jaw tightened, and I stuffed my fists in my pockets. She always had to go one step further, impressing exactly no one in confessing she worked all the time because she had no social life.

"I hope you both got to spend time with your families," Dominic said, reaching out to his framed family photo.

"I did," I said with a smile. "How's Britney doing?"

"She's doing well. Thanks for asking."

I didn't ask after his pregnant daughter for brownie points.

I was actually asking because I knew how excited Dominic was about his first grandchild. Yet the way Taylor's shoulders went rigid did add a sprinkle of pleasure to the situation. I bit back a laugh in her direction since I could almost see the thought bubble, wishing she'd taken a personal interest in our boss's family.

But the Ice Queen didn't have a personal interest in anyone. I doubted she had a heart beneath all the black clothes.

"When is she due again?" I asked.

"May," Dominic answered then slid his attention to Taylor. "Thank you so much for the gifts, by the way. You didn't have to."

My smile dropped as I turned to her. "Gifts?"

The quirk of her mouth was positively venomous. Like I was a trapped mouse. "A little something for the grandparents-to-be."

Dominic found his phone and held it out so I could view the photo of him and his wife, Tamara, wearing matching shirts that read *Promoted to Grandma* and *Promoted to Grandpa*, as well as coffee mugs that I couldn't quite read but were painted with some similar sentiment.

"How nice," I said, feeling her silent vindictive cackle next to me.

Dominic grinned and set his phone back down. "So, I assume you two already know what this is about."

Neither Taylor nor I moved or spoke.

"You two are so incredibly important to our firm. Dean, you've been with us almost since the beginning."

I nodded. Though I had planned to stay in Philadelphia, possibly work at a Big Law firm, my plans changed after Patrick died, and I had tucked my tail between my legs after graduation, returning home. Fortunately, Barbara took care of me, and I was hired at the West Chester office immediately. They'd only opened a few months before, so I had basically been here since the start.

Point for me.

"And Taylor, you've exceeded all my expectations. I know your uncle and grandmother said you were a hard worker, but I honestly didn't think you'd bring in so much business. You are a force to be reckoned with."

I clenched my jaw as she dipped her head slightly. So magnanimous.

Dominic spread his hands between us. "With Reed leaving, he'll be wrapping up as much as he can, and whatever cases and clients are still on his plate will be passed to you. I've told him to give you a rundown on everything."

Taylor and I exchanged tense glances.

"You both know Novak & Novak isn't about competition," he went on, and I heard Taylor's barely audible huff. "We're here to work together, help each other, which is why I need you both to understand that even though titles and distribution of responsibilities are important, they're not everything. We're a team here."

Meaning, we shouldn't be fighting over who was top dog.

Fat chance of that happening.

Dominic looked from me to her then down at his desk, where he unstuck a yellow Post-it, a name and number scribbled on it. "I came into the office to a message from someone named Ariel Gardener." He held it out in the space between the three of us. "She works at Sunset Lounge."

"Sunset Lounge?" Taylor repeated, and Dominic's complexion turned a shade darker on his cheeks.

"The strip club?" I asked. It was located off the highway, in the next town over, and I'd gone there with my friends once we'd all turned eighteen. We'd thought we were big shit.

Nodding, Dominic cleared his throat, eyes averted. "From the little bit of information I've gleaned, it sounds like she's dealing with a hostile work environment. Said she and her coworkers all signed a petition for certain accommodations, and the owner ripped it up."

Taylor took the Post-it from him. "I can handle it."

"You can, though I have a feeling that once you find out more information, it might be a little bit bigger than what you're expecting." Dominic nodded between the two of us. "I'd like you both to work on it."

"Both of us?" I repeated, and he stood up.

"You have more litigation experience," he told me then raised his hand to Taylor when she started to argue, "but you have handled more harassment cases. Plus, I think the workers might feel more comfortable if you take the lead."

I lifted my clammy palms from my pockets to surreptitiously run them down my pant legs. First, we had to work together on this, and now, I was being relegated to taking the back seat after he'd gone on and on about being a team? What the fuck?

"If my instincts are correct," Dominic said before I could interrupt, "this will be going to trial. It would garner a lot of attention for the firm, for both of you."

I felt Taylor turn her hard eyes on me, and I slanted my head to meet her gaze, both of us realizing this was the test even before he said, "Yearly evaluations are coming up in a few months, and we can talk about promotions then, after we see what direction this is going in."

Taylor and I both faced our boss again. With Reed moving on, there was one title for the taking, junior partner, and the only other office besides Dominic's with a door. The rest of us associates were relegated to desks in the open workspace.

The title, that office, was mine.

"It won't be a problem," I said at the same time Taylor took one step closer to his desk, saying, "I'm looking forward to it."

"Good." Dominic smiled, gesturing to his door to dismiss us. "Keep me updated after you speak to Ariel. You two are on point, but I'm at your disposal."

"Thank you," I said and waited for Taylor to walk out in front of me, but she didn't, obviously wanting to be the last to leave the office, just as I did.

"Appreciate you," Taylor told our boss, and *needing* to get the last word in, I lifted my hand to him.

"We'll take care of it."

Taylor grumbled in my direction, though she didn't make a move toward the door. And as if a silent starter pistol sounded, suddenly we were fighting to fit through the doorframe at the same time. Dominic's baritone laugh echoed behind us as we stumbled out into the main office space.

In silent mutual agreement to take this argument out of hearing distance, we stalked toward the break room, which was really more of a big closet, enough to fit a small table with two chairs, a microwave perched on top of a mini refrigerator, and a Keurig on the tiny counter, next to the even tinier sink.

"You're the worst," she started, once her heels clacked on the linoleum floor.

"He made *you* the lead, and somehow you're pissed at *me* about it?" I stole the last chocolate chip Chewy bar from the wicker basket when she reached for it. I knew they were her favorite.

"Oh my god," she groused, "you're a goddamn baby."

I tipped my chin to where she stomped her foot like a child. "You're the one having a temper tantrum right now."

Stepping up close to me, close enough that I observed the golden-red flecks in her brown irises, which I could only assume were a characteristic of the devil, she leveled me with a glare. "I can already see myself in that office. My framed diplomas will look nice on that wall."

"*My* office," I corrected, nose to nose. "*My* wall."

"We'll see about that." Then she spun away, allowing me enough room to finally take a deep breath. I could never when she was so close. I didn't dare inhale that sweet scent of her perfume, which was a terrible mix of warm cinnamon and flowers, like a winter day in front of the fire, wrapped up in a blanket.

I couldn't stand it.

I bit into the Chewy bar as she popped a pod into the Keurig to brew and found her coffee mug in the small pile drying on the rack. Her mug was black with a white interior, but as soon as she poured warm liquid into it, the outside changed to display a picture of her and the person I now knew to be her sister.

With her back to me, she said, "I think it would be best if I called Ariel back first to find out more about what's going on before I bring you in."

Since I was mid-chew, I mumbled my answer. No matter how much I hated that she was the "lead" on the case, it would most likely be easier for Ariel to speak to Taylor. If these women were already experiencing intolerable working conditions, the last thing they'd want would be to speak to a man about it.

"Agree?" she growled, eyeing me over her shoulder.

I swallowed the bar and tossed the wrapper in the trash. "I said, yeah, sounds good."

"Oh." Her gaze dropped, chastened.

"I'm not some ogre."

"You sure about that?"

"I understand why he made you lead," I said, and her eyes flicked up to mine, sizzling with anger.

"Because I'm a woman?"

I shrugged. "Yeah."

"That's not the only reason."

"The only reason that matters," I countered, bending to the refrigerator to find her creamer.

She snatched it out of my grasp, her dark hair whipping back and forth with the movement. "My being a woman has nothing to do with what I've accomplished. You heard him. I've exceeded all of his expectations."

I went in for the kill shot she'd set up herself. "That's because everyone expects you to coast on your name. All you have to do is slightly above bare minimum for a pat on the back."

I thought I earned some steam from her ears on that one, and I grinned, rocking back on my heels. Before she could return the barb, Seth strolled into the room, crowding the already small space by slipping into one of the chairs between us, his attention pinging back and forth.

"Weapons down, please."

I ignored him and grabbed my own coffee mug, nudging Taylor out of the way to put another pod in the Keurig. She deliberately elbowed me as she stirred the creamer into her coffee.

"That's disgusting. I don't know how you drink that stuff," I said, and she passed behind me with a sneer. Her hip—or what I assumed was a hip, but it was hard to tell since she was a human two-by-four—grazed mine as she placed the coconut cream back in the fridge.

"Because you have no taste. I've seen what you eat, food of a third grader."

Seth chuckled at that, and we both turned to him for his two cents. "Maybe not in food, but in women, his tastes are refined."

My neck heated, and Taylor's jaw tightened. Or, at least, I think it did.

"Whatever happened on New Year's?" Seth went on. "You never told me if you sealed the deal."

I fingered the disposable utensils, wondering how much damage a plastic fork could do to an artery. He raised his eyebrows at my murderous expression.

"What?" he asked as if he truly didn't understand what he had done, which was hand over ammunition to the woman vying for my title and office.

She scoffed, and I didn't know if I should defend or explain myself.

"Nothing happened," I said after a while, and out of the corner of my eye, I noticed her shoulders shrink down as if she was relieved. I was too.

Because she wasn't radiating all that combustible tension.

And that crimp in her brow was gone.

"Dude," Seth sighed. "You had her eating out of the palm of your hand."

I took my mug from the Keurig and lifted it to my lips for a scalding sip, buying some time to figure out my answer, my tongue being the sacrifice. I didn't know why I couldn't close the deal, or if I even wanted to.

"I guess I wasn't all that interested in the end," I said eventually.

Seth shook his head like I was out of my mind, but I merely watched Taylor saunter out of the room in her heels and black skirt, her Satan's Mistress voice lingering down the short hall when she said, "I'll email you the details about the case when I have them. I expect a reply."

I flipped the bird at her back.

CHAPTER SEVEN

Taylor

The following Wednesday, I was sitting in my car with the heat on, trying not to freeze my ass off while parked outside of a Perkins restaurant, listening to some last-minute advice from my grandmother.

"They're looking not only for legal advice but for validation," she said as I upped the heat another degree before rubbing my hands together. Nan's voice was loud and clear over my Bluetooth. "They're working in a female-dominated space but managed by majority men. That's how it is across the nation, so, like you said, he told them if they're not happy, they can leave. But where would they go? To another club, where they may or may not be treated like they matter by men who most certainly only see dollar signs."

I agreed with a hum, and my grandmother's voice softened. "You sound muffled. Where are you?"

"I'm sitting in my car, freezing."

"Why don't you go inside?"

"Waiting for Hargrove to get here. He's late as usual."

Nan laughed. "This is the real test."

"Of what? Wills?" I would've liked to say I knew I'd win that one, but I honestly wasn't sure. This tug-of-war game was never-ending, and just when I thought I had the upper hand, he pulled me back into his territory.

"To see exactly how well you can work together."

I huffed. "We don't. That's the whole point of this. Dominic is setting us up to see which one gets the promotion."

"I don't think that's what he's doing," Nan said.

"What else is it, then?"

A moment passed before she answered. "This is your opportunity to truly work with each other."

"We work with each other every day."

"But this is your first case together," she said sagely, and I didn't like the word *first*, as if more would be coming down the pike. "And a little competition isn't a bad thing between you and Dean. It'll force you to be your best. Like your grandfather and me. We hated each other until we realized we were better together than we were separate."

I especially didn't like that leading statement.

"Dean and I are *not* you and Pop-Pop."

"Well, even if this doesn't bring you together on more friendly terms, you can at least learn each other's strengths and weaknesses, so you can help each other better when the next job comes along."

I already knew his weaknesses. His refusal to follow directions, his terrible communication, his typos—Jesus, his typos! A sixth grader could do a better job proofreading his files.

"I'm proud of you," Nan said, and I jerked back at the unexpected sentiment. Not that she hadn't said it before, but that it came out of nowhere.

"Thanks. I'm proud of you too," I replied, and she laughed.

Movement in my rearview mirror caught my attention, and I watched Dean blow out a foggy breath as he shut his car door. He stuck his hands in his coat pockets, lazily making his way toward the entrance of the restaurant.

"He's here, Nan. I gotta go."

"All right. Call me later to let me know how it all went."

"I will," I promised. "Love you."

"Love you too," she said, and the call disconnected. I slung my bag over my shoulder and opened my car door, calling out, "You're late."

Dean held his cell phone out toward me, the time displayed, 9:59. "We're meeting at ten."

"Yeah, and now we don't have any time to prepare," I said, catching up to him at the entrance, where he did *not* hold the door for me. Shocking.

"We've discussed the preliminary information, and all we're doing today is getting to know them better. Letting them get to know us. We're not here to be robots, firing questions at them."

I clenched my jaw, refusing to acknowledge how his words sounded similar to Nan's advice. This was about validation for these women.

"There is such a thing as being overprepared," he murmured to me before smiling at the hostess, requesting a table for five people.

On our way toward the back of the restaurant, I was tight on his heels. "I like being overprepared."

"That's your problem. A lot of this is about being able to talk to people. You can't when you're so uptight, sticking to some script you've written."

I dropped down into a chair. "I've done fine so far."

He only smirked at me, taking his time to remove his coat, draping it over the back of the chair. He fixed the cuffs on his shirt and smoothed down his tie before finally sitting.

"Mirror, mirror on the wall, who's the fairest boy of all?"

His eyes met mine over the plastic menu he held. "You certainly have the lines of the Evil Queen down pat."

I crossed my legs, not apologizing when I kicked the toe of my heel into his shin. He hissed, reaching his hand under the table, and I smiled. "Oops."

"You're such a bitch," he mumbled, gaze down on the menu.

"Thank you," I said, full volume, my attention on the door as three women entered. The one in the front was white with bright-red hair down to her waist, a fuzzy purple coat, and Ugg boots. The Black woman on her left was short with plump lips, a diamond stud in her nose, and sported a leather jacket. The third woman had golden-honey skin with her dark hair in a ponytail, glasses, and a few layers on, including what appeared to be a University of Pennsylvania sweatshirt under her thick coat.

"Ariel?" I asked, and the redhead nodded, leading the way toward our table. "Nice to meet you in person. I'm Taylor Novak, this is Dean Hargrove."

He stood and shook each of their hands then gestured to the table. "Have a seat."

"Thanks for meeting with us," Ariel started after everyone ordered coffees. Even though the trio of women said they didn't want anything to eat, I ordered a few muffins for the table.

"We're here to help in any way we can," Dean said smoothly, folding his hands on top of the table. He flicked his blue gaze to mine, as if asking for permission to begin, and when I stayed quiet, he went on, "Taylor has spoken to you already, and she's relayed the basic facts about what's going on, but before we get into that, why don't you ladies tell us about yourselves? How long have you been working at the Sunset Lounge, and what are you looking to do?"

I flipped open a small pad, but Dean didn't have anything

to take notes, and I blew out a small breath, reining in my irritation. We could argue about that later.

Ariel spoke first, sitting tall in her chair. Her voice was even and smooth, but it was hard to tell how old she was with her whimsical look and the bright makeup around her eyes. She really was like her namesake mermaid princess. "I've been at the Lounge for about ten years. If there is such a thing as seniority, I'm at the top."

I flicked my gaze toward Dean, who briefly met my eyes. Seniority, that was what we were fighting for.

Ariel continued, "I've put too much time and energy into the place to be treated the way I am. Ron's constantly talking to me about my weight, my looks, and it's not right. I take care of all the girls, the regular customers know me. I'm a draw, but he still threatens to take my spots away."

"She's like the mother hen," Julissa added quietly. With her glasses and sweatshirt, she appeared barely out of high school. "She keeps that place together."

"Is that how he acts toward all of you?" I asked. "Does he make comments about your physical appearance?"

Kelly nodded, her hand skimming over her short black hair. She had a '90s Halle Berry vibe about her. "Coming into this, you expect a certain amount of that, right? We're putting ourselves on display for people, of course they're going to comment about what we look like, but we deserve respect from the people who hired and manage us. We deserve to be treated with decency, but Ron sets a tone for everyone that it's okay for them to say whatever, whenever they want. I complained to him about a handsy customer, and he brushed it off. Told me I'd earn more money if I let it go." She tipped her head toward Ariel. "If it wasn't for her, I'd have left a long time ago." Then Kelly shrugged. "The money is good. I don't want to leave, but every night, I wonder if it's what I really want."

"What do you want?" Dean asked.

"I want to provide for my little sister. I want to make sure she has everything she needs. I want her to go to college and not worry about debt. But I also want to be there for her in case of emergencies."

"I know that feeling. I have a little sister too," I told her.

Kelly met my eyes. "I'm not ashamed of what I do. I make a great living, but I want her to have more choices than I had. Then I *have*."

"We will help you," I said, and she smiled, inclining her head slightly.

"What about you, Julissa?" Dean asked.

"I'm paying my way through school. I work on weekends and all my breaks, and I'm relatively new at this. When I started, I didn't know..." Her dark eyes shifted out to the window. "I didn't know what was right or wrong. The customers aren't supposed to touch us, they aren't supposed to get served alcohol if they're drunk, the dancers are all supposed to get breaks and get walked out to our cars." Then she met my eyes. "But none of that happens."

"Or it does after I complain enough, but it only lasts for a few days or weeks, and then the staff gets lazy again," Ariel said. "I even offered to help manage. I told Ron I'd work with him on a schedule that's suitable for all the girls. In fact, I made up a mock one with input from them, but he never even looked at it. He's careless about everything, especially our hours, and over Christmas, Lux's kid was sick, so she needed to go home and be with him, but Ron told her to—" she quirked her fingers into air quotes "—get her fat ass up onstage or leave. So, she walked out. And that was my last straw. It's why I called you guys."

I tapped my pen on my notebook. "When we talked last week, you said you wanted to sue for a hostile work environment, and it sounds like you have a case here, but we never talked about what your long-term goals are."

"Long-term goals?" Ariel repeated as the waitress returned with a pot of coffee and set down a plate of muffins between us.

Dean slid the plate toward her and then Kelly and Julissa, who was reluctant to take one. "Come on. I remember what undergrad living was like. Take one. Actually..." He placed another in front of her. "Take two."

She smiled at him, and he leaned back in his chair before motioning to Ariel. "If you could wave a magic wand, what would you want out of this?"

She tapped her pink fingernail on the table a few times as if deciding whether she wanted to confess it. "I want enough money to open my own place. A club owned and run by women."

Kelly grinned widely, lifting her muffin in a salute. "That's it, right there."

Dean nodded then turned to me in a silent direction to close the deal. I leaned my elbows on the table. "I can't promise you that, but I can promise we will have your back. Everyone has the right to a safe and healthy work environment, and we'll take on this case for you, walk you through it, support you until you have that safe and healthy work environment."

Ariel, Kelly, and Julissa all appeared happy and excited to get started, so over coffee and muffins, we discussed the next steps in filing with the Equal Employment Opportunity Commission and informed them that this would be a long process. They needed to be able to stick with this for any real change.

"That's what I want," Ariel said. "I want an overhaul. I want real change."

Kelly and Julissa both nodded in agreement.

Dean explained, "I know you've been documenting these occurrences, but we will need anyone who wants to be included on the complaint to send them to us."

Ariel already had her cell phone out, typing on it. "I'll let them know."

"As soon as we have everyone's information, we can start working on the filing," I said.

"Then what?" Kelly asked.

Dean idly folded up a paper napkin. "The EEOC will notify Ron within ten days of the charge and investigate whether the claim is reasonable or not. From start to finish, this could take as little as six months or up to two years."

"If Ron is reasonable, this could all go to mediation," I said, and the three women exchanged looks.

"Reasonable is not the word I'd use to describe him," Kelly said.

"But if we do our job right, it would be the better option for him," Dean supplied, crossing his arms like the cocky bastard he was, but it did seem to placate our clients, so I couldn't be mad at him about it.

"And believe me," I said, "we will do our job right."

Ariel smiled and held her coffee mug up toward us. "We're looking forward to working with you."

Dean and I exchanged a look. It was official. We were a team now.

After we finished up with some details and drained the coffee, I paid the bill with the company card, and we walked the trio outside. I pulled my coat tighter around my neck. "As soon as you have everything together, you can email it all to me, and we'll get started."

"Got it! Thanks again!"

Dean and I waved as they drove off, but as I turned to my car, he caught my elbow.

"That went well."

"Yeah. You did good," I said.

"Just what I need, a condescending pat on the head."

I snorted, but I didn't mean for it to be condescending. *This time.* Dean's conversation with Ariel, Kelly, and Julissa was comforting and well-explained. I'd been acquainted with some men in the field who I knew would've been dismissive and made jokes the whole time, but Dean would never do that. He was ever the respectful and intelligent gentleman, much to my chagrin.

I wanted him to be good at his job because we had to work together on this, yet I also wanted him to suck so I could prove once and for all that I should be the one to eventually lead the West Chester office. Although, that wouldn't be happening anytime soon. Goddamn it.

I moved to retrieve my car keys from my purse, but he still held on to my arm. "What?"

His eyes, which were more gray than blue under the cloudy sky, roamed over my face. "Are you okay?"

"Yes." I jerked away, forcing him to finally let go of me. "Why?"

"You look...off."

I huffed. "Such a compliment."

"No, I mean it." He trailed me to my car. "You sleeping all right?"

I unlocked the doors with my key fob and furrowed my brow, lying. "I'm fine."

The last few nights, I'd had headaches and skipped my daily runs. Maybe that was why I'd felt so off, because my routine was out of whack.

"You seem tired."

"Jesus, Hargrove. If I wanted to feel bad about myself, I'd go dig up my middle school yearbook."

He smirked at me. "Sorry."

"Anyone ever tell you not to apologize if you don't mean it?"

He shrugged his answer, standing so close to me his foggy breath broke over my face. It smelled like the mint gum he always chewed.

Even though it was freezing out, my neck heated the longer I stood with him, and I needed to get away. "I'll see you back at the office."

His gaze took one more trip around my face before he leaned in even closer to me. "Last one back buys lunch?"

I forced a laugh at the juvenile challenge then opened my car door. "You're on."

CHAPTER EIGHT

Dean

I'd always loved music. I first learned how to play the trumpet when I was a kid, then taught myself how to play guitar in middle school. It was the latter that led me to forming a band in high school with my best friends. We called ourselves the Anchormen for the Will Ferrell movie that we were all obsessed with. I played guitar, Patrick had been on bass, Gabe on the keyboard, Ethan on drums, and Hank on the mic since he was born for the spotlight. If we got real wild, sometimes Gabe would take out his sax for some sweet '80s melodies, but mostly, we had played covers of our favorites: the Who, the Stones, Zeppelin, the White Stripes, Foo Fighters, Ben Folds Five. All the greats.

Now, we still played our favorites and had expanded to include some others, like Coldplay and Maroon 5, ever since Ethan started urging us to learn songs just so he could impress Laney. As if she wasn't already grinning like a loon from her seat in front of the small stage at Walt's.

After finding Tony and Jerry to replace Patrick and Gabe on bass and keyboards, we accepted a standing gig on the third Thursday of every month. Walt's was a small dive, wide enough for booths on one side and tables next to the windows on the other. The little stage was up a foot off the floor in the corner, while the long rectangular bar took up the middle, and since there weren't many seats open, anyone who needed one would be zigzagging around to the back to grab them.

Hank, in another one of his brightly colored Tommy Bahama shirts, swiped a rag over his forehead, taking his good old time, playing to the crowd like he was the Asian James Brown. He pointed his sweaty towel out to where his wife sat with Laney. "This next one goes out to the prettiest girl in the world, Angela Lau."

Jerry played the first few chords of "True Love" by Pink, which I supposed Hank dedicated to his wife in irony, a song about hating someone so much it could only be true love. Though with the way that oaf acted, like an overgrown teenager, Angela was a saint. She laughed and propped up their two-year-old, clapping little Grayson's hands together.

Once the chorus kicked in, I backed the vocals and strummed away as Hank sauntered out into the crowd, offering his wife a lap dance. She merely blotted his temple with a napkin. It was then, as I tipped my head away from the mic to laugh, I noticed her.

Taylor Novak.

For a moment, I forgot what I was supposed to do, and Hank had to thump me on the arm to get me back into working order, finishing out the song about wanting to strangle someone else while confessing they were in love.

Taylor stood there, eyebrows raised, her dark eyes wide with surprise.

Me too.

I couldn't stop staring. Like spotting a Yeti.

And certainly not because she wore a tight black turtleneck that shaped to her form.

That of a spindly spider.

With legs encased in the tightest pants I'd ever seen. Heels capped it off.

A black widow. On the hunt.

Hank slung his arm around my neck, dragging me out of the trance she had me in. "You might not know this, but this guy right here is the heart of the Anchormen," he said into the microphone. "He first had the idea for us to form a band when we were in high school. A dozen years later, and we're still playing together."

I smiled at my old friend then over my shoulder to Ethan, who lifted his chin to me. These guys were my best friends, my ride-or-dies, and yet that familiar pang in my chest reverberated against my ribs at our missing link, Patrick. I forced myself to keep smiling as Hank went on and on about how we were all in the marching band together and smoked so much pot behind the bleachers one game, we were stripping off our uniforms and trading instruments.

"Since it's Dean's birthday, I'm hoping you'll all join me in singing," Hank said, lifting his arm to the crowd in front of us and launching into "Happy Birthday." Then Ethan counted off with his sticks, and without letting me know what we were doing, they started in on a rendition of the Police's "Every Little Thing She Does Is Magic." It took me a bit to find the right chords before I joined in, but I could barely manage to play as Hank basically humped my leg, changing the lyrics of the chorus to be every little thing *he* does is magic, and had all of Walt's singing along. My gift, I supposed.

It could have been worse.

"And we can't forget about Dean's sister, Laney," Hank said, pointing at her. "This next one is dedicated to you from your lover boy."

Behind me, Ethan pointed one of his drumsticks at her, mouthing something I didn't *want* to comprehend, and led us into an alt version of "Always Be My Baby." I kept my focus on my guitar the whole time so I didn't accidentally find Taylor again.

After the last notes floated into quiet, Hank thanked the crowd and reminded them of our gig next month, and we all waved before starting in on the cleanup from our set. I couldn't help but notice Taylor had found a seat with her sister at the other end of the bar. I tried to ignore how my back felt like it was on fire as I helped Ethan pack up his kit.

"That was great, guys," Laney said, kissing Ethan's cheek and high-fiving the rest of us. "I ordered some food."

I checked my watch. Normally, Ethan and Laney scooted out right after. "You're staying?"

"Yeah. It *is* our birthday. We have to celebrate."

"Thirty, flirty, and thriving," Hank said with a shimmy in my sister's direction. Laney tossed her head back and laughed that annoying, booming laugh of hers. It never failed to call everyone's attention, and when I lifted up my head, I met Taylor's eyes.

Kennedy was saying something to her, but she didn't break our gaze.

I was the first one to blink away.

"What's up with you?" Jerry asked, lightly elbowing my side. "Look like you've seen a ghost."

Tony and Jerry were in their late forties, a bit older than Ethan, Hank, and me, but we got along well enough to play together. Though, we never talked about personal stuff, so I just shrugged and offered to help him with unplugging the cords.

Once the stage was cleared, we settled down at the two tables pushed together, plates of food spread out between us. Yet I couldn't stop flicking my eyes to the back corner.

"Who is that?" Laney asked eventually.

"Some ex-hookup?" Hank guessed.

I huffed. "No."

Ethan looked over his shoulder, and I tossed a fry at him. "Dude. Don't be so obvious."

"What?" He stuffed the fry into his mouth. "I'm trying to see who everybody's talking about."

"We're not talking about her."

"She break your heart?" Tony asked, and a chorus of laughter rang out since I'd be the last person to get my heart broken.

And I needed to shut down this conversation.

"No. It's someone I work with."

Laney zipped her eyes right over Ethan's shoulder. "Oh my god! It's Taylor, isn't it?"

I sipped my beer, suddenly very interested in the muted basketball game playing on the TV by the bar.

Everyone else turned their attention to Taylor, and I dropped my chin to my chest. "You guys are the absolute worst."

Hank took Grayson in his arms, dressing him in a little baby coat, hat, and mittens. The kid fought his dad every step of the way. "You wanna do her, huh?"

I stared at my friend. "No, I don't want to *do* her. I'm only surprised to see her here." I shrugged. "Always weird to see Satan's Mistress in human form."

"Seems like you got some big feelings about her," Angela noted quietly, curiously.

"You're getting as bad as him," I told her while pointing at Hank, but she merely smiled and stood up, accepting Grayson again so Hank could say goodbye to all of us with his usual fervor.

He gave me a bear hug, saying, "You look like you want to fuck or fight. Which one is it?"

I patted his shoulder when my feet touched the floor again, ignoring him. "See ya later, man."

"Fuck, then? All right," he laughed and tossed a small back-pack filled with Grayson's stuff over his shoulder before leading Angela out. "Later!"

Tony and Jerry followed soon after, which left me with my sister and Ethan.

"Stop looking at me like that," I said and stuffed a nacho chip in my mouth.

Laney flicked her fingers toward the restrooms. "I have to go to the bathroom."

Ethan leaned back in his chair, extending his long legs out in front of him, crossing his arms over a Goonies T-shirt, a self-satisfied grin on his face. "You know she's going to talk to her."

"I know. Never minds her own goddamn business," I muttered into my beer, pointedly avoiding the corner where Laney was definitely talking to Taylor. "Bathroom, my ass."

My friend had no qualms about staring at his wife-to-be as she made small talk with my archnemesis. "She's not that bad."

"She is," I said.

"I love her anyway."

I thumped my pint down on the table. "Do you have to be so…" I grimaced. "Happy all the time?"

Ethan chuckled. "I didn't realize it pained you so much."

"Still not used to it."

"It's been two years."

I aimed my thumb over my shoulder. "And she's my sister. My *twin*."

"And I'm going to take care of her. You know I will. She's everything to me."

I nodded as I remembered how I'd found my sister and my best friend in bed one morning, discovering the secret they'd been hiding from me. Secret feelings they'd had for each other since high school. I was a fool for not realizing it. But most of all, I was scared. Laney had just come out of a bad relationship, and I didn't want anything else to bring her down. Not that I'd thought Ethan would, but he was one of my best friends, and relationships were complicated. I had worried that if they broke up, it would shred my friend group even more.

Now, I knew how perfect my best friend and sister were for each other. Sickeningly perfect.

"Less than two months and we'll be brothers. Officially." Ethan tapped his beer against mine, and I gave in to a growing smile.

"You already were," I said, and we both drank from our glasses. I set mine back down on the table, admitting, "I haven't even thought about my speech."

Since I was the man of honor, I'd be standing up next to Laney, along with her three best friends. Ethan's brother, Justin, would be his best man, and we had both been instructed to prepare speeches.

Ethan pushed his glasses up his nose. "You do all your best work at the last minute."

That was exactly correct. I operated best with a close dead-line, which was why Taylor crawling up my ass about how I worked always pissed me off.

At the click of heels next to me, I turned. "Speak of the devil, and she appears."

Taylor narrowed her brows at me while Ethan draped his arm over Laney's chair. "We weren't speaking of the devil."

I shot my gaze to my best friend, Benedict Arnold. He merely grinned at me.

"I happened to notice these two on my way to the bath-room and thought they might want to join us," Laney explained as if no one at this table knew it was all a ruse. She gestured for the sisters to sit, and Taylor dropped into the open chair next to me, her cinnamon-and-flower scent wrapping around me in a vise grip. I refused to look at her. Refused to concede that I had trouble keeping my attention off her.

She didn't greet me, but Kennedy did, smiling widely. "Nice to see you again. And happy birthday!"

I nodded at her. "Thanks."

"Taylor, Kennedy, this is my fiancé, Ethan," my sister said, and he shook their hands with a pleasant smile. "I hope you don't think I'm too forward." Laney leaned her elbows on the table. "But Dean has told us so much about you, Taylor, so when I saw you, I had to invite you to sit with us."

Taylor's mouth quirked in a half smile. "I'm sure everything he's told you about me is how awful I am."

"Pretty much," Laney said.

Taylor opened her mouth, and the sound that came out was...a laugh. I think. I'd never heard it before.

I didn't know demons laughed.

"So, Kennedy, you're Taylor's younger sister?" Laney asked, steamrolling the conversation. As always.

"Yeah. She's been in such a bad mood lately, I had to drag her out of the house."

Taylor sneered at her sister while I eyed my own. Two-on-two here. I didn't like it.

"I'd never been here before," Kennedy went on. "And I didn't know a band would be playing." She elbowed Taylor. "We were both so surprised to see you up there, Dean."

Taylor stared at me over the rim of her glass. Looked like some kind of vodka drink. I smiled at Kennedy. "I'm a man of many talents."

Taylor snorted.

"Well, it's so funny because did you know Taylor used to want to play in a band?"

That had me looking at Taylor. "No. I did not know that."

"Kennedy," Taylor warned.

"She used to be obsessed with Alanis Morissette and tried to learn to play the harmonica, but she was so bad." Kennedy giggled, either unaware or uncaring that her sister clearly wanted to murder her. "She had real long hair and would walk around the house singing... What was it?" She stared off into space. "That one about going down on you in a theater."

"'You Oughta Know,'" I supplied, and Kennedy snapped her fingers.

"Yes! So funny."

"So funny," I agreed flatly, staring at Taylor, who I thought was trying to light me on fire with her mind.

"Do you guys know any Alanis songs?" Laney asked.

"No," Ethan answered, "but we could learn."

And I wanted to light him on fire with my mind.

Kennedy reached her hand over to lightly pat my arm. "So, how old are you today?"

"Thirty," Laney answered before I could. "We're twins."

Kennedy lit up. "Shut up. No way. I always thought it would be so cool to have a twin. Do you guys, like, read each other's minds and stuff?"

Laney and I both shook our heads, but Ethan nodded. "They do." When Laney slanted her gaze to him, he shrugged. "You do. You have these conversations with your eyes, and I don't even know if you realize it."

"What am I thinking right now?" I asked Laney.

"That you want to kill me."

"Yep."

"Good thing I know a lawyer." Laney tipped her chin in

Taylor's direction, and I rubbed at the heartburn lingering in my chest after downing my drink. I caught Taylor's eyes, that unceasingly dark gaze like a fathomless lake threatening to drown me, and her lips parted as if she might say something, but Kennedy spoke up again.

"So, you guys have known each other since high school? That's cool."

I let Laney and Ethan take over the conversation with Kennedy, my mind still reeling over this quiet, almost demure version of Taylor Novak next to me. I don't know if I liked it.

"You all right?" I asked, knocking my knee into hers.

She dropped her attention down to where our legs touched then back up to my face. "I'm fine."

"You're awfully quiet."

"That's how it usually goes with me and my sister."

I crossed my arms across my chest. "Me too."

She wrapped her fingers around her glass, swirling the clear liquid. "I guess I should say happy birthday."

"I guess I should say thank you."

The corner of her mouth lifted, and I shifted in my seat, that hint of her genuine smile doing something funny to me.

"So, you've been in a bad mood lately? Seems like your usual mood to me," I said.

She angled her head to the side like a viper ready to strike but didn't respond, and I took a moment to study her face. She was a bit paler than normal, with dark circles under her eyes. Like she needed a good nap.

"You feeling all right?" I asked, and her nostrils flared.

"I'm fine."

"You sure—"

"I'm fine," she snapped, and I leaned away from her, only now realizing how close I'd moved toward her.

"Maybe your sister was right. You *are* in a bad mood."

"And here I thought we'd play nice since it's your birthday."

"We've never played nice," I said, my gaze slipping to her mouth, where her tongue dragged along her bottom lip.

"You wouldn't know what to do with yourself if I were ever nice to you."

"You're right," I agreed.

She brought her drink to her mouth, polishing it off, her delicate throat bobbing on a swallow before our eyes met again.

"Then again, I don't think you know how to be nice. Women like you don't get where they are because they're nice."

She conceded my point with an unrepentant smile. "True."

"Never change, Novak."

"Don't plan on it, Hargrove."

Then she stood in a swirl of black and slipped into her coat. "Let's go, Ken."

Kennedy offered Laney some parting words, but I wasn't listening, too busy watching Taylor as she paid her bill at the bar. I vaguely waved at her sister, my attention still diverted to Taylor, strutting out of Walt's like she owned the place.

When I finally turned back to Laney and Ethan, they were both staring at me.

"What?"

"Nothing." Ethan shook his head, while Laney threw her head back, laughing.

I pushed away from the table. "I actually do have to go to the bathroom."

"No picking up any strange women," Ethan warned.

"You seem to have me confused with my twin."

"Don't pretend you aren't glad," Laney shouted to my back. "We can read each other's minds, remember?"

And thank god she couldn't. I didn't want anyone to know what I was thinking about. Could barely admit it to myself.

That I'd need to go home and fuck my hand, and it was all Taylor Novak's fault.

CHAPTER NINE

Taylor

I stared into my cup, the coffee long gone cold. My sister had dragged me out to that bar last night in hopes of shaking some life back into me, telling me I needed to loosen up, rid the tension. Little did she know, that last time I'd tried that, I'd gotten pregnant.

I rubbed my fingers over my forehead, willing my breathing to slow down, counting down the minutes until I could leave work and head to the clinic and be done with this nightmare. When my period hadn't shown up, I'd immediately taken a test, already knowing what it would show.

I hadn't felt right, and even though I was on the pill, I'd forgotten one day. One goddamn day, too worked up over my argument with Dean at the Christmas party to take it at the usual time. Then Ace had happened, and when I'd finally realized the next day, I had immediately swallowed down the one I'd missed plus the usual day, like the directions instructed. I didn't get Plan B because Ace had used a condom. Or, at least, I thought he had.

He'd been weird about it, and even though I'd insisted, I guess I should have been more careful. More thoughtful about who I was going home with.

Consequently, I was now the one in one hundred women who got pregnant after failing to take one of her birth control pills. I was a fucking statistic.

Shame washed over me. Again.

It had been trailing me every day since the afternoon I had peed on the stick. After Douchebag McGee had told me I looked tired in the parking lot of Perkins.

I hadn't been able to sleep or eat much, too nauseated from humiliation. It was a mistake. I shouldn't have been so hard on myself. At least, that was what my therapist had said. But I couldn't help it.

I didn't screw up like this. I was the reliable, responsible one. I didn't forget to take my pill. I didn't go home with men I didn't vet.

I didn't...

Closing my eyes, I reminded myself that this was a fluke. One easily remedied.

As soon as the test had turned up positive, I had made an appointment and attended the required "counseling." All I had left to do was to go in today to get the pills, and it would be done.

"Hey, you asleep on the job?"

I snapped my head up to find Dean leaning against my desk. I batted his hand away from where he attempted to straighten my pens and highlighters. "Don't you have somewhere to be? Some puppies to kick?"

"Well, you're over here looking pretty down, so I thought I'd come kick you." He tapped my foot with his, and I angled my chair away from him.

"Go be somewhere else. I have a lot of work to do."

He placed his palm flat on my desk, nudging my planner and pen into perfect parallel lines, and opened his mouth. I stopped him before he could utter one syllable.

"I swear to god." I grabbed hold of my scissors. "If you tell me one more time how tired or raggedy I look, I will murder you right here and now."

He backed away, hands up, the picture of innocence. "For the record, I never said you looked raggedy." He lifted one shoulder, a smirk curving his stupid mouth. "Might have implied it, but never said it."

I slapped the scissors back down and pointed to his desk, a few feet ahead of mine. "Go away."

Instead of leaving, he stood there, one hand in his pocket, the other scratching at his beard, while he stared down at me. "Did you have fun last night?"

"Loads."

He dragged his thumb over the corner of his mouth, like he'd eaten something delicious, and I crossed my legs at the fluttering it sent between my thighs. "You missed us playing 'Devil Woman,'" he said. "I could have dedicated it to you."

"Your hordes of female fans would be so jealous."

"I'd bear it for you."

When I stiffened, he seemed to recognize what he'd said. Not that it meant anything, *I'd bear it for you*. It was clearly a jab at how he'd give up everything else for another chance to insult me by calling me the devil. But the words he spoke didn't jive with the implication. A mistake he tried to rectify.

"Like you say all the time, I do love attention."

It was a halfhearted cover-up at best, and I hunched over my desk, my head in my hands. "I need to get the Sunset complaint in today. I'm waiting on your review of it."

"Yeah, okay," he said, then pivoted around to his desk.

He emailed me the review, and we didn't speak for the rest of the afternoon.

Thank god.

I cut out earlier than usual, a few minutes after Dominic

left for the day, with little more than a wave to Sandy, the office admin. It was raining, and I bundled myself in my scarf and coat before marching out to my car, but by the time I dropped down behind the steering wheel, I was soaking wet. I lifted my chin to peer at my reflection in the rearview mirror and let out a shuddered breath.

I *was* raggedy.

My hair was matted against my head, my skin sallow and makeup smudged. I wiped my finger along my bottom lashes in an attempt to fix my liner, but my eyes suddenly stung with tears, and I blinked a few times to clear them.

More formed, falling over my cheeks, dropping to my lips. I wiped at them, but it was a useless task. I had started and couldn't stop. At least the shield of the rain outside would mask my humiliation from anyone who got within a few feet of my car to witness me crying.

This was what happened. I kept my emotions bottled up, and then they eventually exploded. Normally, I'd cry in the shower, the water washing away any evidence of my weakness. Lather, rinse, repeat.

Unfortunately, I didn't have the luxury of breaking down right now. I had an appointment to get to, yet I couldn't pull myself together. I covered my face, heaving into my palms, my skin wet with my tears.

I didn't know how long I sat there, my hiccupping breaths the only sound to break up the dull pounding of the rain on the roof of my car. Long enough for the office to close, I supposed, because suddenly there was a knock on my window.

I gasped and scrubbed at my eyes, only for my tears to blur my vision at the sight of Dean goddamn Hargrove standing there under an umbrella. He rapped one knuckle quietly, as if asking for permission, and I tried to find a tissue. Coming up empty, I blotted my face with a receipt from the console.

"Open up," he said, and I don't know why I did, turning the engine over to roll the window down. His sandy hair was brown from the rain, his brows wrinkled as he took me in. "What's wrong?"

I sniffled and shook my head.

"I've been watching you out here for ten minutes. You haven't moved."

"You stalking me now?" I tried for arrogance, but the appalling quaver in my voice gave me away.

"Novak," he said in maybe the kindest voice he'd ever used when addressing me, "what's wrong?"

I wiped under my nose. "I...uh..." I cleared my throat and blinked a few times. "Nothing."

"I have never ever seen you cry. *Ever*. It's freaking me out."

I huffed in his direction, my breath forming a cloud in the cold and wet January night.

"Can I help you with something?" he asked, and I don't know if it was the question or *him* asking it that had me breaking down all over again.

A tissue appeared from his outstretched hand, and I accepted it without a word, wiping at my face. "You can't..." I tucked my hair behind my ears in an attempt to look presentable. "I know you're going to use this against me somehow, but I—"

"You think I would use *this* against you?" When I turned to meet his furious gaze, he practically spat his next words at me. "I came to check on you. I was worried. You could just say thanks but no thanks. Jesus." He combed his hand through his hair. "You think I'm that much of an asshole that I'd somehow fucking blackmail you? You really are a piece of work."

More tears sprung to my eyes at how much offense he took at my accusation. We were enemies, and I didn't know what to do with this sudden kindness. "I'm sorry," I said after a while. "I'm...I'm having a hard time right now."

"No shit." He let out a sigh of someone fighting all of their instincts to run. "What are you having a hard time with?"

I didn't want to admit to my struggle. He'd already witnessed my mess. I couldn't tell him my mistake.

He leaned his arm on my open window, drops of rain splattering on the interior of my car. "You're going to tell me what's going on, or you're not leaving here."

"You can't make me stay."

He thrust his hand out and removed my keys from the ignition and pocketed them before I even took my next breath.

"Try again," he said, and I glared at him.

"Give me my keys. I need to go."

"Go where?"

"A place."

He raised one thick light-brown eyebrow. "For an attorney, you're terrible at being cross-examined."

"Don't do this right now," I whimpered, my chin trembling again. I pressed my fist against it to make it stop.

He nudged my hand away and settled two fingers against my jaw, urging me to face him. "Are you hurt?"

I shook my head.

"Are you in trouble?"

I rolled my lips together to keep from frowning.

"I can help you," he said.

"You can't."

"Tell me, and we'll figure it out."

"I can't tell you."

"Can't, or don't want to?" he asked, and I attempted to move away, but he didn't let me, smoothing his hand along my cheek. "What is it?"

I hadn't told anyone I was pregnant. Not my sister, because

she was dealing with enough. Not my grandmother, because I didn't want to disappoint her. Certainly not my mother, because we weren't close enough for that sort of thing. And I didn't really have friends. Acquaintances, sure, but no one I'd consider admitting this to.

So, the only defense I could come up with for the hastily spilled confession was temporary insanity due to the unwavering blue of his eyes that seemed to reach into my chest and pull the words out of my throat.

"I'm pregnant."

He momentarily tightened his fingers along my jaw before dropping them to curl around the open window. He didn't respond, merely stared at me, and the rest tumbled out.

"I'm going to get an abortion, and I'm so embarrassed and ashamed, I haven't been able to bring myself to tell anyone. That's why I've been crying, because I can't stop thinking about how stupid I was. I can't believe I got myself into this situation, and now I'm sitting out here feeling bad for myself and professing all my secrets to the one person I hate." I lifted my chin as high as possible, pretending I hadn't just cut myself open at his feet, offering him a stab at my vital organs, and held my palm up. "That's why I need to have my keys back. I have an appointment."

His eyes narrowed, his bearded jaw moving as if measuring his words, and I prepared myself for some dig or long-winded explanation of how feminism and career-minded women were ruining society. I absolutely was not prepared for his one-word answer.

"No."

CHAPTER TEN

Dean

"No?" Taylor shrieked. "I don't need your permission. I'm going. Give me my keys. Now!"

The tension that had clawed at my throat eased incrementally with every angry word she shouted at me until I almost felt like smiling. I couldn't say what had made me walk over to the office window, where I'd noticed Taylor jogging out into the rain, and I definitely couldn't say what had made me stay there, one arm against the windowsill as I watched her sit and sit and sit in her car.

I'd sensed it. Something was wrong, and when simply standing there, keeping watch, became unbearable, I made my way outside to her. The last thing I expected was to find her crying.

Fucking crying.

It felt like I'd been shot.

Never, in all the years I'd known her, had I ever witnessed anything close to the fear in her eyes like I had when she rolled down her window. And it was abhorrent. I had to do something.

"No, you're not going alone. I'm going with you," I told her, and before she could argue, I opened her car door. "Get out. I'm driving."

Her jaw went slack. "You...can't...what?"

I held up my umbrella so she wouldn't get wet as I wrapped my hand around her arm, towing her out of her seat. She must've been in shock, because she would sooner slice my balls off with her high heel than let me boss her around. "Come on," I said, ushering her to the passenger side and into the seat. "I'm driving. Where do you have to go?"

"Planned Parenthood," she said, looking up at me in bewilderment.

With a nod, I shut the door then marched back around to drop into the driver's seat, fishing her car keys from my pocket. I wiped my wet hands on my pants and found the address on my phone, settling it into the holder on her dash. With one last glance in her direction to make sure she wasn't freaking out, I backed her little Audi out of the parking lot and drove to her appointment.

The clinic was about ten minutes away, and while I would've liked some music or something to take the edge off, Taylor seemed content to gnaw at her nails, her focus out of the window. So, I kept my mouth shut and let her work through whatever she needed to while I silently seethed.

I didn't know a whole lot about Taylor's personal life, thank god, but I could only assume she'd ended up in this situation because of the greasy octopus bartender from the holiday party, and my grip on the steering wheel tightened.

She shouldn't have been going through this alone. She should have told someone, anyone. Christ. She was pregnant and getting an abortion by herself? Not on my goddamn watch.

I had briefly worried there would be protestors outside of the clinic door, but fortunately, I didn't see any. If it was the weather or plain old sensibility, I was glad of it, and I escorted her inside.

I didn't know if I should go with her to the check-in desk or sit down or stand there with my thumb up my ass, so I took to the diligent task of shaking out my umbrella until Taylor finished checking in and found a seat. I slipped into the open one next to her.

"You good?" I asked, and she nodded, barely meeting my gaze.

With her crossed legs and back rigid, she was obviously anxious, while I tried my best to appear relaxed and unruffled. I extended my legs out in front of me and reached into my pocket for my gum packet. When I offered her a piece, she refused with a stiff shake of her head.

"You sure?" I asked, peeling off the wrapper from the green gum.

"Just try to keep your teeth-gnashing to a minimum," she murmured, but it was better than nothing, and I popped the stick into my mouth, making extra noise with it. She rolled her eyes. "What is it with you and gum? You're always chewing."

Although I didn't think I was *always* chewing, I shrugged. "You chew your fingernails. I chew gum."

She rubbed at her temple. "Between your coffee slurping and gum chewing, you're the noisiest eater I've ever met."

"That's because you've never met my friend Hank," I said then knocked my elbow into her arm. "Oh, no, you did. He's the lead singer of my band."

"You say 'my band' like it's actually yours."

"I'm not using that term as in ownership. I say 'my' because it's the band I'm in. You wouldn't tell a baseball player he couldn't say 'my team.'"

"Well, you say it with a tone."

"A *tone?*"

"Yeah, like—"

"Taylor?"

She snapped her head in the direction of the nurse's quiet voice. A second passed when I wasn't sure if she was going to stay or go, but she nodded to herself and stood up, following the nurse through the door then stopped when she realized I was behind her and furrowed her brow.

In response, I gestured for her to keep moving. I'd come here with her and wasn't about to let her go back there on her own. She might've been a frigid bitch, but as far as I was concerned, she was my frigid bitch now.

"I don't need you to come back," she said, and I raised my attention to the nurse, holding the door open. I expected her to wave me inside, but she didn't, so I grasped Taylor's hand.

"I'll be right out here, okay?"

"Yeah, okay," she whispered, the tips of her fingers momentarily wrapping around mine.

I squeezed her hand once. "I'll be waiting."

She didn't smile, but she didn't look scared either, so I took it as a win.

And then I waited. There was a sign about not using phones, so I flipped through an old *People* magazine from the table.

Weirdly enough, Chris "CJ" Cunningham stared back at me from one of the pages. He was an actor turned director and was married to one of Laney's best friends. Ethan had become pretty good friends with him too. He was even going to be at their wedding. I only hoped it wouldn't be a whole thing. A celebrity at my sister's big church wedding? It had the makings of some comedy gone wrong. But Ethan said he was cool, so...

I slapped the magazine down and picked up another one, apparently anxious enough to start worrying about celebrities' lives.

How long did this take?

I read about gluten-free dinner recipes and a trendy new women's hairstyle. Bangs were back in.

I'd just sat down in my chair from throwing out my gum when the door opened, and I jumped up. "Are you all right?"

Taylor stuffed a prescription bag into her purse and frowned at me. "Yeah, why?"

I pointed my finger past her shoulder. "You were in there for, like, an hour."

"It was twenty minutes, Hargrove. Chill out."

I patted my tie back into place and willed my nerves to subside, lest my bones turn into goo and I melt to the floor. I thanked the nurse at the check-in with a wave and kept my hand wrapped around Taylor's elbow as we hustled back outside.

"I don't need you to put me into the car."

"Shut up and get in," I muttered, closing the door after her.

Once I was back out on the road, I chanced a glance her way. "Everything go okay?"

She kept her focus out of the windshield. "Yeah. I took one pill in there, and I have more to take when I get home."

"And that's it?"

"Yeah. It's a medical abortion."

"Right." I nodded and made a mental note to read up on the process as soon as I could. I should have before, and I felt like a dick for not being more informed. Laney would be ashamed of me. But I'd figured voting for it would have been enough. Now I knew it wasn't.

Not when I was sitting here, next to my frigid bitch, trying to make her feel better while in the middle of an abortion.

"Where are you going?" she asked when I made a left turn.

"Home."

"I'm not going home with you," she bit out.

"Obviously." I leaned my elbow on the car door, rubbing my forehead. "I'm taking you home."

"But this isn't..." She flapped her hand between us. "You have to go back to the office."

"Why?"

"Your car. This is my car!"

"I can hear you fine when you use your inside voice."

She growled.

"Though, you could work on your inside voice too. Make it less screechy."

"I hate you so much," she said.

I hit her with a smile and patted her knee. She batted at my hand.

"I'll take you home and get an Uber or something back to the office for my car," I told her once she settled down. "Does that satisfy you?"

She didn't answer. Only folded her arms over her chest.

"You live on Mills, right?"

She slanted her head in my direction. "How do you know?"

"Stalking."

She rolled her eyes.

"I don't know," I said. "I heard you talking about it before. How does anyone learn anything about a person they work with?"

"We aren't friends. We don't talk."

"A normal person would say, 'Yeah, Dean, that sounds great. Thank you so much for driving me today. It was so nice of you.'"

"I'm not a normal person."

"Oh." I forced a laugh. "I know that."

Our argument faded into silence as I drove to her apartment on the other side of town. West Chester, Pennsylvania, was a college town, so housing was always expensive and in demand, but Taylor's building wasn't part of the short-term rentals college kids used. It was what looked to be an old mansion renovated into separate apartments.

"Wow," I said, taking in the gray stonework and arched doorway.

"What?" She met me out front of the car, seeking shelter under my umbrella.

"It's gorgeous."

"The building? You like it?"

Her tone of surprise irked me, and I afforded her an annoyed look. "Old buildings can be gorgeous."

"I know. I agree with you. There're too many luxury apartments and new, cookie-cutter homes. I like things that have history and a story to tell." When I huffed, she wrinkled her nose. "What?"

"Nothing. I...I agree with you."

She clucked her tongue. "Is that the first time?"

I stared off into space. "I think so."

She hummed and then backhanded my chest. "Okay, well, thanks for everything. I'll see you on Monday."

I tailed her to the door of the building, and she spun on me when we reached the overhang. "What're you doing?"

I closed the umbrella. "Going in with you."

Her eyes bugged out of her head. "Absolutely not."

Since I hadn't handed her keys off yet, I ignored her and found what I presumed to be the correct one to unlock the door. Lucky guess that it was, I opened it and grinned, waving my hand for her to walk in.

"You don't need to do this whole chivalrous thing." She marched inside and up the stairs.

"No, I don't," I agreed. There were four apartments, and hers was on the second floor. She sighed and tapped her foot while I studied her keys again. As I held up a brass one, she nodded, and I unlocked her apartment door. This time, she stalked inside, probably hoping to shut the door in my face, but she couldn't with my fingers still on the handle.

She stuck out her hand. "Keys."

I deposited them into her palm and shoved my way past her to inspect her place. It was as chaotic as her desk at work. Not dirty but stuff everywhere. Random potted plants, shelves overflowing with books and papers, an abstract statue of what I *believed* was a flamingo. For all the black she wore, her apartment was a shock of color, from her jade-green sofa to her bright-yellow lamp to the framed art on the walls. I couldn't believe Satan let her decorate like a rainbow splattered on her walls.

"All right, well, now that you've forced yourself in here, you can see yourself out."

"Where's your sister?" I asked, turning toward Taylor.

"Work."

I checked the time. It was after seven. "On a Friday night?"

She retrieved her prescription bag then tossed her purse and coat down on a velvet chair that looked straight out of 1928. "Yep."

"What does she do?"

She dropped her head back on her shoulders. "Why does it matter?"

I stuffed my hands into my pockets. "I'm curious."

"She does a lot of things. Right now, she's picked up a few shifts at a bar by the college."

"When will she be back?"

"I don't know." Taylor shrugged. "After two, if she comes home at all."

I didn't like the sound of that and curled my fingers into fists.

"You done with the deposition?" She kicked off her heels

and stomped over to her kitchen, where she filled up a glass with water. I watched as she opened up the bag and set down a packet, counting out four little pills.

"Do you need to take it with food or something?" I asked.

"No."

"Do you—"

"I don't need you looking over my shoulder about this."

"I'm not looking over your shoulder. I'm asking if you need anything."

"I need you to leave," she said and finished off the glass of water before swiping the pills into her hand. She pivoted, clomping down the small hall without looking at me. "I'll see you Monday, Hargrove."

A door closed quietly behind her.

And I blew out a breath, dropping down onto her green couch.

CHAPTER ELEVEN

Taylor

I didn't wait to see if Dean left. I knew he would. He'd done his good dead for the year, soothed his wretched soul or whatever he was trying to do. I didn't care.

I only wanted to complete this process. The doctor had explained I could take the four pills orally if I waited twenty-four hours, but I didn't want to. So that meant I had to insert them into my vagina then lie down for thirty minutes.

After stripping off my clothes, I took a shower, waiting for the tears to come, but they never did. Probably because I'd cried them all out in my car. In front of the last person on earth I'd ever want to.

And yet some small part of me, some atom-sized part of me, was...happy?

No. That light feeling threatening to curl the corner of my mouth couldn't be happiness.

Gratitude? Sure.

Relief? Yeah.

But happiness?

It couldn't be.

Dean Hargrove was my direct competition. The antagonist in my nightmares. The infuriating voice in the back of my head. There was no way I even held an electron's worth of happiness that he was there with me today. I assumed the stress of the whole situation was getting to me, and I turned off the water to wrap a towel around myself, tucking the end in by my armpit before sliding an elastic headband around my hair. Then I shoved the pills up.

The doctor warned me the process could start as little as thirty minutes after, though it would most likely last a few hours. So I tossed my work clothes into the hamper and stepped across the hall to my bedroom to find my comfiest clothes, and I stuck an extra-large maxi pad in my underwear before lying on my bed.

When the thirty minutes were up, I figured I should eat something and made my way to the kitchen. I gasped at the familiar figure standing there, and he whirled around, a soapy sponge in one hand, a pot in the other. He took an immediate step toward me. "Are you okay?"

"Am I okay?" I repeated. "What the hell are you still doing here? I told you to go home."

"No one else is here, so I thought I'd stay."

I licked my suddenly dry lips and rubbed at my forehead. "I'm fine, really. You need to go home."

He turned back to the sink to apparently finish doing the dishes.

"I..." I trailed off, unsure what I was even about to say.

I can do it.

I'm fine on my own.

I don't need you.

None of them felt right.

"I know you can do it," he said, and I wondered if I'd voiced my thoughts out loud. "But I saw them sitting here and had to do something. This place is a mess."

"It's not a mess."

He tipped his head toward the table, where mail had been stacked into a neat pile, then nodded his chin to the counter, where all my bits and bobs were lined up like tiny kitchen soldiers. "Random pieces of mail and salt and pepper shakers on a counter are not a mess."

"It's clutter."

I took the clean pot from him and dried it off before putting it away. "I don't need you to do any of this."

"I did some reading. Google says you might feel nauseous, so you should eat something light." He dried off his hands and pointed to a steaming bowl of soup on the table in the living room, along with a plate of apple slices.

I bit into my lip to keep my chin from quivering, and I breathed through my nose a few times. "Thank you, but I'm fine on my own. I planned it this way. It's the weekend, and I can be home by myself."

"Why?" He strolled over to the couch, and it was only now I noticed he'd ditched his shoes, tie, and coat. His checkered button-down was rolled up to his elbows, and I didn't know if I'd ever noticed his forearms before. Or the indentation of his collarbone, which peeked out at the top of his shirt.

"Why what?" I asked, blinking away from his throat as he plopped down on the couch.

"Why do you need to be home by yourself?"

I swiveled my head side to side, searching for a hidden camera. I didn't know what game he was trying to play, but he wasn't going to win. "Why do you insist on being here? I didn't ask you to do this."

"I know, but I'm not leaving you to go through this alone. I shouldn't be the one to be here, but..." He lifted his arms, eyes wide, as if to say there was no one else, and my skin heated.

"I have people," I snapped, striding over to him, kicking his foot so he'd stop manspreading. His knees knocked back open.

And the asshole set his arms out on either side of him on the back of the cushions like it was *his* fucking couch.

"Why aren't they here?"

I hated him. I hated him so goddam much for not only making me say this out loud but for everything else I had divulged to him today. "Because I don't want them to be here! I can't let them…" I swallowed the lump in my throat and shoved the heels of my hands into my eyes until my vision cleared. "I don't want them to know."

"To know what? That you're not perfect?" He snorted and typed out something on his cell phone. "No one is perfect, Novak. Not even you. Now sit down and eat."

I followed his direction but slapped at his thigh as I sat on the floor. "Get your disgusting feet off my coffee table."

He heaved out a sigh, placing his feet back on the floor.

"I helped myself to a sandwich," he said after I swallowed my first spoonful of chicken noodle soup.

"A sandwich?"

"Yeah, something people make, usually with two pieces of bread and meat, although some people like to add vegetables or—"

I thumped him with the side of my fist, and he laughed. A genuine laugh. It was nice.

I hated that too.

"Google also says to take some pain relievers." He pointed to the two small pills next to a glass of water.

"Did Google also say to make yourself at home in *my* apartment?"

"No, that was my idea." And to prove it, he shifted, nestling down farther into the couch, then reached for an open soda can. "You need to get some coasters in here. You've got rings on the tables." He lifted the small wooden side table. It was barely big enough for maybe two drinks and a candle, and the surface was covered in multiple ring stains. "See?"

I shrugged. "Furniture is meant to be used."

His lip curled in disgust as he set the tiny table back down. "When was the last time you cleaned your car?"

I swallowed down the pills. "Last year sometime."

"I knew it," he mumbled. "I didn't want to say anything before because I'm a gentleman, but your back seat is gross. And the floor?" He pretended to gag. "There was a green stain."

"That was a Shamrock Shake."

"From last March?" He slapped his forehead. "Jesus, Novak, that's disgusting."

"It's my car. I don't care what you think of it."

"You should, though," he said, thrusting his hand out in my direction. "You spent money on it. Or do you not care because you have so much of it? You can go buy a new one whenever you want."

"Don't act as if you don't also come from money. You're not some street urchin begging Scrooge for money."

He shook his head. "Scrooge would treat his possessions with a little more respect."

I swallowed some soup then stuck the spoon in the air. "Funny that you speak of respect when you're not respecting my wishes for you to leave."

He combed his fingers through his short hair, the front sticking up, before dragging his hand down his face. "Listen, I know you don't want me in your business, so I won't ask why you didn't tell your sister or anyone else, for that matter, including whoever the guy was." His shoulders rose, his jaw clenched for a brief moment. "But I'm going to assume it's because of some warped sense of pride, and although I would love nothing better than to knock your sense of self-impor tance down a few notches, I'm not here to fuck with you. I'll stay until your sister gets home. Or, whoever else you want here."

His words were so sincere I easily ignored the dig about my pride and supposed self-importance, but I couldn't meet his gaze when I told him, "My grandmother calls me the rock. I've been the steady, unmovable force in my family for so long, I'm not sure I know how to be anything else."

He didn't say anything, so I went back to eating, and it was a long time before he finally said, "Paper covers rock."

I set my bowl down from where I'd been lapping up the last of the broth. "What?"

"In rock, paper, scissors, paper covers rock. It's not unbeatable."

"I have no idea what you're talking about." I scooted up onto the couch with the plate of apples and held it out to him.

He bit into a slice, speaking around it. "You might be a rock, but that doesn't mean you're supposed to withstand everything. You're strong—really strong—but sometimes you get beat by being covered with paper."

"And let me guess—in this analogy, you're the paper."

He took another apple slice from the plate with a gruff sound. "You can't even admit that was a really good philosophical metaphor." Then he tossed a blanket over me. "Soulless demon."

I smiled into the cream knit blanket and laid my head on the end of the couch, while he aimed the remote at the TV. "What do you want to watch?"

"I don't care."

He scrolled through my streaming apps. "What's your favorite movie?"

I leaned over to set the empty plate on the table then burrowed back down in the blanket. "I don't know."

"You don't know?" He eyed me suspiciously. "How do you not know?"

I shrugged.

"What is it?"

"I don't know, maybe *Donnie Darko*," I said.

He tapped his finger on the remote a few times. "*Donnie Darko* is your favorite movie? The one with Jake Gyllenhaal hallucinating with the rabbit and the end of the world?"

"Yeah."

He huffed a laugh. "That's not your favorite movie."

I sneered at him. "Yes, it is."

"No, it's not."

"Yes, it is," I bit out. "You can't tell me what *my* favorite movie is."

He sent me a reprimanding glare. "*Donnie Darko* isn't your favorite movie. That's the movie you say when people ask what your favorite movie is, but it's not *actually* your favorite. I want to know what your real favorite movie is, the one you watch whenever it's on cable. The one you know all the words to and makes you feel good."

I sat stone silent.

"What is it?"

"I don't know," I said.

"Yes, you do," he countered.

"No, I—"

"Taylor, stop fighting with me over this and just tell me what your favorite fucking movie is." He dropped his elbow on the back of the couch to hold his head up like I was giving him pains. "Christ, everything is an argument with you."

And I didn't know what shocked me more, the fact that he used my first name or that I told him, "*Parent Trap*. The Lindsay Lohan version."

Without a word, he lifted the remote and found it on the

streaming service. Then he folded his arms over his chest, lowering down to rest his head on the back of the couch.

I studied him for a minute. How he wetted his lips with his tongue. The same tongue that mere moments ago formed my name. We'd never first-named each other to our faces. It was always our last names or "demon spawn" or "asshole." Never Taylor or Dean.

Calling me by my first name felt intimate. But I supposed what we were doing now, sitting here in my darkly lit living room after he escorted me to a clinic to get an abortion, was more intimate than anything I'd ever done in my life.

It was more than I'd shared with anyone else. Ever.

"Thank you," I said, and he turned his gaze to me, the colors of the television flickering over the planes of his face. His forehead that often wrinkled in thought, his nose that was ever so slightly upturned, giving him a boyish air, his square chin and angled jaw covered by the neatly trimmed beard, it all came together in the exact right amount of handsomeness. Not stop-dead hot, but the kind of handsome that eased you in, lulled you into comfort. He was the kind of handsome that would age well.

How unfortunate.

Though he didn't verbally respond to me, he slowly reached out his hand as if asking permission. When I didn't stop him, he placed his hand on my leg, patting it over the blanket, and left it there.

Until the cramps started, and I sat up, curling over.

"You okay?" he asked, and I shook my head, breathing through the twisting pain in my abdomen and back. "No, of course you're not okay. That was a dumb question. What do you need?"

I winced, pressing my hand against my stomach. "I have a heating pad in the closet in the bathroom."

He immediately hopped up, his footsteps fading and then returning. "Where do you want it?"

I set it under the waistband of my lounge pants, but he stopped me. "Wait. Wait."

He searched through the drawers of my kitchen, finding a dish towel. "Use this so you don't get scorched." He kneeled on the floor, telling me, "Lie down." When I complied, he lifted up my sweatshirt a few inches and laid the towel across my torso before setting the heating pad on top of it. He tucked it back under the band of my pants. "How's that?"

"Good." But I grimaced.

"What else do you need?"

"Nothing."

We sat in silence for a few moments, his mouth twisting to the side, until he broke up the quiet with a question. "Why didn't you tell him?"

I didn't need to know who *him* was, and I shook my head. "You think I should've had a baby with a guy I met at a Christmas party?"

"No, but he should be here. At least."

I swiped my hand over my clammy forehead, breathing through a fresh wave of cramps. "So he could be about as useful as he was that night? No, thank you."

Dean smirked. "It was terrible, huh?"

"Really? You think *this* is the time for jokes?"

He tucked a few strands of hair behind my ear, and if his fingertip lingered at the bottom of my lobe, I was sure I was hallucinating from the pain. Another reason why I couldn't keep my stupid mouth shut. The honesty tumbled out like I was under some sort of spell. "I forgot to take my birth control pill that day. Which I don't ever forget to do, but I guess I was distracted."

"By the octopus tattoo? Understandable. Distracted me too."

An agonized moan escaped my throat when my stomach constricted, and pain shot down the backs of my legs.

Dean wrapped a gentle hand around my arm, squeezing it reassuringly. "You don't have to explain it to me, but if it'll make you feel better..."

I angled my head, meeting his gaze to admit yet another truth I'd buried. "I don't know for sure that he used a condom."

"*What?*" The single word echoed through my apartment.

I grimaced in discomfort but also in embarrassment. "I saw it. I watched him open it and put it on, but it was after he was like 'Are you sure? We don't need it.'"

Dean dropped his chin toward his chest, folding his hands in front of his face, mumbling something I couldn't hear.

And I kept right on going as if we were best friends. "I can't be sure he kept it on. I was..." I didn't want to tell Dean I had been so busy trying not to envision *him* while having sex with another guy that I wasn't paying attention, so I hedged. "After it was over, I didn't see it, and I was... I just wanted to leave. But I should have been more careful. I should've—"

"Don't say it," he seethed, his lips curled up so I could see his perfectly straight and white teeth. "Don't say it's your fault. Forgetting to take one pill in your entire life is an accident. Purposely removing a condom is sexual assault."

My eyes stung. I hadn't wanted to acknowledge the possibility of someone intentionally doing that to me. Or how I felt like my body wasn't my own for days after. I didn't want to face reality. "I did it to myself," I said quietly, curling up on my side, keeping one hand on the heating pad, and bending my other arm to cradle my head. "I wasn't as careful as I normally am."

"So is that what this is?" he asked in a near whisper. "You're punishing yourself by going through this alone?"

For the first time all day, I felt my mouth threatening to curve up into a smile. "I'm not alone. You're here."

He laid his hands on the edge of the cushion by my head, one on top of the other, and propped his chin on them, our faces so close, I could count each individual whisker in his beard. He let out a deep breath that sounded irritated. "We could sue."

"Who? Ace?"

He rolled his eyes. "I can't believe you had sex with a guy named Ace. What the fuck is wrong with you?"

I rolled my eyes right back at him. "First of all, I already thought about my options, and it's impossible to prove anything, and there are no laws on the books about stealthing in PA."

"There should be," he muttered.

"And second of all, I don't go around judging your sexual partners."

"Yes, you do. You're always disparaging them. At the party, you were talking shit about Shauna."

"She was wearing a light-up sweater." That alone was deserving of scorn.

"This from the girl who nearly bit my head off for judging your bartender?"

Our gazes clashed in the thick silence between us, neither one of us conceding *this* truth. That we were highly aware of everything the other did, both in and outside of the office. And now certainly wasn't the time to explore why. Especially when it felt like someone had their fist twisted around my insides and was pulling them out.

"I have to go to the bathroom," I mumbled, clumsily standing up from the couch.

Dean held his hand out to steady me, and I waddled to the bathroom, bent in half. Closing the door behind me, I sat on the toilet and threw away the soiled maxi pad then breathed through the waves of cramps. I was sure Dean could hear my muffled groans of pain, but I was too uncomfortable to care.

After I didn't know how long, I finally cleaned myself up, put on a new pad, sucked down a few more painkillers, then swiped a cool washcloth over my sweat-dampened skin before opening the bathroom door. The hall was dim, but Dean's dark form was there, on the floor, back against the opposite wall, legs outstretched, arms folded, chin down.

"Wh-what are you doing?"

He tipped his head up, momentarily stunned, like a guard caught falling asleep on duty. "Everything all right?"

I rubbed at my still-cramping stomach, though it had lessened quite a bit, and I shrugged my answer.

He pushed up to his full height. "I was making sure you were okay."

"On the floor?"

His gaze shifted behind my shoulder to the bathroom. "You were in there for a long time. I got…" He rubbed his hand over his jaw. "I was worried, but I figured you wouldn't want me knocking on the door, so I thought I'd sit here and listen in case you needed anything."

"You didn't have to," I said, even though everything in me wanted to wrap my arms around him and bury my face in his neck.

So I did.

He tensed, arms frozen in understandable shock, but after a beat, he dropped them around me, holding me tight. As if he knew I needed someone—him—to hold me together. I felt his hands lock at my lower back, his biceps tugging me closer, and while I usually took evil pleasure in seeing eye to eye with him in my heels, I was appreciative for the few inches of difference between us now. That I could fit against him snugly, inhale the clean, starchy scent of his clothes, feel the bristles of his beard against my temple when I ducked my forehead against his throat. He was my enemy, and yet I was safe and warm and content.

"You gonna cry again?" he asked.

"No." The one word was muffled against his throat.

"Good. You're an ugly crier."

I pushed away to find him grinning brightly even in the dark, totally unapologetic. He pulled out his cell phone from his pocket, the screen lighting up his face. "It's almost eleven," he told me. "Are you tired?"

"Not tired, but I could lie down."

He put his phone away. "You want me to tuck you in?"

"No." *Yes.*

He pressed his hand to my lower back, his fingertips slipping beneath the hem of my sweatshirt. "Come on."

He pointed to the door across the hall and threw a questioning glance over his shoulder, before leading me into my bedroom.

"I don't want to hear it about what a mess it is," I said when he flicked on the light.

"I'd never."

I huffed and slunk over to the bed, rolling under the covers with all the dignity of a drunk sailor. With a slow spin, he didn't hide his inspection, but he didn't utter a word. Not even when he used his index finger to lift up the bra I had hanging on the closet handle to dry. He merely replaced it and walked out of the room.

I curled on my side, trying to find a comfortable position, though that seemed like a useless task, and after another flip flop, Dean shuffled back into my room. He set a glass of ice water on the table next to me, along with a mug of tea, crackers, and my cell phone, which I'd left in the living room when I'd originally stumbled my way into the bathroom.

"I like blue Powerade when I'm not feeling well, but you don't have any." He plugged in the heating pad and handing it to me. "Should probably add it to the grocery list."

"I'll get right on that." When I tried to sit up, he dropped down to the bed by my hip and helped to prop me up against the pillows. He held out the mug of steaming tea. "My sister was always drinking tea when she didn't feel well."

I accepted it carefully and sipped on the chamomile drink. He'd even added a squeeze of lemon.

What an aggravating puzzle this Dean Hargrove was.

He watched me take a few more sips then took the cup from me. After he set it back on the table, he shifted, allowing me to lie back down, and he did indeed tuck the covers in all around me.

He settled a hand on either side of my waist, leveling his face over mine, his eyes making a circuit of my features. He frowned at whatever he saw there. "Are you still in a lot of pain?"

"Some."

He nodded and stood. When I thought he was finally going to leave, he didn't. Instead, he rounded the corner of my bed and flopped down next to me, crossing his legs at the ankles.

"Are you serious right now?" I said, though it didn't have any of my normal bite.

He readjusted the angle of his head. "You need firmer pillows." He whacked the one beneath him. "I'll need to see a chiropractor after this."

"Feel free to leave anytime."

He didn't look at me. Didn't even acknowledge my words.

But he did curl his arm behind his head and take out his cell phone. "You like the Stones?"

"The Stones?"

He slanted his gaze to me, eyebrows pinched together. "The Rolling Stones."

"Oh yeah. I guess."

"You guess," he huffed and pressed play on some music app so soothing tones filled the space between us, Mick Jagger crooning on about wild horses not being able to drag him away.

Next to me, Dean scrolled on his phone, his foot absently keeping time with the music, and I moved closer to the middle of the mattress, closing my eyes. When the song ended, I asked, "Play it again?"

And he did.

CHAPTER TWELVE

I was normally the first person into the office, after Sandy, but this morning, I lagged behind. Not because I was still a little tired or recovering, but because I was afraid to face Dean.

At some point in the middle of Friday night, I'd fallen asleep with Dean still in my bed. When I had woken up, it was a little after seven in the morning, and the left side of my bed was cold. The only evidence he had been there at all was the indentation in my "flat" pillow and the texts on my phone.

> Some Asshole: Your sister came home around 3, or at least I hope it was your sister.
>
> Some Asshole: Otherwise, sorry you were murdered in your sleep.
>
> Some Asshole: I didn't know if or what you were going to tell her, so I waited until I heard her bedroom door close and snuck out.
>
> Some Asshole: Hope you feel better today.

I was too tired and still too embarrassed about falling apart in his presence to text him back, but now it was Monday, and I couldn't avoid him.

I had to face him. Face the man whom I had ever only thought of as my adversary. Face the man whom I'd told *everything* to.

Gritting my teeth, I opened the door to the office, well aware I was the last one in. With a wave to Sandy, I strode into the open work area, noting Seth at his desk, his head down over his keyboard. The intern, Ayaan, was here today too, at a tiny desk in the corner, and I offered him a tip of my chin as I hung up my coat and purse then sat down at my desk with a long exhale. I was saved from seeing Dean, for a few more minutes, at least.

As my computer booted up, I checked my planner for my meetings and appointments then read through my emails and made a to-do list for the day. Now that Reed had officially handed over his files, my days mostly consisted of sorting through all the information, finding out which clients needed immediate assistance and which simply needed me to check in with them.

I was on the phone when Dean strolled to his desk, a cup of coffee in his hand. His eyes stayed on mine for a second longer than normal—or what was normal previous to Friday—as he dropped down into his seat. Since I was behind him, I had a perfect view of how he held a pen in his right hand, idly spinning it between his fingers, a trick I'd never learned to master, but one that I now assumed was due to his dexterity from playing guitar. As I finally hung up with the client, Dean scratched at the back of his head, fingers scrubbing through the neatly trimmed hair above his shirt collar, and as if he knew I was gawking, he spun his chair, dragging his gaze to the side.

I dropped my chin, scribbling nonsense on a piece of paper like I was in the middle of something super important before slowly lifting my head back up to find his eyes on me, the cap of his pen between his teeth.

He tilted his head to the side, asking a nonverbal question with a brow raise. *How are you?*

I offered him a half smile. *Okay.*

He nodded and swung his chair back around.

So, for the first interaction since...everything, it wasn't so bad. I got back to work—actual work, not pretend scribbling—for the next half hour until Dominic called me into his office. I sat down across from him, and we spent a few minutes chitchatting before he got down to business.

"I know Reed put you on the Mackenzie suit, but I just got off the phone with Chris Raber."

"Chris Raber?" I'd spoken to him this morning. He was my first phone call, and I thought it went well, especially since I wasn't fully present, with my attention lingering on the back of Dean's head.

"Yeah, listen," he started, readjusting his position in his chair, and I knew whatever he was about to tell me wasn't going to be good. "Though I don't agree with his decision, and I did try to talk him out of it, he wants someone else on the case."

My jaw flapped open. "But...I...we've... Everything was fine. We'd emailed a few times, and I thought..."

Dominic rubbed his hand along his cheek. "I know. This isn't your fault. This is an old boys' club thing."

I leaned forward in my chair. "Dom, you can't do this."

"I'm sorry. I don't want to. I hate to, but we can't lose them as a client."

"This is bullshit."

He nodded. "It is."

"So, you agree, but you're still not going to fight for me?"

"I did try to talk him out of it, but I think he assumed you were a man from your email signature."

"That's not my fault. I'm a woman, and I'm also a Novak." I shot up from my chair, extending my arm toward the door, as if the sign for the office was right outside. "Doesn't that mean anything to him?"

Dominic held my gaze. "This is nothing against you."

I opened my mouth to keep arguing, but it would only prove Raber right. Whatever backward ideas he thought about me, about women, that we were too emotional or too dumb, I wasn't going to spend any more time arguing against them. They weren't true, and my worth wasn't based on one man's stupid fucking opinion. Instead, I gave Dominic a nod and held my head high as I marched back to my desk to get back to work.

That was my only choice.

A few minutes passed before Dominic called Dean into his office, and I only needed one guess to know what it was about. Five minutes later, Dean walked back out and sank down into his chair. He didn't bother to look at me, and I was glad. I wouldn't have been able to hold my tongue.

After working for a few minutes, Dean made his way to Seth's desk, where I heard them murmuring about the Mackenzie case. Seth had been assisting Reed with it, so I supposed he'd now be helping Dean, and I could feel the title of partner slipping through my fingers.

I whirled away, traipsing to the break room, needing a few minutes to grind my molars in peace. But, of course, I couldn't even get that.

"I'm sorry," Dean said behind me.

I sighed out my irritation. "It's not your fault."

"But we've done this before. You're going to blame me."

I refused to turn around to face him and reached for the open box of grocery store donut holes.

"You gonna talk to me?" he asked, voice laced with frustration.

I forced myself to swallow the stale donut hole. "About what?"

I heard him exhale, his shoe squeak on the floor, the brush of fabric. "I don't know. This. Friday. Everything."

Intellectually, I knew Dean didn't have anything to do with Raber changing his mind, but it was a harder pill to swallow emotionally. Dean had been there for me, had taken care of me, but now we were back to our regularly scheduled programming.

He could have refused to take the case, though if it were me, I would have happily accepted the client. I couldn't fault him. But I was still pissed about it.

We'd gone from enemies to...not quite friends and back to enemies, and I had whiplash.

I wiped my fingers off on a napkin and slowly turned. We had barely a few inches of space between us, and I folded my arms to keep myself together. Keep any more secrets from escaping. Keep the caress of a gaze away from me.

"Guess we're back to where we started, huh?" he said after a while.

"Guess so."

Out of the corner of my eye, I noted Seth pop into the room, take one look at us, then spin right back around. "Try not to get any blood on the floor when you stab each other."

Dean let out a noisy breath, nostrils flared, his jaw tight.

"I guess I should say thank you," I said. "For Friday."

He nodded once.

"And fuck you for today."

He stepped away from me, lips pursed, holding back whatever he wanted to say. I moved to brush past him, but he caught my arm, stilling me.

"I liked you better when you were honest with me," he grated, close enough that I could smell the mint of his gum.

I ripped my forearm out of his grip. "I liked you better when you didn't steal my clients."

He pivoted us and crowded my space, forcing my lower back against the counter. "This is a shitty situation, but I can't tell what's bothering you more. That you lost it because you're a woman, or that you couldn't keep it, even with your last name."

I pushed my palms against his chest. "How does it feel to win by default?"

"Feels like a win no matter what." He grasped my hips with his hands, and I hadn't realized until then that my fingers were still on him, curling into the fabric of his shirt, the same sky blue of his eyes.

My focus unintentionally dropped down to his throat, where his Adam's apple lifted on a swallow. Where I'd rested my forehead days ago. I wasn't only fighting for a promotion but against the pull of his fingers on my waistband, against the urge to lay my head on his shoulder and give in.

But that was not who I was. That was not what I did.

I was the rock. A fighter. I never yielded.

And I wouldn't start now.

I shoved away from him. "You better get back to work. Mackenzie goes to arbitration in a few weeks."

I rushed back to my desk and worked with earbuds in for the rest of the day.

By the time I got home, Kennedy was on her way out.

"Where you going?" I asked, setting my keys on the table by the door.

She looped her purse across her body. "Meeting Jordan."

"I thought you were taking a break."

She shrugged, a half smile crawling across her face. "I'm just too lovable."

I playfully elbowed her. "You coming back tonight?"

Again, that secretive smile. "Maybe."

Obviously not. "Be safe."

She waved her hand over her shoulder, and I shut the door behind her before heading to my room to change. Growing up, I'd been a cross-country runner. Being outside with my feet slapping the trail in a constant rhythm was like meditation for me. I still ran, but in the winter, I needed to use a gym treadmill, which wasn't at all close to the peace I had running miles outside, but I had to take what I could get.

Bundled back up in my parka, I braved the bitter winter wind. Only a few more weeks until the temperature would rise and the sun lingered a little longer in the sky, and I could finally get back to my normal routine. At the gym, I nodded to the girl at the desk, dropped my stuff off in a locker, then made my way to my favorite treadmill in the corner, already sticking my earbuds in. I couldn't stand the clatter of the gym bros dropping their weights and the chatter of the people on the cardio machines while they talked on the phone. Like, are you working out, or are you gossiping?

But as I neared *my* treadmill, my steps faltered.

Because Dean fucking Hargrove was on it.

I stomped over to him, mashing my fist on the stop button. He stumbled, barely catching himself before he fell off. His blazing eyes found me. "What the fuck is wrong with you?"

"What the fuck are you doing at my gym? On my treadmill?"

He wiped sweat away from his forehead with the sleeve of his shirt, though it was already soaked through at the neck. With him in his shorts and tee, I couldn't avoid looking at him.

At his veiny forearms, which might as well have been crafted just for me. At the breadth of his shoulders under the cotton. The sprinkle of light hair on his legs.

"So, you own the gym now?"

I cocked my hip, crossing my arms. "I'm here almost every day, and I've never once seen you here."

He shrugged. "I just joined."

"Why?" I nearly whined. "Can't you find somewhere else?"

His eyes coasted around the whole of the gym. "From all my stalking, I figured you'd be here."

My jaw went slack, and he smiled like I was too easy to rile up. Obviously, I was.

"I picked the place closest to my house, Novak. I have better things to do than play detective about where you work out."

I didn't call attention to the fact that he sought me out Friday in my car and then forced his way to my appointment and into my apartment.

"Fine." I stepped up onto the treadmill next to his. "Let's see if you can keep up."

He breathed out a miffed sound and started his machine again, peering over at my speed, which was barely a jog, then dialed his to the same rate.

"Easy," he murmured.

"It's only the warm-up."

"I'm already warm. I've been on here for ten minutes."

"Big, tough man," I said in a baby voice, and I didn't need to see his eye roll. I could feel it.

Three minutes later, I increased my speed to a fast jog, so Dean did the same.

"I ran cross-country in high school," I told him conversationally. "Were you an athlete?"

"Nope."

I angled my head ever so slightly to check out his form. It was crap. "I can tell."

"Fuck off," he said, fighting a smile.

After a few minutes, I upped the speed once more, finding my rhythm now. I gave myself over to the reverberation of the strides, sank into my breaths, and let the tension drain from my body. From my mind.

"I needed to find something else for my stress," Dean said after a while. "Before, I would work on my house and play music and..."

I was curious about the dangling thought but was too scared to know the answer. Fearful it would be the same as mine. That he fucked his stress away.

"The past few months, it hasn't been enough," he went on. "My sister talked me into yoga, but that wasn't for me."

"Me either," I agreed. "It's too slow for me."

"I need something loud and hard to get me out of my head."

I almost tripped over my feet when my focus darted toward him. He needed something *loud* and *hard*.

Oh god, my mind was in the gutter.

I swept thoughts of echoing moans and stinging thrusts out of my mind. "So you're here at the gym?"

"Apparently trying to race you." He turned his eyes on me and grinned.

I raised my brows then increased my speed and incline to a full-out run, and Dean followed, although I could immediately tell he couldn't keep up.

"Jesus, woman," he panted after a minute. "What are... what are you trying to do to me?"

"You give up?"

He pressed his index finger into the button to decrease the

speed to a walk and bent his head, breathing heavily. When I laughed, he muttered, "Fuck off."

I decreased my speed to a jog. "You have to build up your stamina."

I didn't miss the way his eyes raked over me. "Guess so."

"It'll take a few weeks."

"You gonna train me?" he asked, and even though I could tell he was joking, I lifted a shoulder.

"I'm here every night after work until it gets warmer out. Then I run outside."

He merely nodded.

And that was how we started running together every day.

CHAPTER THIRTEEN

Dean

I had a problem. Besides the desperate need to gulp down air, I had trouble keeping my attention ahead of me.

For two weeks, the evil woman next to me had worn leggings and a bra to the gym every single day.

A *bra*. That was it. A few inches covering her chest, leaving a large expanse of skin open along her torso and back. Of course, they were always black, but today, her bra was shiny with a little Nike swoosh in the corner.

I didn't know when I started having a thing for women who were straight as a board with a distinct six-pack, but here I was, trying not to slobber all over Taylor fucking Novak.

"You giving up already?" she asked.

I took my treadmill down to a slow walk. "I gotta head out early." When she arched her brow, I explained, "Poker night."

"Poker night?"

"Yeah." I planted my hands on my hips. "Something I do with friends. You have heard that term before, right? *Friends*?"

"Vaguely." A ghost of a smile graced her lips.

Not that the two of us often gossiped together, but I racked my brain for any time I'd heard her talking about friends, and I couldn't think of any.

"What are you up to this weekend?" I asked in an effort to find out more. "Big plans? Sleepover and pillow fight with your girlfriends?"

"If this is your piss-poor attempt at an invite, it's not working," she said, keeping steady pace as she ran. She was like a goddamn greyhound, barely broke a sweat. I didn't know how she did it.

"So, you are having a sleepover? What would one wear? Something slinky?"

"You wish. And no sleepovers for me. That stopped in middle school."

As I was a thirty-year-old man, my memories of what my sister did in high school were hazy, but I was sure she was still sleeping at her friends' houses then, and I was unable to stop the question before it came out of my mouth. "Seems young to quit sleepovers with your friends."

"My dad got sick when I was fourteen. Staying up late, talking about boys, seemed insignificant when your father's dying."

She said it so evenly, so plainly, it knocked the wind right out of me, and I turned the treadmill off. I couldn't keep walking with that revelation sitting right there. I'd known the family history, that Barbara's elder son, Samuel, the one who would've taken over the Philadelphia office, passed away from brain cancer.

"Was high school hard after that?" I asked because I'd almost dropped out of law school when Patrick had died.

She kept right on running as she answered. "Most people probably think his dying made me a bitch, but I was one before that. I never had much patience for people. Never felt the need to belong or join or whatever."

"Can't picture you as a Girl Scout."

She snorted a laugh. "Definitely not." She hit the console to lower her speed to a brisk walk. "After my dad...the few friends I had stopped inviting me. Nobody wants to be friends with the sad and angry girl."

After a moment, I stepped off my treadmill and stood next to hers, curving a hand around the frame of her machine. "So, what's your excuse now?"

"For what? Not having friends?" She swiped the back of her hand along her forehead then sipped from the water bottle she had placed in the cupholder. "I'm still the sad and angry girl, and I'd rather not like anyone to know."

"You let me know."

She stopped her machine and hopped down to the floor right in front of me. Without her heels, she actually had to lift her chin to meet my eyes, and I took endless joy from that. She smelled of sweat and her godforsaken cinnamon-and-flower scent. I was now convinced hell didn't smell of fire and brimstone, it smelled of Taylor Novak.

"Because deep inside, you're a sad and angry boy too," she told me, and I ticked my head to the side, wondering if Satan had granted her superpowers when he set her free on earth. In answer to my silent question, she said, "You put on the show that I refuse to."

If I weren't already hot and sweaty, I would have become so. "I have friends. I like my friends. Love them."

"So, why don't you tell them?" she asked casually, as if she hadn't punched me right in the throat. She strolled away, toward the wall, where she sat down, stretching out her legs, reaching her fingers to her toes.

I shadowed her. "Tell them what? That I'm sad and angry?"

She nodded, and my hamstrings cried out as I tried to touch my toes. I held the position for a few seconds then relaxed. "I'll tell them when you tell yours."

Her mouth teased a wicked grin. "But I don't have friends to tell."

"You have me."

"You aren't my friend," she said, leaning back on her hands.

"No? Then what are we?"

She squinted, toggling her head back and forth. "I'm not sure. Maybe frenemies."

"Frenemies?" I repeated with a laugh, and when she nodded, I held out my hand. "Okay. Frenemies."

She met my handshake, palm to palm, her eyes holding mine, and I swore I could feel her trying to mentally burrow into my mind. I let my index finger drift to her inner wrist, dragging along the soft skin over her pulse point, and I could see into her mind. Into the simmering emotions she kept tightly locked up, and how she hated that I'd witnessed her break-down. She only ever showed the world how strong she was, but I—the guy she supposedly hated—got behind her walls.

I was the enemy in foreign territory, and I probably should have run screaming. But I was willing to let her break me and carry me back to her lair.

Which was why I needed to leave before she could.

I stood abruptly. "I'll see you Monday."

She offered me one heartbreakingly tender smile. "Have fun with your friends."

Then I got the hell out of there.

I was late getting home, so I sped through a shower and change of clothes, and by the time I trotted downstairs, Hank and Ethan had let themselves in.

"Where were you?" Ethan asked, setting out the black folding chairs for the table we used.

"The gym."

Instead of helping set up, Hank sat on his ass on my couch with a bag of chips. "Since when have you started going to a gym?"

"Since a few weeks ago."

"You turning into a gym rat?" he asked, crumbs falling all over the floor.

"Come on, bro." I stole the bag out of his grasp and stomped into the kitchen to retrieve a bunch of paper plates, handing him one. "Act like a human."

"Plates and utensils are a modern invention. We don't actually need them."

"And I don't actually need you at my house," I said, pointing at the table, a silent direction for him to eat at it.

"You're touchy today." Hank plopped down on one of the folding chairs. "Shouldn't you be less stressed after being at the gym? Or is it all that testosterone making you angry?"

I didn't answer and lifted my gaze to Ethan, who had his head tipped to the side as he mindlessly flipped poker chips between his fingers.

"I'm not angry," I told him quietly, and he nodded.

"Never said you were."

Taylor's words echoed in my head. *Because deep inside, you're a sad and angry boy too.*

These guys were two of my oldest friends. I could tell them the truth. I should tell them the truth.

That I felt like I'd been standing still for years. No matter what I accomplished, no matter how many "adult" things I checked off the list, I still felt as if I was that twenty-four-year-old in the middle of my apartment staring at the dead body of my best friend. Despite everything I'd tried, I still felt frightened and alone, guilt-ridden and pissed at myself, knowing I should have done more to help Patrick. To save him. I was sad and angry that day, and I couldn't do a goddamn thing about it.

So, I took the beer offered to me and downed about half of it in a few gulps, right in time for Seth and Nadir, a neighbor from down the street, to show up.

I'd started hosting these once-a-month poker nights about three years ago as a way to fill up the time and space of this house, which, at the time, was in need of a major renovation. But now, I was starting to see, no matter how hard I'd tried to show my friends—the world, really—that I was fine, I had moved on, I hadn't. I couldn't move on. I didn't know if there was such a thing as moving on from grief.

Because for the last six years, I'd been standing still.

And in the middle of a game that I'd all but forgotten about, I picked up my phone and texted Taylor.

> I was thinking about what you said.

BEELZEBUB

Oh yeah?

BEELZEBUB

You're going to take it easier on the Axe?

> It's NOT Axe. I told you.

BEELZEBUB

Well, whatever it is, you don't have to bathe in it.

> It's beard oil.

BEELZEBUB

The three whiskers on your face barely qualify as a beard.

> Stop pretending you don't love it.

As I recall, you had your face all up in there last month.

BEELZEBUB

I don't remember. I was in a bad place and nearly delirious.

I remember.

It took her so long to respond, the current round had ended with Seth taking the pot, and Nadir had already dealt a new hand.

BEELZEBUB

Is there a reason you're texting me right now?

BEELZEBUB

Shouldn't you be talking to your friends?

I have a question.

BEELZEBUB

So get on with it, Hargrove.

Do you think it would have been easier or harder for you if you'd hung out with your friends after your dad died?

Another long while passed, another hand completed and begun.

BEELZEBUB

I couldn't say. Why?

Just thinking that it hasn't been any easier for me, even when I make sure to keep my friends together. Fill up my time.

BEELZEBUB

I'm sure it's like the truth. It lies somewhere in between.

You're probably right.

Her next message was a screenshot of my text to her. **You're probably right.** With the time stamp.

BEELZEBUB

Evidence.

I laughed and placed my phone down to find Ethan, Hank, Nadir, and Seth all staring at me.

"What?"

"Who have you been texting this whole time?" Hank asked.

Nadir tsked. "We should implement a no phones at the table policy."

Seth tapped his cards on the table. "Is it a chick?"

I didn't answer, and Hank slapped my back. "Of course it is."

I shook my head at Ethan's steady gaze on me. "Don't you start."

"I didn't say anything."

"Yeah, but you're taking mental notes so you can run home and tell Laney everything."

"You're so pussy-whipped," Seth said with a chuckle, and Ethan's jaw popped.

"So?"

"So..." Seth looked around at the rest of us. "Who wants to be wrapped around their girl's finger like that?"

Nadir, who was married with three kids, Hank, and Ethan all raised their hands. I laughed into my beer, and Seth sucked in air through his teeth.

"You guys are pathetic. Never find me simping for a chick."

Ethan glared at him. "If you were blessed to be with anyone half as good and perfect as Laney, you'd be on your knees *simping* any chance you got."

While I generally wasn't a fan of hearing all the ins and outs of Laney and Ethan's relationship, I had to give it up to him. He'd promised he'd take good care of her, and he was.

Seth grumbled something incomprehensible and slumped back in his chair.

"So, Dean, baby," Hank started, a pretzel stick hanging out of his mouth like a cigarette, "who're you talking to now?"

"Somebody from work," I said, and Seth's mouth dropped while Ethan set his cards down on the table.

"Taylor?" he asked, a little too interested.

"We're friends," I replied immediately, which clearly was too defensive because Seth smacked his hand to his head.

"You're kidding."

"No. We're...getting to know each other." I tried and failed at a casual explanation.

"But she's a bitch. What more do you need to know?"

I shifted so fast in my chair, I rattled the table as my spine snapped ramrod straight. "Don't call her that."

Silence descended.

Seth's cheeks colored. "But she is. You said it yourself."

I was the only one she permitted to see behind her frigid bitch mask, and I was the only one allowed to call her that. "Say it again, and we're going to have a problem."

He let out a breath and tossed his cards on the table before raising his hands. "Whatever, man. I thought you hated her."

"I do."

"Don't sound very convincing," Ethan said quietly, and I ignored him.

"Maybe you should fuck it out," Hank suggested, and Nadir snickered behind his cards.

"I'm not fucking Taylor."

Hank tried on a deliberate look of scandal. "I didn't mean Taylor. I meant Seth."

"Shut up," I said, and all of us broke up into laughter, cutting the tension.

Though I was still tempted to punch Seth in the face. The kid could do with a punch in the face from someone, anyone. Knock some sense into him.

Taylor would definitely enjoy doing it.

And I'd applaud her from the sidelines.

That was the scariest thought of all. I had no interest in standing in front of her anymore. I'd much rather stand next to her and give her whatever made her happy, including violence.

CHAPTER FOURTEEN

"Are you sure you don't want to take any of this food home to eat?"

I shook my head, holding up my hand. "I'm sure."

My grandmother couldn't blame her cooking skills on her age. She had never been great at it. Her chicken had always been dry.

Nan shrugged and wrapped up the leftovers in tinfoil then stuck them in her refrigerator before sitting back down across from me. She had a box of mixed chocolates and lifted the lid, silently offering them to me. I helped myself to a raspberry-cream-filled one.

"Who'd you get these from? Your boyfriend?" I teased.

She studied the label before choosing a dark chocolate piece with caramel. "Joseph. He lives upstairs."

"Joseph," I repeated with a raise of my brow.

"Stop it, you. He's only being nice."

"Oh yes. I am always gifted chocolates by men who are only being nice."

"As well you should be," she said, completely ignoring my sarcasm. When I didn't respond, she wiped at her bottom lip with a napkin, then sipped on her water. "Why aren't you receiving more chocolates and gifts?"

I pointed to my face.

She reached for me as if I had some confidence issue. "You have a lovely face."

"I have what is colloquially referred to as resting bitch face."

"Oh." She nodded sagely. "I also have that. Though I don't believe it had a name when I was younger."

"But Pop-Pop didn't mind your RBF."

"RBF." She laughed in delight as if I'd made that up all by myself. "No, he didn't mind. But he was also more evolved."

"In that regard," I said, leaning back in my chair, "men have not made much progress in the last fifty years." I shook my head when Nan offered me another chocolate. "But you should try this one." I pointed to an oblong-shaped chocolate. "Coconut cream inside."

"Yum." She picked up the candy with her long, refined fingers. Though they were now weathered and pale with years, she still got her nails done weekly.

"Have you thought about moving in with Uncle Kevin any more?"

She leveled me with a reproachful frown. "Is that why you're here? To talk me into it?"

"No." I tried my best to appear offended, although I had been tasked by my uncle with persuading her. "This is our monthly dinner."

She crossed her arms, the picture of stoic independence. She had been born and raised in Philadelphia and always said she never planned on leaving. After my grandfather had passed, everyone assumed she'd move out of the house they'd lived in, but she was steadfast and determined to stay. It was only three years ago we'd convinced her to sell their house and move in to this apartment, where she would be surrounded by people if she needed anything. I talked to her every day, and Uncle Kevin was with her as often as possible, but we walked a fine line of supporting her and pissing her off by being too overbearing. She had a pretty good cold shoulder when she wanted to.

"I'm not going to move in with someone else to live like a pet."

"Nan, come on, that's hyperbolic. You'd have just as much independence there as you do here, but if you needed something, Uncle Kevin would be right there."

"Yes, because I'd be in a rocking chair like some old crone, knitting."

"Do you even know how to knit?"

She waved the question away. "I'm staying here. End of story."

"Whatever you want to do," I acquiesced, noting the time. It was almost nine, and I'd been there since six. "I guess I better get going."

"Next time, see if Kennedy will come," she said, standing up when I did.

"I'll try, but you know her." My phone buzzed. "Speak of the devil."

"It's your sister?"

I nodded as I read the text message from her informing me Dean was at her bar. I answered absently as I put my coat on.

OK. Why are you telling me?

KENNEDY

IDK. Thought it might be of interest. It's a bachelor party.

"What's she saying?" Nan asked, shoving the box of chocolates at me.

I shook my head and stuffed my phone into my coat pocket. "Nothing. Letting me know she saw Dean at the bar she's working at."

"Oh?"

I pointed a stern finger at her. "Don't get any ideas in your head. Nothing's going on. We're..." I nearly choked on the word. "Friends."

"Friends?" She walked with me to the door. "Well, that's an improvement."

"It's tenuous," I said, leaning in to kiss her cheek. "I love you."

"Love you too, honey. Call me when you get home."

"I will." With a wave, I made my way out to the elevator and down to the main floor, where I said goodnight to the woman at the desk. My phone buzzed again with another text from my sister.

KENNEDY

There's a group of college girls that won't
leave them alone.

On my walk to my car, a grainy photo appeared. It was of Dean and a group of men, a few of them I recognized from the night we saw his band play. He had his head tipped back in laughter, his arm around one of the guys, a drink in the other hand. They appeared out of place in their button-downs at the cheap bar, like they'd come from a nice dinner. It was also impossible to miss the young girls next to them.

By the time I started my car, Kennedy had sent yet another photo. This one of a girl with her head on Dean's shoulder, her hand on his chest. His head was cocked back at a funny angle, like he was trying to get away from her.

> Why are you sending me these?

KENNEDY

Isn't this right up your alley? More ammunition
for your fights?

I didn't respond, and I was on I-76, driving back home, when her next text popped up.

KENNEDY

Maybe you guys should fuck it out of your
system.

I guffawed but waited until I was off the highway to message her back.

> Coming from the girl who doesn't know what
> "just fucking" means.

KENNEDY

We're talking about you. Not me. That's what
you do, right?

KENNEDY

So do it.

There was no way I was going to "fuck it out" with Dean. We were barely even friends now, and I wasn't about to make it any more complicated than that. Though, if I was being honest, if he fucked as good as he fought, it would be a damn fine night with him.

But since I wasn't going to imagine that, I poured myself a glass of wine before I sat down on the couch in the living room to watch another Lindsay Lohan classic, *Mean Girls*.

Absently scrolling through my phone, I pulled up my last text message to Dean from yesterday.

> Did you ever follow up with the state about the Sunset filing?

Of course, he hadn't answered, so I texted him now.

> Next time I ask you a question about a case we're working together, it would be really great if you responded.

Seconds later, he did.

SOME ASSHOLE

Jesus, Novak. It's Saturday night. Stop working and get a life.

> I have a life, and it doesn't revolve around getting drunk with underage girls.

SOME ASSHOLE

Neither does mine.

SOME ASSHOLE

Have you been spying on me?

> No. My sister is. She's working at the bar.

> Though that sounds like an admission that you are getting drunk with underage girls.

SOME ASSHOLE

You sound jealous.

> Nope.

SOME ASSHOLE

How bout now?

A moment later, a photo came through of Dean and Kennedy. He was leaning over the bar, his arm around Kennedy's shoulders. His eyes were wide and twinkling, his mouth curved into an absurdly happy grin.

> How many drinks have you had?

SOME ASSHOLE

A few.

He sent another photo, but this time, he was kissing my sister's cheek.

SOME ASSHOLE

This is what people with lives do.

> I had a lovely dinner with my grandmother, and now I'm having a drink and watching a movie in peace.

SOME ASSHOLE

Sounds terrible. You should come out.

> No, thank you.

SOME ASSHOLE

I promise I'll send the underage girls away

> You admit it?

SOME ASSHOLE

Why do you care so much?

> So I know what kind of criminal case I'm dealing with.

SOME ASSHOLE

Your sister is the one checking IDs. You think she'd let underage girls in?

> There is a reason she can't hold down a job.

SOME ASSHOLE

Ouch, Nov.

SOME ASSHOLE

Harsh even on your own sibling.

It's nothing she doesn't already know and nothing we haven't talked about.

SOME ASSHOLE

You gonna go find a kids bball game to berate the kids who miss?

Probably.

SOME ASSHOLE

Take me with yu.

SOME ASSHOLE

you*

How drunk are you?

SOME ASSHOLE

Enough to admit I'd pay to see you yell at a preschooler for not coloring in the lines

I only yell at adults.

SOME ASSHOLE

basically me.

Basically.

SOME ASSHOLE

Your obsessed wit me

you're*

with*

SOME ASSHOLE

You admit it?

Go home. You're drunk.

SOME ASSHOLE

can't go home yet we still have another bar to hit up

SOME ASSHOLE

enough time for you to get your ass out here

My ass is home and comfy in my pajamas.

SOME ASSHOLE

take them off!

SOME ASSHOLE

I meant take them off and put pants on

SOME ASSHOLE

I don't want to see you without pants on

SOME ASSHOLE

swear

SOME ASSHOLE

are you still there?

SOME ASSHOLE

well I didn't want to talk to you either

I laughed and tossed my phone to the chair in the corner, so I wouldn't be tempted to return any more of his drunken texts. I was too close to walking into my room to put on my pants and meet him. So, no, I'd stay right here, in my pajamas with Lindsay Lohan and my glass of red wine.

Much safer that way.

CHAPTER FIFTEEN

Taylor

When Monday morning rolled around, Dean and I avoided talking about his drunken text messages to me. I didn't even mention how he still looked hungover.

Because I was a nice person.

Though, he didn't have any hesitations about calling me Satan when I made fun of him until he sped up his treadmill to full-out running and then had to hop off because he was heaving like he might puke.

"It's almost like you're dehydrated. Wonder why," I teased.

He only flipped me the bird, and I laughed.

And that was how we spent the rest of the week, in this place somewhere between friends and frenemies, pushing each other at work and afterward at the gym, never once acknowledging the growing ease between us.

I certainly wasn't going to be the one to blink first.

Though I came close Thursday morning because Dean Hargrove was using *that* voice. The take-no-prisoners tone which he reserved for the toughest clients and cases. Currently, he was using it against Ron Singer's lawyer. Ron, the owner of Sunset Lounge, was sleazy, so it was no surprise he had a sleazy lawyer, Larry del Vecchio, who was attempting to push off the state's investigation, while Ron was threatening the girls who worked at the lounge at the same time.

"Need I remind you," Dean growled into the phone, "if any one of those women are let go for seeking legal help in improving their working conditions, we'd have a great time putting together a wrongful termination suit on top of the complaint we already have in with the state. You wanna go two for two?"

I curled my lips between my teeth to keep from laughing as Dean nodded at whatever del Vecchio was saying.

"Well, that's good to hear," Dean replied eventually. "I'll be following up to make sure it stays that way. I won't make this phone call twice. Next time, your client will be served more papers."

When he hung up, I slow clapped a few times. He swiveled around to face me and scrubbed his hand over his head, the front of his hair sticking up from the movement. "I'd like to nail them both to a cross."

"We will." I tipped my head toward the break room, so he'd join me. "Thanks for calling him."

He waved off my gratitude. Larry del Vecchio, much like Chris Raber, who refused to let me take over his case, had a problem with women in positions of authority, and del Vecchio hadn't returned either of my two calls. So, as much as I despised it, I had to bring in my backup.

"You sounded good," I said before I thought better of it. "I mean, what you said to him. It was good."

A self-satisfied smirk curved his lips. "Glad to be of service."

I shook my head at him and washed out my coffee mug before placing it in the Keurig with a new pod. Dean handed me my creamer. "I can't go to the gym today."

"Why not?"

"Gig at Walt's."

I folded my arms, hoping my disappointment wasn't written all over my face. "Again?"

"We have a standing date there. Every third Thursday."

I nodded. "That's great."

He tidied up the counter as if he needed something to do while my coffee finished brewing, and then he slipped his mug into the machine to replace mine. After he had the pod in, he turned back to me. "What are you doing tonight? Pajamas and *Parent Trap?*"

I leaned against the counter, holding my mug in both of my hands. "You got a thing for my pajamas, huh?"

He skimmed his hand down his slate-gray tie. "Yeah. I always figured when you went to bed, you peeled off your human mask to reveal your true form."

"Which is?"

"A demon."

"Of course."

"And demons don't wear pajamas because they don't sleep."

I hid my smile with a sip of coffee. "Of course."

"So, what are you doing tonight?" he asked, removing his full mug from the Keurig.

"Definitely pajamas and maybe some coloring."

His brows rose over the rim of his cup, and he coughed on his sip of coffee. After setting it down on the counter, he stepped right in front of me. "You color?"

"Yeah." I set down my mug too. "It's really relaxing." When he bit back a grin, I rolled my eyes. "What?"

"Nothing. You coloring... It's adorable."

I shoved at his shoulder, and he caught my wrist. "Why don't you save your coloring for tomorrow and come to my gig tonight?"

I didn't fight against his hold on me. Not even when he tugged, forcing me to bend my arm when he pulled me closer to him. "You want me to come to your gig?"

His eyes, his stupid, pretty eyes, completed a circuit of my face, and the way he studied me never failed to make me feel as if he really enjoyed what he was looking at. An obviously practiced action. No doubt the reason he had so much luck with women. "Sure. Why not? You need to learn how to live, Nov."

"Like you?" I said, finally breaking free of his light grasp. I shifted away from him, keeping my hands behind my back. "You want me to get drunk and pick up underage girls?"

His hand landed on the counter, right next to my hip. "I can't help but point out how you keep harping on all these girls you think I'm hooking up with. I haven't been with someone in months."

I shouldn't have been happy about that. I had no right. Especially when I had been with Ace in December. Although, I would have rather erased that from memory. But this wasn't a game, and I didn't care about notches on his bedpost. Just like he didn't care about mine.

At least, I didn't think he did.

"Yeah, maybe I will," I mused. "I did notice the bartender there was pretty cute."

His eyes narrowed. "Which one?"

"I don't know his name." I shrugged, like I didn't care. "He had gauges and tattoos."

Dean was so close to me, I could feel the heat radiating off him, note the individual flecks of gray and blue in his eyes. Hear his low exhale. "What's with you and tattoos?"

I pretended my skin didn't feel tight. Pretended I didn't relish his sudden interest in what I supposedly wanted. "I like them."

The space between his brows crimped. "Why?"

I tipped my head to the side, pretty positive Dean Hargrove had exactly zero tattoos. "I like a certain type of guy, and that certain type of guy usually has tattoos."

"A certain type of guy?" he repeated.

My neck and cheeks heated, and I took sudden interest in the scuffs on the linoleum floor.

"Certain type of guy in bed?" he asked after a moment, his voice a shadow of its normal self.

I nodded.

"Taylor."

I automatically raised my gaze to his, powerless when he rasped my name like that.

"What do you mean?" he asked.

I licked my dry lips, and his eyes zeroed in on the motion. "I can't talk about this with you."

"Why not?"

I darted my gaze to the door, where no one was coming to my rescue. No one to interrupt us. I met his eyes once again and cleared my throat. "Because we're friends."

He hummed curiously. "I thought we were frenemies. I'm moving up the ladder."

"And we're going to stop the escalation right there."

With a shake of his head, he pressed in closer to me, the corner of the counter biting into my lower back. Both of his hands were on either side of me now, caging me in. "You have to tell me."

"I don't have to tell you anything," I said, though my voice wavered.

He bent his head, his voice becoming so low it wound under my clothes and brushed along my skin. "I won't be able to work. I won't be able to concentrate. So, unless you want me imagining the worst, you better tell me now."

I closed the distance between us and rested my forehead on

his, our breaths mingling for a brief moment while I gathered up my wits, remembered *this* wasn't what we were.

"No," I told him, pushing my hands against his chest. "You couldn't handle it." I grabbed my coffee and shouldered past him. "Might expire on the spot."

"I could handle it," he said to my back.

"Well, you won't ever find out. So, I guess you won't have to worry about it, Hargrove."

———

It was Satan. That's the only logical explanation for why I found myself at Walt's later that night.

Dean often joked that I was from hell, but that couldn't have been true, because I wouldn't have fallen prey to whatever evil tricks got me here. So, it must have been Satan. Obviously.

I entered the bar behind a couple holding hands and shivered. Though it was the third week in February and we'd had almost no snow this winter, the wind had been crazy lately. I combed my freezing fingers through my hair before blowing into my cupped hands.

"Taylor?"

I spun toward Dean's voice, flattening my hands together.

"You actually showed up," he said in obvious surprise.

"I had nothing better to do, so..."

"Figures." He gave in to a smile and dragged his attention over me. "You cold? Come on away from the door. Come sit down."

Without a word, I followed him to a table by the bar, where Laney was seated, laughing at something a guy—I think I recalled his name was Frank—said. When Laney spotted me, she grinned widely. I was curious what their parents looked like because these two were like an Abercrombie advertisement. Wonder Bread Twins.

"Taylor! Hey!" She pulled out the chair next to her.

"Hi." I offered her a small smile, and since Dean had disappeared, I sat down, looping my purse around the back but keeping my coat on, rubbing my hands together.

"I don't know if you remember anyone from last month. This is Hank," she said, pointing to the guy on the other side of her.

Hank, not Frank, waved. "How's it going, Taylor?"

"Good."

"You know," he said, leaning on an elbow, "you're not what I expected."

"Not what you expected from everything Dean has said about me?" I stuck my hands between my thighs. "You expected horns and a tail, huh?"

"Pretty much." He laughed at himself. "I told him you guys should fuck it out, you know?" He pumped his fist. "Get the resentment out and move on—"

Laney smothered a hand over his mouth. "Dear Lord in heaven, I don't know why we keep you around."

He nuzzled into her, wiggling her fingers away from his mouth. "Because you love me."

"Not really," she said, looking around. "Where's Angela? She needs to collar you."

"Grayson's sick."

"Oh, really?" She smacked his shoulder. "Why aren't you home with them?"

"She told me to come."

A glass of amber liquid appeared in front of me, set down by Dean's hand, and I tipped my head up in question. "Whisky," he told me. "Warm you up from the inside."

"Thank you."

He nodded at me then turned to his sister and friend, as if he'd heard their conversation. "I told him he should've stayed home. I could do the vocals."

"Yeah, but I think our fans would miss my stage presence."

Laney gestured to the whole of the bar, to the few patrons, most of whom appeared not to care less about the band. "Your fans?"

Hank stood up in a huff. "You just wait, Delaney doll, I'll have them eating out of the palm of my hand."

I had a feeling Hank was living out some schoolboy fantasy with this band, and I bit my lip to keep from smiling as he paraded to the stage like he was Mick Jagger. Dean shook his head then peered down at me. "I can't believe you're here. Of your own free will."

"Me either."

"Well, do Hank a favor and, even if you're bored, pretend you're not, all right?"

"Sure." I crooked my fingers into quotation marks in the air. "Hank."

Laney hooted, pointing a long finger at her brother. "You're so transparent."

He batted at her finger then made his way to the stage, placing the strap of his guitar over his shoulder, and I *knew* I shouldn't have come tonight. Because I was getting that tight feeling along my skin again, goose bumps racing down my arms, and I peeled off my scarf and coat.

Once the band was all set up, some of them testing out their instruments, the drummer, Laney's fiancé, hopped off the stage and laid a smacking kiss on her cheek. "Got a new one for ya, tonight."

Laney's returning smile could be described as nothing less than radiant. "Another Coldplay?"

"Nope." He kissed her on the lips then glanced my way. "Hey, Taylor. Nice to see you again."

"Yeah, you too," I said and took a sip from my glass, the liquor burning on the way down. When I cringed, Ethan laughed softly.

"That whisky?"

I nodded. "Dean gave it to me."

"That must mean he really likes you. It's from his special stash. They keep a bottle of some fancy stuff in the back. He always has one drink of it before we go on."

I swirled the glass in a circle, the small amount of liquid splashing up on the sides of the tumbler. "For good luck?"

Ethan seemed to chew on the inside of his lip for a few seconds before finally answering, "He's never told us, but I think it has to do with Patrick."

"Patrick?"

Ethan's eyes cut toward Laney, and this time, she was the one to explain, "He was our friend since we were kids. He was originally in the band." She inclined her head toward the stage. "But he passed away when we were twenty-four."

I mentally connected the dots. This Patrick must have been the friend who died around Christmas, the one my grandmother briefly told me about, whose death had made Dean change his whole life plan.

And I was drinking his special whisky.

Dean allowed me on in that relationship, even if he hadn't informed me what it meant.

I took another sip, but this time, it wasn't only the drink warming me from the inside out.

"All right, gotta go." Ethan, like he was a magnet with Laney, kissed her again then pushed his glasses up his nose. He tapped the table once and jogged up onto the stage with long-legged strides, settling behind his drum set.

Hank, in another brightly colored shirt, introduced the band, and Ethan counted them in with his sticks high in the air.

The Anchormen started with a rendition of "Fell in Love with a Girl" by the White Stripes, and I tried not to be conspicuous as I watched Dean. I knew nothing about guitars, but his looked pretty classic, a shiny black-and-white body hanging across his torso by a thick black strap. He wore a fitted Henley, the sleeves pushed up to his elbows, the veins in his hands and forearms taunting me as his fingers so expertly played the instrument he held.

It was practically pornography.

Laney leaned in toward me. "I'm glad you're here. I never miss a show, and sometimes I'm their only groupie, so I sit here like a loser by myself. And there's only so many times I can listen to them play Ben Folds Five."

Laney was warm and welcoming and could probably make friends with a tree, but I was happy she was here too. I had planned on finding a seat in a corner somewhere, but this was much better. Especially if she was going to run the conversation. I had no problem being the introvert.

"They always play the same songs?" I asked.

"No, but there's a steady rotation."

And that rotation was quite an eclectic mix, from Haim to Cheap Trick to the Who. At the end of the set, Ethan pointed his drumstick at Laney as he beat out a rhythm on his kick drum, and she tossed her head back, laughing and clapping.

Eventually, the rest of the band joined, and Hank began singing. Laney did too, her arms up, her voice so loud it almost drowned out Hank. Ethan looked like he had a hanger stuck in his mouth, and I glanced at Dean, who was shaking his head in amusement.

When his gaze met mine, he cocked his head in their direction, rolling his eyes, like we had some inside joke. Like I knew his friends well enough to be in on it.

Finally, once they hit the chorus, I understood. Because even Ethan started sing-shouting the lyrics to "Let's Get Married" from behind his drum set.

"We play this song every morning," Laney told me, mid-shimmy. "It's going to be our first dance together."

She was so full of joy, and Ethan was practically bursting with it as he drummed. It was impossible not to smile. The rest of the patrons at the bar were getting in on it too. The love between the drummer and the loud blonde in the front too obvious to ignore.

When the song ended with only Ethan on the kick drum again, Laney leaped out of her seat, hooting and hollering. I threw in a wolf whistle just because.

Dean shot me a look, and I shrugged.

He was the one who'd invited me.

Once the bar patrons settled, Hank introduced each member of the band then thanked the crowd for coming out. Ethan promptly left his spot and charged at Laney, hoisting her clear off the floor and spinning around.

"I'm gonna marry you so hard," she said between kisses.

"That's my girl." He set her down with a kiss to the top of her head before heading back to the stage to disassemble his drum kit.

"You two are really sweet together," I told Laney. "I'm happy for you."

She pressed her hand to her collarbone. "Thank you. It feels..." She closed her eyes and smiled. "It feels like everything is exactly what it's supposed to be."

Last week, while we were running at the gym, Dean had relayed to me how Ethan had been one of his best friends since high school and that he'd had feelings for Laney for a long time. "Dean said you two were together when you were kids."

"That's a long story," she said with a laugh. "Maybe I can tell it to you over a bottle of wine."

"I do love wine."

"Me too." She brightened even more, if that was possible. "I used to live in San Francisco. I was so spoiled with all the wineries out there."

I tucked my fist under my chin. "I bet."

"What do you like? Red or white?"

"Both, as long as it's not sweet."

She nodded, about to open her mouth, when Dean interrupted. "I don't really like what's going on here."

I angled my head back. "We were having a really nice conversation until you got here."

"My sister and my mortal enemy conspiring against me, I see."

Laney snorted a laugh. "I was about to invite Taylor to the wedding."

"*What?*" my question was echoed by Dean next to me.

Laney grinned at me. "Please come. Dean needs a date, and we're giving out little bottles of wine as our favors. Special ordered from my favorite winery. Dry red blend, you'll love it."

I started to argue, tell her there was no way I could intrude on her wedding, but Laney merely exchanged a look with her brother. I tipped my head back, meeting his gaze.

He shrugged. "You want to come?"

CHAPTER SIXTEEN

Dean

I hadn't known until that moment that I did indeed want Taylor to be my date to Laney and Ethan's wedding. Until I saw her sitting there smiling as she chatted with my sister, her dark sweater pulled down over her hands like she was still cold.

She stared up at me now with wide eyes, silently asking for help. But I wasn't going to get her out of this situation my sister had cornered her into.

Because I wanted her to come with me. I wanted to spend time with her outside of work. I wanted time with her that wasn't sweating and swearing at the gym or based around a doctor's visit. I wanted to have fun with her.

More fun than I'd already been having.

"I need someone to drive my car to the reception anyway, so you'd be helping me out."

"You asshole," Laney said, punching me in the arm. She turned to Taylor. "Don't listen to him. You don't need to drive his car like some chauffeur."

"You're right. I could drive it myself." I leaned my hand on the table, bringing me closer to Taylor while focused on my sister. "But you're the one who wanted us all to ride in that stupid trolley."

"You're getting a trolley?" Taylor asked.

"Yes, and oh my god, it's so cute. I can't wait. I'm sure it'll still be a little cold out, but—"

"A little cold out," I interjected sarcastically. "You're getting married in the beginning of March. You'll be lucky if it doesn't snow."

This time, Taylor was the one who punched me. "Don't piss on your sister's wedding joy."

I scowled at her. "Since when are you into wedding joy?"

"Since always. You don't know everything about me," she snipped, and I flapped my hand at them.

"Whatever. I gotta finish packing up my gear." I spun away, but Laney's voice carried behind me.

"Listen, I'd love for you to come. Like I said, there's an open seat for you. Think about it, okay?"

I couldn't hear Taylor's response as I stepped back onto the stage, fixated on winding up all the cords and not on how Laney and Taylor had their heads bent together.

Taylor was right. I didn't know everything about her. I assumed she'd hate weddings and anything romantic. She wore black all day, every day and was basically the walking equivalent of frostbite, but then again, she knew all the words to that dumb *Parent Trap* movie and she colored. *Colored!* Beneath her hard exterior, she was actually rather soft and sweet, and my curiosity about that side of her grew every day.

By the time I returned from taking my guitar and amp out to my car, Hank had already left, and Tony and Jerry were on their way out. I gave them each a fist bump then slid into the open seat at the table. Ethan had his arm around the back of Laney's chair while he chugged down water. When he finished, he set down the glass and smiled at my sister. "Ready?"

She nodded and gathered her coat and purse.

I tossed my hand in the air. "You guys are leaving too?"

"Gotta go de-stress my lady," Ethan said with a lascivious smirk, and I covered my ears.

"Nope, nope, nope."

Next to me, Taylor raised her glass, still nearly full of the pour of whisky I'd given her. "Have fun."

Laney waved her fingers in our direction, laughing. "We're going home to color, Dean. Relax."

Ethan shook his head, his hand slipping down Laney's back toward her butt, and I would seriously never get used to *that*. "Leave now. Goodbye. Never speak to me again about this."

Taylor dug her bony elbow into me. "You're so uptight. Maybe you should color too."

I angled my chair toward her. "Only if we're still using that word as code for fucking."

The tops of her cheeks reddened, and I slid my foot alongside hers, our calves touching, but she didn't back away. "Don't get all shy on me now like some blushing virgin, when a few hours ago, you were telling me I couldn't handle whatever it is you like in bed."

She pursed her lips, and I curled my hands into fists to keep from tracing her mouth with my fingers.

"It's really not that big of a deal," she murmured. "I don't know why you're so interested."

I inhaled deeply, trying to rearrange my jumbled thoughts about the woman in front of me. "I'm a guy. I'm always thinking about sex."

Her long lashes lifted, revealing those dark, enigmatic eyes that could cut a man to ribbons with one look. "Sex with me?"

I nodded. When a person came to an impasse, sometimes it was best to go right through it. "Ever since you went home with that octopus-tattoo douchebag."

"You go home with a lot of women, but I'm not hammering you about it, cornering you in the break room, which, might I add, should be an HR complaint."

"Go ahead," I dared her, shifting so I was in her space, her leg between both of mine, my forearm draped across the table in front of her, my other hand gripping the back of her chair. "Go tell Dominic how you silently fume whenever I bring up other women, how your breathing speeds up when we're this close, how you wonder what my beard would feel like against your thighs."

She shot her eyes up from my mouth. "You're such an asshole."

"You going to come to the wedding with me?"

"Why?" she countered.

"Why not? It's open bar, and they're having bacon-wrapped scallops," I said, because who didn't like bacon-wrapped scallops?

She considered me with a tilted head, rubbing her index finger along a dent in the wood of the table. "But *why*?"

I knew what she was asking. She didn't want to be an afterthought or a pity invite. She was too proud to be anything other than anyone's first choice.

"I told you I haven't been with anyone in a while, and even if I had been, I wouldn't invite them to my sister's wedding. I don't date, so the only person I could bring would be a friend. And since we're friends now, I'd like you to come with me."

She weighed my words, her eyes squinted as if trying to see inside my head. After a moment, she pushed the whisky toward me. "Tell me about this."

"It's from Japan."

"Okay, but Ethan said you've never given it to anyone else. Why is it so special?"

I tugged on my ear, dropping my gaze to the floor. I hadn't

thought twice about giving her some of the drink, which should have set off alarm bells in my mind, and yet I'd felt nothing other than a desire to help when she walked in. A little something to warm her up, to take the stiff edge off, a gift for being brave enough to do something she wasn't used to.

I hadn't consciously thought about what it meant that I was giving her something I'd never offered to anyone else. Never even spoke about to anyone else, for that matter.

"It's, uh…my friend Patrick, we'd been friends since first grade. We did everything together, and he was at my house a lot 'cause he didn't get along real well with his family. His dad left when he was a baby, and his mom worked double shifts, blamed a lot of shit on Patrick. They lived with Patrick's grandparents in this little house by the school we went to. His grandma was a strict church lady, and…" I shook my head, letting a smile grow as I remembered how he'd convinced his grandmother his pot was oregano.

"Anyway," I went on, blinking up to Taylor, finding her sitting forward in her chair. "He was really artistic, always drawing and into Japanese culture. He loved anime and Kurosawa films. We both went to college in Philly and lived together through undergrad and when I started law school."

I attempted to clear my throat of the gravel stuck there, and Taylor's hand found mine, her fingers settling over mine with a gentle squeeze. The silent gesture was enough to make my eyes sting, and I lifted my other hand to my beard, subtly trying to clear my eyes, but if her teasing smile was any indication, I was doing a shit job. So, I blotted at my eye with the back of my hand, tugged on my earlobe again then dropped my hand to my thigh, running it up and down my leg a few times.

Once I knew my voice wouldn't crack, I continued, "He found out about this whisky. It's called Yamakazi and is one of the best in the world, aged for twelve years. Costs two hundred bucks a bottle."

When she huffed, I nodded. "I know. We were two kids in college and ordered this fancy-ass whisky from Japan, but he was so excited. We opened it on his twenty-first birthday and allowed ourselves a tiny pour. From then on, we drank a little bit anytime we were celebrating something or needed a pick-me-up, but only ever an ounce or so. We didn't have enough to keep buying more bottles, so we had to make it last."

"How many did you go through?" she asked, our knees touching, her fingers intertwined between mine.

"I don't remember, but I know when I got accepted into law school, we had a bit more than a few ounces and polished off the last of the bottle, so I replaced it as a gift to him when we graduated."

"And you kept up the tradition after?"

This was where it got tough, and I took a deep breath. "Yeah, but when I started law school, I didn't have a lot of time. You know how it was." When she nodded, I tossed her a grin. "Plus, there was this brown-nose girl who kept getting all the top grades. She was a real pain in my ass, competitive witch."

She inclined her head with a smile, but my humor eventually faded, and I licked my lips, forcing myself to go on. "Patrick was hit by a car while riding his bike." Taylor gasped quietly, and I had trouble meeting her gaze again. "He had a couple of broken bones and was prescribed Percocet. At the time, I didn't think anything of it. During high school and college, we all drank and dabbled in some stuff, but I should've known..." I curled my fingers into a fist, digging it into the top of my thigh. "I started dating this girl, and we were pretty hot and heavy. Believe it or not, before..." I swallowed thickly. "Before Patrick died, I was really into monogamy. I was with my high school girlfriend, Kayla, for a long time, even a couple years into college. And then I started dating Marin, and between her and all the work in school, I wasn't home a lot. I didn't see..."

I closed my eyes, grimacing at the memories, and Taylor's voice settled over me like a warm blanket. "It's okay," she said. "It's not your fault."

"It is," I ground out, bending my head, so she couldn't see when tears formed in my eyes. "He was addicted, and I didn't see it. I should have noticed, questioned why he always needed money, talked to him more about why he wasn't sleeping. But I was too..." I jammed my fingers into my eyes, and Taylor let go of my fingers to wrap her hands around my head and neck, forcing me to look at her.

"It is *not* your fault. I know it's hard to accept, but it isn't your fault. There is no use thinking about all the what-ifs because they will go on forever." Her fingers dug into the skin at the nape of my neck, anchoring me to her. "You can't keep blaming yourself."

I let my forehead drop to hers, closing my eyes, and everything else disappeared except for her and me. I didn't hear the clink of glasses or shouts from patrons anymore. Only Taylor's slow and even breaths. "I came home from taking my last exam right before winter break, ready to celebrate with our whisky, but when I opened the door to our apartment, he was there, on the floor."

"I'm so sorry," she whispered, her lips ghosting over my temple as she pulled me into her, holding me close.

I inhaled her scent, finding comfort in the least likely of places, her arms, and I was wrecked. Completely and utterly wrecked.

Which was why I never told anyone. Remembering it was hard enough. To speak of it was like going into battle. Without any armor. Just me, standing there with my arms wide open, asking for their arrows.

Sometimes, I thought that might be easier.

I eventually backed away from Taylor, blinking a few times, and she curved her hand around my jaw. Her fingers were chilled, but I gave in to the touch anyway. She scraped her thumb over my beard as she offered me a kind smile. "So you still drink a little bit of this whenever you have something to celebrate?"

I nodded. "Although there hasn't been much to celebrate the last few years. I keep a bottle here, in the back, and have a drink before we go on. If he were here, I know he'd be the one offering me a shot before every show, so…"

Taylor lifted the glass and took a sip then held it out to me, and I tipped my head back, letting her give me the last of it. And then she set the glass down on the table and kissed me.

Her lips weren't cold and thin like I had always assumed. They were warm and lush, gently urging me to give in to her, but I was shocked into immobility. Even as my heart pounded in my ears and my skin itched, my hands remained firmly planted, my mind spinning off too fast to give any orders.

Something had changed between Taylor and me over these last weeks. I wasn't sure when exactly, but the fire of animosity had burned off, so only the crackling heat of need remained.

Need to win her over.

Need to shelter her.

Need to burrow under the thick shell she wore and uncover all the soft, sweet places she had yet to show me.

So much fucking need.

It all boiled over, and my body burst to life. I threaded my fingers into her hair, holding her to me, taking control, testing her. Finding out exactly how much she'd give me.

I licked into her mouth. She tasted of the whisky, of my pleasure and pain, and I drank in more. Nipping at her lip, I curled my hand around her neck, squeezing ever so slightly, and she moaned into my mouth, opening wider, allowing me to learn the texture of her tongue, scrape it with my teeth.

I angled my head, aiming to discover all the hidden corners of her mouth, when a glass smashed and we both jerked away from each other.

"I'm sorry," she said behind three fingers over her mouth. "I just…"

I shook my head, but by the time I reached for her wrist, she was jumping out of her chair, tossing her coat over her shoulders as she practically sprinted away.

"Sorry. I gotta go."

Then she was gone.

CHAPTER SEVENTEEN

Taylor

I didn't know what the hell I was thinking.

I wasn't thinking.

That was the problem.

I was running solely on emotion. Listening to Dean tell the story about his friend cracked something wide open inside me. All those jabs we'd exchanged over the years about projection. They were true.

All that hate and anger, it was because we saw the things in each other that we hated in ourselves. All the grief and guilt, all the broken bits we hid from other people. I saw it in Dean, and he saw it in me.

When no one else did.

I was grateful. I could stop pretending. Finally.

So, I kissed him.

Like an idiot who based decisions on emotions. No, that wasn't right. It wasn't even a decision. It was pure need. Some base instinct calling to the only other person who knew me.

Of course, he had kissed exactly the opposite of what I'd anticipated. He wasn't lazy or soft or any other stereotype of a rich white guy who wore loafers. After getting over the initial shock of my pouncing on him, he gripped me tight, holding me to him in a way that let me know he was in charge.

I could have died on the spot.

Especially with the way his teeth grazed my tongue and lips. God, I wanted him to bite me. To hold me down and do whatever he wanted to me.

And I did the only rational thing. I got the fuck out of there.

Like a coward, I called out of the office, working from home on Friday. Dean texted me to ask if I was okay, but I didn't answer him. Saturday and Sunday were sunny, and I spent a few hours each day running outside in the cold, hoping to knock some sense of reality into me. I might have wanted Dean, but I couldn't act on it. We worked together. Not to mention, we were competing against each other for the same promotion.

There was no way we could continue down this road. Only a dead end lay ahead.

Since it was Presidents' Day, the office was closed Monday, so I went out with Kennedy, shopping at the King of Prussia mall for clothes I didn't need. But it was successful in keeping my mind off Dean Hargrove and his godforsaken hands.

Tuesday couldn't be avoided, so I trudged into the office, determined to keep it completely professional. I avoided any extra eye contact and didn't walk past his desk unless absolutely necessary. And it worked.

At least, for a few days.

He'd become good at popping up when I least expected it, but I always found some excuse to wiggle away from him. Until Friday night, when I stayed late, finishing up all the work I'd missed, an unfortunate side effect of hiding away from Dean.

The office was empty save for me and my terrible mistake, who was currently stretching in his chair, his tie loosened, like he was planning to stay the night. Well, I wasn't leaving until *after* he left. This was one game I was determined to win.

"It's six," he said, absently swiveling back and forth in his chair, though he didn't face me. "You need some help with something to get you out of here?"

"Nope. I'm good. I'll see you Monday." I kept my focus down, refusing to look up when I heard the squeak of his chair as he rolled it to my desk. Then his arms were there, one on top of the other.

"If you're planning on staying here a while, we could order dinner. You need to eat."

My eyes went unseeing, as they had all week when I was forced to make up some lie. "I'm not hungry."

"I could hear your stomach growling from over there."

"Go home," I told him, finally meeting his gaze. He smiled in return. The gall.

"I thought I'd keep you company."

I frowned at his smacking gum. "I don't want you to."

"Then why don't you be honest and tell me what you do want," he said.

"I want you to leave me alone and go home."

"Do you, though?"

"Stop," I said, but when he tipped his head to the side like a begging dog, I had trouble keeping my mouth set in a straight line. "Go home."

"See. Here's the thing. I've been patient with you all week, but I'm tired of being ditched and avoided. We need to have a conversation."

"Nope." I closed my planner and shut down my computer. Whatever I didn't finish, I could do at home. There was no way I was staying here to listen to this. "We don't."

I stood and grabbed my coat, but he was on me, snatching it from my hands.

"Hey!" I took it back, though he didn't let go, starting a tug-of-war game.

"What are you so afraid of, huh?" he goaded.

I yanked on my coat in an attempt to get him to release it, but he barely moved. With a devious smile, he leaned over and pulled, forcing me forward. My heels didn't help, and I skidded right into him, chest to chest, nose to nose.

"Since when do you run away from a fight?"

His heat, his scent, the fan of his breath across my lips, it was all so familiar, I nearly gave in. Instead, I closed my eyes, whispering, "I don't want to fight with you."

"What was that?"

I knew he heard me fine. He was only being an asshole. "I said, I don't want to fight with you."

He wrapped his hands around my waist. "But you're so good at it."

I couldn't help how my spine turned soft under his touch. How I let him back me up to the wall. "That's what you're going to compliment me on? Fighting with you?"

"I doubt you'd believe me if I gave you any other compliment."

I lifted my chin. "Try me."

His low hum sent goose bumps across my skin. I squeezed my thighs together at the flutter between them. As if he could tell, the corner of his mouth kicked up.

"You're smart," he said, and I nodded.

"I know."

"And humble."

I dropped my head back, realizing too late the mistake I'd made in exposing my throat to him. He took advantage, his tongue licking my pulse point. "You taste good."

I inhaled an uneven breath. "Dean."

He froze, body tense, but after a moment, he brushed his lips over the spot below my ear. "Say it again."

My back arched at the feel of his teeth on my earlobe. "Dean."

He dropped his forehead to my shoulder, exhaling harshly, almost painfully. "You sound so good saying my name."

Flashes of naked skin, scratching fingernails, lips, and moans entered my mind, swirling into a fog until all I wanted was this man over me and in me, growling in my ear. I squeezed his bicep, finding the tiny piece of sanity lingering in the back of my brain, and forced the words out of my mouth. "We can't do this."

"You also have impeccable timing," he said, still complimenting me, and I smothered a laugh against his neck.

The tip of his nose skimmed the shell of my ear, and I allowed myself one more deep inhale of him before pressing my hands against his chest, pushing him away. "It's too much."

He eyed me, his hands in the air between us like he wanted to touch me but was stopped by an invisible wall.

"I'm sorry I kissed you," I said, willing my heart to stop beating so hard, my skin to stop aching with desire. "I shouldn't have."

His jaw worked, but he didn't argue, didn't try to convince me otherwise.

"We're finally friends." Which was the truth.

He nodded. "Right."

"Besides, it'll be hard enough for you when I'm your boss."

He guffawed. "Not gonna happen, Novak." He tipped his head back in the direction of Reed's former office. "It's mine."

I flicked at his tie. "We'll see about that."

Then I slid on my coat and snagged my purse as I rounded him, careful not to let any part of me touch any part of him.

I was halfway to the door when he stopped me. "Hey."

I spun to face him.

"I would really like it if you came to the wedding with me," he said softly. The tops of his cheeks flushed. "It's..." He tugged at his ear, a sign I'd come to learn was his emotional tell. "It's hard, these big life events. I've convinced myself I'm fine always being the one alone, but..."

I waited until he met my gaze. "You need a rock?"

His smile grew slowly. "I'm a flimsy piece of paper sometimes."

"Yet paper beats rock."

He shrugged, arms flopping at his sides like he had given up. Like he had nothing to lose. "I covered you, now I need you to hold me steady."

Well, fuck.

Momentarily transported to that Friday night when he'd stayed by my side, comforted me, covered me, I found myself grinning like a lovestruck idiot.

And I had to lock that down. Immediately. I masked my face into something I hoped was indifference as I pointed a stern finger at him. "I do not 'YMCA' or 'Cupid Shuffle' or whatever other stupid song they always play at weddings."

"Me either, but I doubt there will be any of that. Ethan has spent weeks putting the playlist together."

"And don't expect me to be in pictures."

He cocked his head. "Do demons show up in photos?"

I bared my teeth. "We'll see how much blood you have left at the end of the night."

"You think that scares me?"

"It should."

He took one step toward me, and I reflexively took one step back, even though we were separated by at least fifteen feet. "Nothing you could do or say would ever scare me away."

That scared me. This thread that had formed between us over the last few weeks, the knowledge that he and I were more alike than either one of us had wanted to admit, the fire that was feeling more and more like lust had only brightened. It all scared me.

Yet, I nodded, agreeing to be Dean Hargrove's wedding date.

Satan help me.

CHAPTER EIGHTEEN

The morning of Laney and Ethan's wedding was hectic to say the least. Gabe arrived back in town Thursday night, and I'd taken off work Friday to help with last-minute stuff my sister needed me to take care of before the rehearsal. Which mostly involved keeping my mother settled.

This wedding was huge, almost three hundred people, most of whom Laney and Ethan only knew tangentially, but when your father was a well-known orthodontist and your mother was basically the Don Corleone of a national human resources firm, it wasn't just a wedding. It was an extravaganza.

Saturday, I was up early, or at least I thought I was until I was greeted with a text from Taylor at six in the morning.

BEELZEBUB

Don't fuck up today. Everyone will be watching.

For the last two weeks, I'd played it cool with her. I had kept my hands and dirty thoughts about Taylor's moans and lips and teeth to myself. I was basically an altar boy around her. Then I'd go home, recall whatever

158

fucking bra she wore to the gym that day, and beat off in the shower.

I couldn't fault her for pushing me away that night in the office when I'd basically begged her without words to kiss me again. She was right. It was too much to digest whatever we were: friends, enemies, or something in between that felt like wanting to peel off my skin every time I was around her.

I didn't quite understand it myself—the urge to bend her over my desk and fuck her while she called me names and threatened to cut my balls off. All I knew was that it was a *terrible* idea. Yet it was all I wanted. All I could think about.

And I was going to bring her to my sister's wedding and... not do anything.

It was going to be great. *Great!*

I texted her back.

> I do my best work with people watching.

BEELZEBUB

> Don't be gross.

> You're the one reading innuendo into it.

BEELZEBUB

> How does it feel to be so transparent?

> I got a hotel room with two beds, so don't get too excited.

BEELZEBUB

> I still don't see why you need a hotel room.

> Since you've apparently never been to a wedding before, it's usually an event where a lot of drinking happens, and I am not going to drive home.

BEELZEBUB

> Rideshare.

> Everyone is staying there. We're having brunch the next morning. You'll thank me when all you have to do is take an elevator to your bed instead of waiting for some stranger to pick up your drunk ass and drive you home.

BEELZEBUB

I'm not going to get drunk.

> Great, then I won't have to hold your hair back.

BEELZEBUB

But I'll have to hold yours?

> Now you get it.

> Also, why are you up so early? I didn't know the devil worked this early.

BEELZEBUB

Yeah. He needed help with some contract negotiations.

> Figures. That guy can't do anything on his own.

BEELZEBUB

A lot like you.

I sent her the middle finger emoji, and she messaged me a selfie, flipping me the bird at the gym. She was sweaty and flushed, her six-pack on display as she lay on a mat. Fucking hell.

Now I had one more thing to add to my task list: masturbate to this photo.

> Picking you up at noon.

> Leave the horns and tail at home.

Her only response was the devil emoji.

I laughed but then scrolled back up to the picture she'd sent me. It was the only picture I had of her, and I stuck my hand down my pants, already half hard after texting a few barbs back and forth.

I was pathetic, really. Like Pavlov's dog. One sharp word from her, and I was drooling.

I swiped my thumb over the tip of my cock, imagining it was her tongue, as I studied the photo. The slight curve of her breasts in the tiny triangles she called a bra. She'd worn it before. I knew the three straps on either side crisscrossed along her back, and I closed my eyes, picturing how I might pluck at those little straps, leave tiny red marks when they slapped her skin, how I knew she would like it.

I thought about running my hands over her flat and hard stomach, licking at her belly button that always teased at the top of her leggings. I licked my lips now, my hand speeding up, already close. Staring at the photo again, I focused on the beads of sweat on her collarbone, how her body was twisted to the side, like she was in the middle of a stretch, and fuck, I would twist her that way too, hold her legs tight and move her which way I wanted, finding and hitting the angle that was perfect for both of us. She'd beg. I'd make her beg me to let her come.

And that was the thought that finished me off. Her voice, full of smoke and lust, *begging*.

With a stiff shake of my head to bring me back to reality, I slunk out of bed and into the shower, scrubbing away the evidence of my orgasm, though I knew those fantasies would stay with me all damn day.

I dressed and made my way to Ethan's house, where all the groomsmen, and Leah, his sister-in-law and groomswoman, were gathered, along with Trace, his six-year-old nephew. We hung out for a while, eating the breakfast Leah had prepared because she was a literal angel sent from above. Ethan's brother, Justin, who had been diagnosed with Huntington's disease, worried about speaking at the reception since his speech had become quite slow, so we went out back to practice a few times. He kept it short and sweet, and I reassured him that it didn't matter what he said. Whatever it was, Ethan and Laney were happy to have him there. Then I handed him a Yuengling, saying, "If there was ever a day for a morning beer, it's today."

He saluted me, and I thought my job here was done, so I gave my future brother-in-law a hug and a smacking kiss on the cheek, made sure I had his gift for my sister, and then I was off to my parents' house.

"Dean Nicholas Hargrove! Why aren't you dressed?"

I jerked back, not having even made it three feet inside when my mother started screeching at me from her perch at the eat-in kitchen counter. My parents' home was open concept, and she had a clear view of me even from the back of the house.

"Mom, you gotta relax. We have hours."

She checked the slim silver watch on her wrist. "Two hours and thirty-six minutes until the trolley will be here."

"And I only need sixteen of those minutes to get dressed."

She scoffed at me as my dad ambled into the house from the garage. I raised my hand to him in greeting. "Hey. What are you up to?"

"Trying to stay out of the way," he grouched.

My father, in full retirement mode now, didn't know what to do with his house overrun by so many women. I heard them upstairs cackling. One, who I assumed was a hair stylist, popped her head around the staircase, a blow dryer in hand as she banded a cord around it. "Mrs. Hargrove, we'll be ready for you in about half an hour."

My mom acknowledged her with a wave then added more champagne to her already-full mimosa.

"Is everybody decent upstairs?" I asked the hair stylist before she could turn around.

"Yeah. You need to come up?"

"To talk to my sister."

"Oh, you're the elusive Dean," she said, eyeing me over her shoulder as we made our way up the carpeted steps.

"I wouldn't say elusive."

"The bride's twin brother who is her man of honor and the guy running errands all week for her. Seems like a stand-up gentleman to me."

I grinned at her. "I try."

She smiled and pivoted, ushering me down the hall to my parents' bedroom, which was big enough to fit the girls, their dresses, and all the other...stuff.

"How goes it in here?" I asked, stepping into the lace and tulle war room.

"Hey!" Laney beamed at me. "Did you see Ethan? Did you bring your suit to get dressed here? Are you hungry?"

"Yes, no, and no," I said, making my way over to her. "You're babbling a little bit."

"Am I?"

"A smidge." I smiled and bent to kiss her cheek, which was still clear of makeup, though her normally curly hair had been smoothed out and pinned up with a sparkly clip. "Happy wedding day." Her friends, Gem, Bronte, and Sam, were in various states of halfway ready, though they all wore matching robes and drank out of matching Golden Girls mugs. I greeted them then held out Ethan's gift to my sister.

She accepted the small package. "From you?"

"Ethan."

The girls all gathered around as she unwrapped the tissue paper to reveal an old photo of Laney and Ethan from when we were at Senior Week, a tradition for East Coast high school graduates to spend a week sans parents at gross beach rentals where they'd all get sunburned and drink cheap beer. In the picture, Ethan had his arm slung around Laney, and she was turned to him, her head tipped back as she laughed. I could almost *hear* that photo, and I choked up, thinking of us as kids, of all the fun we'd had with our friends, and of course, the shadow of grief that always followed me around.

"Oh my god. So sweet." Bronte sniffed, dabbing a tissue at her eyes.

Sam took the photo to study it. "That's so thoughtful."

"What's the card say?" Gem grabbed at the accompanying envelope.

Laney ripped it open, reading out loud, "This is our beginning, but our journey is far from over. See you at the end of the aisle. I love you. —E. PS: I hope your dress shows off your tits."

"Jesus Christ," I growled, slapping my hands over my ears as all the girls howled in laughter, Laney the loudest.

"Oh god, I love him so much," she said eventually, pressing the card to her chest, the picture set up on the vanity in front of her. "I can't wait to marry him."

"Well, then let's get you ready," another woman with a tool belt of brushes said, nudging me out of the way.

I stepped back, afraid to interfere anymore, and was about to leave when the hair stylist stopped me. She slipped a business card into my hand. "If you ever need a haircut."

Then she winked.

I didn't know how to respond and darted my gaze to Laney, who had witnessed the exchange. She pushed Gem toward us. "See if you can do anything with this bedhead, Bonnie."

Taking the hint, Bonnie set to work on Gem's hair, and I tipped my chin to my sister. "I'll be back in a bit."

"You going to pick up Taylor?"

I nodded and turned to the door, my sister's voice trailing me. "I made a bet with Ethan about you two. He owes me ten bucks!"

"Make sure you cover up that zit on your chin!"

She gasped. "Rude!"

I waved my hand behind my head, then promised my mom I would be back in plenty of time before jogging out the front door and back to my car.

At home, I showered again and carefully trimmed my beard. I kept it short but made sure it was always soft and well-groomed. It was light brown, a few shades darker than my blond hair, which I had just gotten cut yesterday, ironically. I smoothed it with some product before spritzing myself with cologne.

My stomach roiled with nerves. It wasn't even my wedding, and yet my jitters grew with every minute that ticked closer.

I packed an overnight bag, dressed in my gray tuxedo, and double-checked that I had everything before heading out with my guitar case slung over my shoulder. I had about half an hour to pick up Taylor and get back to my parents' house, which was cutting it close, but a leopard couldn't change its spots, even for my sister's big day.

I parked right outside of Taylor's building and found her waiting inside the small lobby. My jog slowed when I spotted her until I outright froze, the door halfway open, my breath rushing out of me like I'd been punched in the gut.

She had punched me in the gut.

Her dark hair was pin straight as usual, but it gleamed almost black, and she had the side clipped back, revealing diamond earrings dangling down the slope of her neck. She angled slightly in profile as she checked her mailbox, so I could see how her dress—Jesus, her dress—was completely backless yet clung to every part of her like it was painted on. With long sleeves and a hemline that hit at her knees, it was so tight, I didn't know how she could walk. I clutched my chest, forcing myself to breathe, hoping she couldn't hear my heartbeat. Because it was surround sound to me.

Once I stepped inside, the door swung closed, and she pivoted to face me. I was struck all over again.

God, she was gorgeous. I wasn't sure if I'd ever noticed before. The gentle slope of her cheekbones, the length of her eyelashes, the bow of her top lip.

I swallowed past the desert in my throat. "You look…"

She inclined her head, probably waiting for some disparaging comment.

"You look beautiful."

Her normally cold expression melted into something warmer. With her amber eyes soft and berry-painted mouth curving from its usual hard slash, I had a glimpse of the first flower peeking up through the last frost of springtime. "Thank you."

"Are you ready?"

She nodded, and I bent for her bag then waited as she wrapped herself in her coat, covering up that second skin of a dress. It wasn't too terribly cold, though it was overcast with a slight breeze. I held the door open with one hand and offered my other arm. The corner of her lip twitched as she curled her hand around my elbow.

"This is the gentleman everyone is always talking about, huh?"

"You didn't believe he existed?"

She shook her head as I opened the passenger side door of

my car. I'd had it cleaned and washed yesterday. It was smelling extra nice, and I pointed it out to her. "Just for you."

"I feel like that is some backhanded way of telling me I need to get my car detailed."

"It absolutely is."

"So, not one hundred percent a gentleman."

I bent down to her level once she was seated. "I don't think you'd like me to be one hundred percent gentleman."

Her eyes, with those forever-long lashes, flicked up to mine. "No," she said barely above a whisper, and I couldn't help myself. I lifted her hand to my mouth, brushing a kiss across her knuckles then rotating it to scrape my teeth along her inner wrist.

Her lips parted on a quiet gasp, and I smiled into her palm before placing it back in her lap.

The car ride to my parents' house was silent, save for her informing me her seat warmer was too hot. To which I replied, "I thought it would remind you of the temperature of your home."

She sent me a narrow-eyed glance. "And yet you invited me with you. It's almost like you want me to drag you to hell."

I settled my elbow on the console between us. "In that dress, I'd follow you anywhere."

Like the queen she was, she raised her brow, assessing me. Seeming to deem me worthy, she offered me a smile, though it bordered on waspish. "Careful. It almost sounds like you like me."

CHAPTER NINETEEN

Taylor

I didn't want to go in and meet the Hargrove family. It felt too... relationship-y, but Dean practically dragged me out of his car. As soon as he strode in the front door, a photographer knocked into him.

"Oops, sorry 'bout that," they said, finding a better place to change out a lens.

Dean held his hand up. "No problem."

"There you are!" a blond woman, who had to be Mrs. Hargrove, shrieked from her spot by the fireplace. "You were supposed to be here at 12:45."

Dean held up his wrist, displaying his watch. "And it is exactly 12:45."

"See," I muttered, "being exactly on time is not an asset. It's anxiety-inducing."

"For you. Not for me." He tossed me a cheeky grin as he took my hand to lead me farther into the house. My heels clicked on the wood floor until my feet met the plush carpet of the living room, where the bride and her bridesmaids were lined up.

"There he is!" a dark-haired one chirped, and they all swung to Dean, who waved.

"Everybody, this is Taylor. Taylor this is my mom, Gem, Sam, Bronte, and you know my sister."

All the women smiled at me, though Mrs. Hargrove appeared a bit frazzled, and Dean walked over to her, sliding his hand along her shoulders. Her shoulder-length honey-colored hair was down and curled, accentuating the wide neckline of her sparkly blush gown.

"You look great, Mom," he told her, and she immediately relaxed a little.

"Dad!" Laney yelled. "Come on!"

Mr. Hargrove, a stocky gray-haired man made his way downstairs, fiddling with his cuff links. His tuxedo was black, his boutonniere a sprig of green, his teeth immaculately white. No wonder this whole family could have been on a billboard. They were like a commercial for laundry detergent or toothpaste or some other *after*effect of a product.

Laney was radiant in a lace and satin gown that was fitted to her hips and bust with a daring display of her generous cleavage. Her bridesmaids wore matching burgundy satin gowns. The shortest one with a pixie cut—Gem, I thought— appeared a little tipsy already. Sam, the one with rose-gold hair, bent down to adjust Laney's shoe, while Bronte conversed with a second photographer.

I watched from the corner as pictures were snapped in different poses and sets of people, before Laney waved me over. "Come on, get in this one."

"I don't think..." I trailed off, my eyes finding Dean's. He made no motion one way or another, and everyone's eyes landed on me. My skin heated, knowing the longer I argued and deliberated on how I was not part of the family or wedding party and, therefore, should definitely *not* be included in photos, the more I delayed the proceedings. So, I felt compelled to trudge forward. Laney tucked me in right next to Dean, grinning.

"I'm so glad you're here."

"Thank you, and you look stunning."

"Thanks." She fingered the long veil draped behind her shoulders. "I'm anxious to get this all over with, so I can see Ethan."

I startled when Dean's hand found my lower back as he leaned behind me to speak softly to his sister. "We could be done with these pictures whenever you say."

"Whenever *I* say?" she said through clenched teeth, her eyes pointedly landing on their mother.

Dean sighed then pulled me closer to him, his mouth by my ear. "Don't worry. We won't hang these photos over the mantel or anything."

I jabbed his side, and he breathed out a laugh that skittered goose bumps along my neck and shoulders. He tightened his fingers on my waist as the two photographers wrapped up and the group started toward the front door. Dean dug into his pocket and held up his car keys.

"Don't scratch the paint, Novak."

I accepted them with an open palm. "Screw your paint job. I'm going to Mexico."

He turned so his back faced Laney and her friends assisting her out the door, making sure her veil didn't drag on the floor. "Seriously," he said, "you're really helping me out. I couldn't bring my guitar with me, and you driving my car is a big help."

"I won't let anything happen to your precious baby."

He'd told me that he'd had his acoustic guitar since he was a kid, and that it was really special to him because Patrick had drawn some art on the body of it. Dean had brought it to play a song for Ethan and Laney as his gift to them. I told him that he should have gone with a toaster oven instead.

We were the last ones out of the house, and Dean locked the door behind us before he escorted me to his car and opened the driver's side door. "I'll see you at the church."

Even though he didn't need it, I smoothed my hand over his collar and tie, and Dean held very still at my ministrations, his eyes boring into me.

"Thank you," he said after a moment, his gaze raking like sandpaper over my skin.

"Couldn't let you go without making sure you looked perfect. I know how vain you are."

I felt his smile against my temple. Then he gently nudged me into his car, and after situating myself, I finally peered up at him. His eyes were unwavering on me. "You have to stop staring at me like that. You're giving me a complex."

"I didn't realize your self-esteem was so weak," he goaded.

"No more than your dick," I volleyed back.

His lips twitched in amusement even as his eyes narrowed. "Watch your mouth, Novak, or you might not like where I put my dick."

I forced out a laugh, though it was little more than a puff of air. "I'd like to see you try."

He bent, squeezing my chin between his thumb and forefinger. "Don't tempt me."

With a rough flick of his fingers, he straightened and closed the door, sealing me inside his car that smelled of him. I watched him climb into the old-fashioned trolley, where I could see him through the windows, addressing the group like he was the king of the castle. And it wasn't even his wedding.

What an asshole.

I smiled and turned the ignition over, following my phone's GPS to the church, where I snagged a program and was ushered to my seat by a clean-cut dark-haired white guy, who looked like he'd have trouble fitting through the doors, his suit doing nothing to mask his muscles. Another guy, who I swear was CJ Cunningham, the famous actor-director, was walking back toward me after helping an elderly woman to her seat, and I had to blink a few times, clearing my eyes to make sure I wasn't seeing things. The third usher was a tall and drop-dead gorgeous blond man. He escorted a woman to a front pew on the groom's side, her long, dark hair flowing halfway down her back, her shawl matching her dress, and I flipped through the program, reading their names and making mental connections to who everyone was.

The ushers were married to the bridesmaids. The woman, Marcela, was going to be doing a reading, and I blew out a breath at the sheer length of this wedding.

I wasn't religious and knew next to nothing about Catholicism, but I suspected the ceremony would take a while. I crossed my legs, trying to find a comfortable position on the hard wooden pew, then resorted to counting all the pink and white flowers that decorated the aisle while the church filled up with more and more people. I spotted some familiar faces seated on the groom's side. Seth was invited because he attended their monthly poker nights, and there were the two guys who played the keyboards and bass from the Anchormen, but with so many people in attendance, I doubted even Laney and Ethan knew everyone all that well.

A violinist played classical melodies, and at some point, the murmurs quieted. A priest in long robes took his place at the altar, and Ethan and his groomsmen lined up next to him. The first people down the aisle were Ethan's parents then Dean, accompanying his mother, followed by Gem, Sam, and Bronte, who was already crying. According to the program, Trace, the ring bearer, was Ethan's nephew, and the little boy appeared as if he might sprint down the aisle if it weren't for the pretty Black woman holding his hand. She was Trace's mom and a groomswoman. She wore the same silk dress as the brides-maids and reached out to squeeze Ethan's shoulder as she and Trace passed.

Then the music changed to the traditional wedding march, and we all stood. Ethan fixed his glasses on his nose as if he wanted to be able to see everything perfectly and blew out a big breath when Laney appeared on the arm of her father. A rippling gasp swept through the attendees, as if no one could get over how beautiful the bride was, and I peeked over to the altar in time to catch Ethan drag his knuckle over his cheek, wiping away a tear, but I didn't miss how Dean tugged on his earlobe, his focus on the floor. The softy.

At the end of the aisle, Laney and Ethan held hands, and the priest began with a blessing. For the next hour and a half, there was a lot of sitting and standing and doing what the priest instructed. Poor Trace had trouble sitting still. Then again, I was a grown adult and struggled too.

Dean turned over his shoulder, stretching his neck, his eyes searching. I sat taller, and when our gazes met, he tipped his chin to me, a silent message. *We're almost done.*

Though the vows had been exchanged, like, thirty minutes ago, it felt like thirty hours from the way this priest droned on and on. He finally invited the bride and groom back up and said one final blessing before introducing the new Mr. and Mrs. Marrero. They shared a kiss to an excited round of applause and practically danced down the aisle together, followed by their wedding party. When Dean passed me, he winked, and I pretended it didn't wake up a few butterflies in my stomach.

A short receiving line formed in the vestibule, and I offered Laney and Ethan each a hug. Dean wrapped his hand around my elbow, reintroducing me to Hank and then to Gabe, a groomsman and friend from high school, as well as Justin and Leah, Ethan's brother and sister-in-law. But I barely had time to exchange a few words with them before we were shepherded outside to see off the happy couple.

This time, Dean and I had no sarcastic comments, only a squeeze of our fingers. I took part in blowing bubbles like the rest of the crowd as the trolley took off down the street, to wherever the bridal party was headed for photos.

I hopped back into Dean's car and drove to the reception. According to Dean's instructions, I was to leave everything in the car and head inside to the happy hour. He said he'd take care of everything else. So, I grabbed a glass of red and found my seat. Without knowing anyone, I pretty much kept to myself. Though I did have a short conversation with Seth. He seemed rather suspicious of me and my presence here, but I didn't give a shit what he thought about me and went back to sipping my very pleasant red blend.

An hour later, the wedding party was introduced, and Laney and Ethan had their first dance to the same song the Anchormen had played at their gig a few weeks ago. Dean appeared at my side.

"Hey, Nov. You having fun?"

"Your sister was right. The wine is delicious."

"See? I told you it wouldn't be bad."

No, it wasn't bad. Not when I was tucked up against his side, his fingers skirting over my back. I both loved and hated this dress. I loved the way I looked in it. Hated the way Dean had an all-access pass to my skin. Because I was on fire wherever he touched me.

As if he knew, he drew the tip of his finger down my spine, from my neck to my tailbone, and I shivered.

"You cold?" he asked, smirking.

"One of these days, someone is going to come along and smack that cocky smile right off your face."

He lifted his hand to my neck, curling around it possessively, and that did more for those stupid butterflies in my stomach than anything else he could've done to me. Especially when he leaned into me, his nose in my hair, his lips against my ear. "Don't threaten me with a good time."

I couldn't hold in my laugh and turned into his side. His fingers at my neck tightened ever so slightly, and I tipped my head so we were within kissing distance. He didn't move. Neither did I. A standoff between a rock and paper.

The song ended as people all around us clapped for the bride and groom, and I blinked back into awareness before taking my seat again, this time next to Dean. We were at a table with Laney's bridesmaids and their husbands, and the man across from me was mostly definitely CJ Cunningham.

I found my phone in my purse and texted Dean.

\Why is CJ Cunningham here?

When Dean didn't move, I placed my hand on his thigh. He lurched slightly under my touch but relaxed after a moment and placed his arm on the back of my chair, brows raised.

"Check your phone," I told him.

"I am not working at my sister's wedding. Bad form."

I sent him a bland look, and he removed his phone from his pocket, his thumb scrolling over his screen as he typed a message back to me.

SOME ASSHOLE

Married to Bronte.

Are we not supposed to acknowledge he's famous?

SOME ASSHOLE

Never thought you'd be a fangirl.

> He was nominated for an Oscar, and he's just sitting here. Eating a dinner roll.

SOME ASSHOLE

> He's also really good friends with Ethan and is married to one of my sister's best friends.

SOME ASSHOLE

> Stop drooling.

I dug my fingernail into Dean's thigh, and he hissed. "Jesus. Put the claws away."

The salad course was served, and I mostly kept to myself, though Gem, Bronte, and Sam pulled me into their conversations about Gem and her children with her husband, Jason. Sam talked about the backpacking trip she'd taken with her husband, Mike. And Bronte and CJ were in the middle of some story about their dog when the DJ's voice came over the microphone, inviting Justin to deliver his best man's speech.

Ethan's brother looked nothing like him, and Dean filled in the gaps for me, explaining that they were both adopted, and Marcela, the woman who'd read during the ceremony, was Ethan's birth mom. Justin's speech was short and a bit halting because of his Huntington's disease, and when he finished, both Ethan and Laney gave him teary-eyed hugs. Then it was Dean's turn.

He strolled over to the DJ's booth, where he'd hidden his guitar. He settled the strap over his shoulder and stood at the microphone with a smile. "Hello, I'm Dean, Delaney's brother and one of Ethan's best friends. I've had the distinguished pleasure of seeing two of my favorite people grow from idiot kids in love into...relatively smarter adults in love."

That earned laughs from the crowd, and I leaned my elbows on the table, sinking into this drunken feeling like I could listen to him forever.

"In lieu of a speech and in place of a toaster oven, I have something else for you," he told the bride and groom. He plucked a few chords on his guitar, and Ethan held out his hand to Laney, guiding her back out to the middle of the dance floor once again. Dean sang in a surprisingly smooth voice "You Can't Hurry Love" as they swayed.

I found myself grinning like an idiot kid in love, even when Dean's eyes met mine over the expanse of the dance floor. His smile grew as his hands continued playing that sweet song about being patient to find love, and it felt like he was singing directly to me.

With the last notes of the song, Ethan dipped Laney back and kissed her throat to raucous applause, for not only the couple but for Dean, too. He lifted his hand in recognition, set his guitar back down, and made his way back to the table. He was greeted by backslaps and fist bumps, but when he sank down into his chair, he wrapped his hand around my neck again, asking softly, "So, how'd I do?"

My attention slipped to his lips for a moment before I forced it back to his eyes. "I think you need to be very careful who you point that guitar and charisma at, Hargrove."

He grinned and squeezed my neck then let his hand drift down my back.

I didn't know what I was more afraid of. The way he had looked at me just then, like what I thought about him really mattered. Or the way he touched me, like he already owned me and he'd have me, no matter what.

Either way, I was pretty sure I lost the game.

CHAPTER TWENTY

Taylor

We ate and danced and drank to our heart's content. As Dean had promised, there was no "YMCA" or "Cupid Shuffle," but there was quite an assorted playlist. Some for the older crowd, some classic rock sing-alongs, and some that had me clinging close to Dean, his hands branding my back with his finger-prints. I didn't know if I could ever wear this dress again.

If I did, it would only remind me of the night I learned Dean Hargrove was heart-wrenchingly sentimental with his friends and family and also quite territorial with me. After a few rounds of shots with his high school buddies, he'd found me chatting with a man named Declan, who was one of Ethan's cousins...I thought.

But with the way Dean's eyes narrowed on us, he might as well have been an interloper stealing the wedding gifts. Dean slid his hand around my waist. "I've been looking for you."

"Yeah? Not real hard, then." I gestured to the space around me. "I've been right here."

Declan chuckled, but Dean silenced him with a glare then looked back to me. "Making friends?"

"We were just chatting," Declan offered.

"Yeah, I had to keep myself occupied."

Dean's brow rose. "You ever hear the phrase, you dance with the guy who brung ya?"

"No, and as I've repeatedly informed you, you need to work on your grammar. It's atrocious."

Declan snickered, and Dean aimed another scowl his way. "Excuse us."

With his palm between my shoulder blades, he steered me away from Declan and to the dance floor, where I let him lead me in a slow dance even as I said, "That was rude."

"I don't care. I know for a fact that guy has so much sex I'm surprised he doesn't have the clap."

"That's the pot calling the kettle black."

He slanted his head back to meet my gaze. "I've never had the clap."

"Not the point," I muttered. "I was talking to him for, like, five minutes. There is nothing to be jealous of."

"I'm not jealous." He held me closer as the song changed to a faster-paced one, while we still slowly rotated, dancing to our own melody. "I've never been jealous in my life."

I snorted at the lie.

"I haven't."

"Except for right now," I said.

He adjusted his hold on me, letting go of my hand to fit both of his along my lower back. "Your words are saying one thing, while your tone is telling me something completely different."

"If my tone is telling you you're a jackass, then that's what I'm trying to convey."

A few strands of my hair caught on his beard as he shook his head, his jaw scraping along my cheek. "It sounds as if you *want* me to be jealous."

With my heels still on, we were the same height, but I rested my chin on his shoulder, admitting, "I don't know what that feels like. I've never been with anyone long enough for them to be jealous."

He let out a harsh breath that tickled my neck. "Growing up with a twin, I always sort of felt like I wasn't wholly me. I had to share, if not DNA, then something else. The world has some weird obsession with twins, they want to put us in boxes, but I was me."

With how he was rambling, I had no idea where he was going with this, but I understood there was truth to be discovered in his drunken rant.

"Even being fraternal, everyone wanted us to be exactly the same. Our family, my parents. We had to do everything together, and that's why I learned to be possessive about what was mine. I wanted to keep what I had separate. I was me, and she was her, and my stuff was my stuff, my friends were my friends. I think that's why accepting her and Ethan was hard. He was my friend first."

My fingers found their way into the hair at the nape of his neck as he spoke, his own hands gently curling and uncurling against my spine like he was trying to dig into me. As if, maybe, he was looking for something. The same something I was looking for in him.

"I have a tendency to get weird about people touching my stuff," he said. "I've worked hard my whole life to get what I have—my job, my house, my car, and I do everything I can to keep it all pristine. I'm not going to let my stuff go to shit after I spent so many years to get it. I'm the same way with women."

"You treat them like your *stuff?*" I asked, leaning away from him, but my mocking smile faded when his hand coasted up to my neck.

"Never." Then his hand slid up into the back of my hair, gripping it roughly. "But when I work hard for something, I won't let it go. I won't let anyone else have it."

"Women aren't objects. They aren't yours to own," I told him, though there was no heat in the reprimand because I liked the hint of danger in his words. Because I knew, had already experienced, how safe I was in his hands, and desire pooled deep in my belly at his delicious promise.

"Something tells me you'd like to be owned, at least for a little while." His lips ghosted over my cheek, and my heart beat in my ears. "You're always going on about needing something special, needing a certain type of guy."

"You don't know what you're talking about," I whispered, having trouble regulating my breathing.

"Don't I?"

I shook my head, though it was nearly impossible with how he held me, and the slight tug on my hair sent a ripple of heat over me, settling between my legs.

"I think I do," he said, tilting my head back to skim his nose along my pulse. "And I think you like it."

I gulped down air, my chest heaving with the action, but Dean didn't care. In fact, he pushed me away from him, holding on to one of my hands, and then twirled me into him like a rag doll. My body was so confused, it didn't know whether to laugh or cry or strip naked right then and there.

I did none of the above as the DJ handed off the microphone to Laney and Ethan, who each took turns thanking everyone for coming then introducing the last song of the night, "Sunday Morning" by Maroon 5, which was apparently one of Laney's favorites. They took to the center of the dance floor, scream-singing the lyrics, and I took the opportunity to snag an untouched glass of champagne from a random table. I downed it, but it did nothing to soothe my wretched nerves.

As Dean cupped his hands around his mouth to shout something to the bride and groom, I coasted my gaze around the ballroom, wondering how I got here, to this literal and figurative place, at a wedding, contemplating having sex with the guy I'd hated since law school.

What the fuck have I been doing with my life?

But I didn't have long to assess the possible damage because the lights of the ballroom turned up. It was eleven o'clock, and though we didn't have to go home, we couldn't stay here.

Dean, with his tuxedo jacket over one arm, his vest open, his tie long gone, slung an arm around my shoulders, the alcohol evidently hitting hard now. Seemed like once the party ended, so did his tolerance. He leaned into me, and I struggled to keep him upright as we made our way toward the elevator.

"I told you," he said. "Isn't it so much easier to go to our room instead of drive home?"

"At the moment? Not really." I grunted and paused to hitch him higher. "You are suspiciously heavy for such a short guy."

"Fuck you, I'm perfectly average. Except my dick. That's above average."

I snorted, and he yanked on my hair.

"Ow!" I elbowed him, and he staggered into the wall, laughing.

"God, Novak, if we're going to wrestle, I'd rather it be naked."

"I could take you and what is certainly your below-average dick."

"First of all," he started, holding up his finger like he was in front of a jury, "it's not very kind to dick-size-shame. Everyone knows the average vagina can only take three or four inches anyway."

I dug my hand into his pants pocket for the key card to our room, grateful that he'd brought our bags up earlier. I wouldn't have been able to handle them and him. "I don't need you mansplaining my own anatomy to me."

He went on as if I hadn't spoken. "Second of all, I'm not talking shit. I'm being real. My dick is above average."

I propped him up against the wall as I opened the door, and he all but tumbled inside then immediately started unbuckling his belt.

"Oh my god, Hargrove! I don't need proof. I believe you."

From where he sat on the edge of the bed closest to the door, he gazed up at me with pink eyes and red cheeks. "I need to take a shower."

He bent over and untied the skinny laces of his dress shoes and threw each one to the corner of the room while I carried my bag to the other bed. I wasn't going to undress while he was right there, so I kept myself busy, drinking some water and downing Advil. I'd had a few drinks but was nowhere near as drunk as he was. I was downright sober comparatively.

With a groan, he flopped back on the bed, one sock on, his vest off, and belt unbuckled. "I feel like I'm going to puke."

"You need to drink water." I brought him one of the bottles, along with some crackers I'd packed. "Here."

He opened one eye to me, and when I held them out, he struggled up to a sitting position. Like a toddler trying to solve a puzzle, he couldn't even manage to open the crackers, so I sank down to the bed next to him with a sigh and opened them for him.

"Look at you," he crowed. "Tearin' through plastic wrap like the best of 'em."

"It's the top skill listed on my résumé."

"As it should be." He stuffed a cracker into his mouth. "You have fun?"

"I did, yeah."

"I'm glad."

I sipped my water as he polished off the crackers in contented silence, and after he finished the entire bottle of water, he swiped his hand over his face. "Thank you for coming with me. I wasn't lying when I said you are the only person I'd bring."

"Because it's impossible to form an attachment to the devil, right?"

He tossed the empty bottle to the night table, and it landed on its side. "You'd be surprised."

"Yeah?"

He turned to me, his eyes significantly clearer than fifteen minutes ago. "I hate that I like you."

I didn't know how to respond, but he didn't seem to care. He scrubbed his hands over his face once again before standing up to remove his clothes. I twisted away, tucking my shoes into my bag and removing my earrings and hair clip. After the trill of a zipper sounded, Dean padded in the opposite direction of me, and I checked over my shoulder to make sure the bathroom door closed.

I dropped down to the bed, using a wipe to remove my makeup, listening to the shower run, and my mind absently wandered into the garden of dicks and Dean's supposed above-average one. I truly didn't care about the size of my sexual partners—as long as they could get me to orgasm, I didn't care how they did it. But now I was curious about Dean's. About the length and girth and if it hung to the left, and when the door opened again a few minutes later, I reflexively lifted my attention to it.

Dean slumped out, a small towel in his hands as he wiped it over his hair. He wore only black boxer briefs, and I absolutely tried to see what was beneath them, but with the low light and his walking around his bed, I couldn't tell. Though the rest of him was up for consumption. He was tanned and trim, but not overly muscular, with a bit of sandy hair on his chest.

"Done?" I asked, holding my toiletries and pajamas in my arms.

He nodded and opened up another water bottle. "All yours."

I scooted into the bathroom, where I washed my face, brushed my teeth, and changed into a T-shirt and lounge pants, which took all of five minutes. Ten, at the most. Yet when I walked back out, I found Dean already fast asleep, his arm thrown over his face, the sheets pulled halfway up his body.

I tossed my dress into my bag before curling up on my bed, easily drifting off to sleep.

Only to be shocked awake in the middle of the night by snoring. I flipped over, blinking into the darkness of the room, and pushed up onto my elbow. Feet from me, Dean was sawing wood, adrift in peaceful slumber, totally unaware that being in the same room with him was like listening to the *Wheel of Fortune* wheel spin without the chance of winning a prize.

"Dean." When he didn't answer, I sat up. "Dean!" That rattling snore reverberated again. "You've got to be kidding me." I threw one of my pillows at him, but he kept right on going. "Wake up!"

I flopped back down and covered my head with another pillow, though it barely muffled the maddening sound. "Dean!" I jumped out of bed and leaned over him, waiting for my eyes to adjust to the dark. Once they did, I saw his mouth was wide open, his naked chest expanding with every snore. I shook him. "You need to wake up."

He jolted and tossed his arm away from his face, almost hitting me in the process, as he blinked up at me.

"You're snoring like a goddamn bear," I told him, and he mumbled an apology. I moved to step away from his bed, but his hand closed around my wrist and he pulled me down to him with a startling amount of force for his being half asleep. In shock, I fell onto his mattress as he turned on his side, and I peered over my shoulder. "What are you doing?"

This prick was asleep already, unconsciously cuddling with me.

"Dean." I dug my elbow into his stomach. "Dean!"

His face was buried in my neck. "Hmm?"

"Wake up and let go of me."

He didn't, but he did drape his leg over me. With his arm around my middle, his thigh holding me in place, and his steady breaths against the back of my head, I was trapped.

I sighed. "I hate that I like you too."

Then I hunkered down and made myself comfortable, falling asleep in the cushion of Dean's arms.

CHAPTER TWENTY-ONE

Dean

My fingers twitched as my body whirred to life, my brain like coffee beans in a grinder, and I shifted, barely aware. I inhaled cinnamon and flowers and comfort, my arms constricting around something soft, and I nuzzled my face against the pillow. A growing heat spread from my arms and legs to my groin, and I unconsciously ground my erection forward as my mind sputtered and chugged awake. I flattened my palm against my bed...

But my bed moved, and I blinked, forcing my eyes open, even as my head protested. I lifted my arm, only now realizing what I thought was my bed was a person. A dark-haired, sharp-tongued, remarkably soft person.

I blinked, fully awake this time, and leaned back as I yawned. The inside of my head clamored for more sleep, but the woman next to me rolled over, revealing a face so serene I almost couldn't believe it was real.

I rubbed the heels of my hands into my eyes, clearing the sleep from them, then studied her more closely. Morning sunshine spilled in from the curtains on the other side of the room, lighting the room in a muted glow. Taylor's hair was a mess, chunks of it across her cheek, and I used the tip of my finger to push them behind her ear, then traced down her jawline. When she didn't wake up, I touched the bow of her top lip, gently rubbing side to side, and I didn't know why or when she'd gotten in my bed, but I really liked waking up to her.

Which was a surprising but not completely unwanted feeling.

Pieces of the previous day filtered through my memory. Her dress, her breath on my neck when we danced, her soft gasp when I squeezed her neck, her eyes sparkling with desire when I called her out for wanting me to be jealous. I might have drunk a lot at the reception, but I recognized blatant craving when I saw it. And she wanted me as badly as I wanted her.

Which was why I had this raging hard-on the longer I looked at her.

I woke up with morning wood all the time, but not like this. I stared down at the steel pipe in my underwear and dropped my head back to my pillow. "Fuck me."

Taylor didn't move, still fast asleep, and I carefully extricated my left arm out from under her then snuck out the other side of the bed. With the door to the bathroom closed, I bent over the counter, trying to get a hold of myself and my hangover.

I drank water straight from the tap and found a bottle of pain relievers, swallowing down three of them before brushing my teeth. I stared at myself in the mirror, my mind inundated with flashes of my hands on Taylor, on her bare back, on her neck, her chin. Blood rushed south, swelling my already hard cock, and I gripped the edge of the sink, spitting and then rinsing my mouth out.

I was so hard, so painfully hard, I had to do something about it, and I couldn't even wait for the shower to warm up. Instead, I shoved my underwear to the floor and wrapped my hand around my length, gripping it tightly, as I closed my eyes, remembering how Taylor shuddered when I skimmed my fingers down her spine, how her pupils widened when I not-so-playfully threatened to put my dick in her mouth.

Grinding my molars, I imagined the shape of her lips around me, how she'd use that tongue for something else besides trying to take me down a peg. God, I'd love to see her on her knees.

My ears buzzed with white noise, my mind going blank except for the picture of Taylor's mouth, the feel of her tongue when we kissed at the bar, and what I was *desperate* to do to her.

Heat singed my skin, light sparked behind my eyelids, and I jacked my hand harder as I spilled my orgasm into the sink, grunting a low curse.

Only to hear it echo next to me.

My eyes flew open, and I found Taylor plastered to the doorframe, her hand at her throat, her mouth open, cheeks stained red.

I wanted to say something, but I couldn't. Not when I was stark naked with my dick in my hand, my body still coming down from the high of release.

"I...uh..." Her attention caught on my softening cock, and her throat worked on a swallow. "I wo-woke up, and I couldn't..." She blinked a few times before pulling her gaze up to my face. "I didn't know where you were and I called your name, but you didn't answer. I thought maybe you went down to breakfast already."

As if she hadn't walked in on me masturbating, I told her, "I wouldn't go without you."

Her focus drifted down again, and I sniffed a laugh. "Eyes up, Novak."

She jolted as if electrified, face flaming. "I'm sorry."

I tilted my head to the side. "Are you?"

That delicate throat of hers bobbed on another swallow, and I took a step toward her, needing to wrap my hand around all that pretty pale skin. I didn't think twice. I just did it, and she let out a breath, dropping her head back against the wall inside of the door.

"I don't think you are sorry," I said. When she didn't answer, I squeezed slightly. "Are you?"

She shook her head.

"With words, Taylor."

I felt her next swallow under my palm. "No, I'm not sorry."

"No, of course you aren't. You don't apologize for anything, do you?"

"No," she rasped.

I inched even closer, my stomach pressing along her side, my dick that had been out of commission mere moments ago already finding life again. "And you won't apologize for barging in here. You won't apologize for liking what you saw, will you?"

"No."

Jesus, she was perfect, and I smiled against her temple. "No, because you enjoyed it. You enjoyed seeing my hand wrapped around my cock while I thought of you, huh? You love knowing what you do to me."

She nodded, and I tightened my fingers where they were wrapped under her jaw. "Yes," she corrected. "I like it. Love it."

The buzzing was back, the clawing need raging through me. "And you love my hand around your throat, around your neck."

"Yes."

I coasted my mouth along her jaw. "And if I were to slip my hand inside your underwear right now, I'd find out how much, huh?"

"Yes."

I nipped her ear. "Tell me to stop."

"No."

And that was all I needed. I pushed the elastic of her pants out of the way, barely restraining myself from ripping them all the way off her legs to get to her flimsy underwear. I snapped the waistband once, eliciting a needy little gasp from her. "I know you better than you think I do, and I know you like a little pain." I curled my fingers and thumb through the leg holes of her underwear and bunched the material together, yanking it between the seam of her pussy. "I know you like it rough."

She inhaled sharply and reached for me, but I shook my head as I pulled up on her underwear so it would scrape against where she wanted it, yet not get her anywhere close to what she needed. "Take off your shirt."

She obeyed, and I rewarded her with a scrape of my teeth over her collarbone as I lowered my hand from her throat to her breast. She was flat-chested, but her nipples were pert and golden brown and begging to be bitten. So I did.

She cried out, and I yanked on her underwear one more time before releasing it. "You're soaked, aren't you?"

She nodded. "Mmhmm."

"Mmhmm," I repeated, finally pushing her pants down to the floor, her thin, wet panties immediately following, and I stood back to admire her. Without her heels, she was a few inches shorter than me and had to tilt her chin up to meet my eyes. I offered her a half smile. "Look at you, all flushed. Almost as if you like this. Like *me*."

She didn't answer, so I twisted her nipple, earning a moan and an even deeper blush, though she still didn't admit it.

But I'd get her to.

Drifting my hands over the lines of her muscled thighs

from all that running, up over her hips to her flat stomach, I traced the indentations there. "So strong." I moved my palms to her shoulders and traced the slope of her biceps to the crook of her elbows and her forearms, to where I finally gripped her wrists, holding them above her head against the wall. I stared down the length of her body, arching toward me. "So stubborn."

I dragged my tongue up her neck and sucked hard on the skin below her ear, making sure to leave a mark. Her hair would cover it, but even if it wouldn't, I didn't think she cared from the way she writhed in my hold. "Open your mouth," I instructed, and I stuck my index and middle fingers in, dragging them along her tongue. "Suck."

She closed her lips around my fingers, and my dick swelled at the wet heat and suction, sure that once she put her mouth on me, it would be my end. But at least I'd go to my death happy.

She swirled her tongue, her eyes never leaving mine, and I pulled my fingers out with a pop then dragged them down her chin and throat, leaving a wet trail to her nipple. I pinched and pulled on it as I bent to suck the other into my mouth until her breathing stuttered. "Have something to say?"

She shook her head. "No."

When I lifted my fingers up in front of her face again, I didn't have to ask, and she immediately sucked them into her mouth, this time dragging her lips up and down. "You're good at this. I think maybe you want something else stuffed in your mouth." Her teeth grazed the pads of my fingers in answer, and I ground my cock against her hip. "But not yet. Not until you're begging."

She released my fingers from her mouth, her brow raised in a challenge. "I don't beg."

"That's what you think now." Without warning, I spanked

her pussy, the soft crack of her skin releasing a beast inside me. "Spread your legs." She didn't even try to argue, and I smacked her again, my wet fingers meeting her flesh with a possessive clap, and she shuddered. I skimmed my nose over her cheekbone. "Not so tough without your black clothes and heels." I spanked her again, this time lower, directly between her thighs, and she gasped, her skin breaking out in goose bumps. "That armor you put on every day won't save you from me." Another smack. "You want it rough. I'll give it to you rough."

I parted her with my fingers, sliding through her red and swollen pussy with ease, her arousal coating even the tops of her thighs. I dipped my fingers inside her then dragged them up to her clit, and she whimpered yet still didn't say anything, so I pulled my hand away from her and spun us both around to face the mirror.

"Hands on the counter," I instructed, kicking her feet wide as I held on to her throat with my left hand, squeezing ever so slightly. Her mouth was open, dark eyes bright and pleading. She tipped her ass up, pushing back against me. So wanton. I leaned into her, my hard length settling against her backside. "Look at yourself. Look at how you're breathing, you can barely stand it."

I roughly handled one of her breasts and then the other, biting her shoulder, and she moaned. Peering over her shoulder, I noted her white-knuckled grip on the counter, so I doubled down, biting and sucking on her neck while I alternately worked her nipples until she was grinding back against me. "So fucking desperate. Tell me you like this. That you want to come."

I slid my hand down her stomach and parted her swollen flesh with my fingers, though I did nothing but simply hold her hot, wet pussy open. Her teeth bit into her bottom lip, keeping quiet. "So fucking stubborn."

Releasing my hand from her throat, I gently slapped the side of her breast, and she jerked. "Oh god."

"That's more like it."

"You're such a prick." She breathed out a laugh, bending farther toward the sink when I pinched her nipple, while I kept my other hand frozen on her. I was positive the cool air against her wetness was torturous. Good.

"One word, and I'll help you out. I'm sure you're aching. I'll take it away. All you have to do is say please."

She briefly dropped her chin, so I plunged my fingers into her sweet heat, and she let out a groan, her eyelids flying open to meet my gaze in the reflection of the mirror, but just as she rolled her hips, I removed my fingers, lightly teasing her clit. She curled her hand into a fist and thumped the counter.

"One word, Novak." I dragged my wet fingers between her breasts and circled one of her nipples. "One itty-bitty word."

"If that was some double entendre about the size of my tits, I don't appreciate it."

I hummed, kissing across her shoulder blade to the other side of her neck, then palmed one of her breasts. "These tits? They're perfect."

"I also don't appreciate lying."

I flicked her nipple. "Me either. So stop pretending you don't want this, don't want *me*, and give in."

I didn't know why it was so important for me to hear how much she wanted me, but I craved it as much as I craved her body, feeling her shiver, hearing her whimper. I couldn't be the only one fucking dying inside. If I was going down, I was taking her with me.

Gripping her hair, I tipped her head back so she was staring up at the ceiling as I slapped her clit. She moaned, and I circled my fingers over the tiny bud, listening to how she gasped for breath, her pulse slamming under her skin against my tongue.

She was cracking, her knees starting to give out, and I plunged my fingers back into her over and over, the sound of her wetness utterly crude and perfect to my ears. But as I felt her starting to tiptoe over the edge, I pulled out of her and cupped her pussy.

"Oh, come on," she whimpered, and I let go of her hair to wrap my arm around her shoulders, leaning her back against me so we stared at each other in the mirror. With her legs splayed wide open, one of my hands between them, and my forearm across her body, she was mine.

"I told you how I don't like to share, and this orgasm is mine. But if you use your sweet manners, maybe I'll give it to you." I licked the shell of her ear. "Let me hear it, Taylor."

She finally—blessedly—gave in. "Please."

"Please what?"

She growled, closing her eyes. "Please make me come."

"Now, watch us in the mirror. Look how good I can make it for you." I gave her pussy one more smack for good measure as her eyelids popped open, then I trailed my fingers over her clit and pushed into her, charting the same journey, in, out, over, until she was grinding against me. "So pretty," I husked, my voice failing me as Taylor and I both watched her muscles clench, her skin flush red all over, and I worked my fingers inside her, pressing my palm against her clit, letting her ride my hand, chase her high. "Such a needy pussy you have, don't you?"

She couldn't answer, her head thrown back, lost to herself as she pulsed on my fingers, and I didn't know if she heard me, or if she even cared, but I said it anyway. "I'll take care of it. I'll always take care of you."

Once her orgasm subsided, she sighed and draped herself on the counter, covering her face with her hands, and I smoothed both of my palms over her sides, across her hips and ass, up her back, until she lifted her gaze to mine in the mirror.

I was about to ask if she wanted more when a knock sounded on the door. "Housekeeping!"

With a blink, I shook myself out of my Taylor Novak stupor and realized we were late. It was time to check out, and the breakfast was almost over. "We gotta go."

CHAPTER TWENTY-TWO

Taylor

Dean and I dressed in a fury, tossing toiletries into bags, bumping into each other in the bathroom, both of us ignoring how he'd made me come so hard I saw stars. How I watched him masturbate with his above-average cock.

Son of a bitch, I hated him.

Hated how he could read me like a book. How he knew exactly what I needed without my having to ask, and he was good at it too. Good at touching me, at whispering his perfectly arrogant and filthy words over my skin until he had me begging.

I hated that I loved it.

And now I hated that I had to face his family. We ran down to the little room by the lobby, where a buffet was set out, alongside a dozen or so tables and chairs with small vases of pink flowers from yesterday. Luckily, no one noticed that we were late or that I had a hickey on my neck. Dean was careful that the red bruise barely showed under the length of my hair, but it was there all the same, and I hiked my scarf up higher around my throat.

With a scoop of eggs, a few slices of bacon, and a heaping pile of fruit on my plate, I dropped into the open seat next to

Dean. Across from us, Gabe looked especially hungover, his shoulder-length hair down and wet, probably from a recent shower. His sweatshirt was on inside out, and he had sunglasses resting on top of his head, while his boyfriend, Pavel, appeared to be asleep with his head in his hand.

"You guys driving home today?" Dean asked, and Gabe nodded, sipping a coffee.

"How long is the drive? 'Bout six hours?" I guessed, since they were headed back to Boston.

"Yeah, as long as there's no traffic."

"I wish you could've stayed longer," Dean said, after downing an entire glass of water.

"Maybe we'll make a trip down this summer, or," Gabe said, his red-rimmed eyes bouncing between Dean and me, "you guys can come up to visit."

We both answered at the same time.

"I don't—"

"We're not—"

"Yeah. Right. We weren't either." Gabe laughed, but his smile quickly faded as he rubbed his temples. "Oh my god. I'm too old for this shit."

I chanced a glance at Dean, who was shoving sausage links into his mouth like they were the last ones on earth. I poked his side. "You're going to throw up, eating so fast."

"I'm starving, and I need something greasy in my stomach." He held up his fork with a link across it.

I bit into it. "You're not as hungover as I thought you'd be."

His eyes landed on my mouth as I chewed and swallowed his bite of food. "Funny, isn't it?" Once his morning-blue eyes made their way back up to mine, he offered me the rest of the sausage. "Almost like I had a really good wake-up call or something."

I darted my gaze across from us. Although Gabe was too

busy waking up Pavel to take note of our conversation, I lowered my voice anyway. "The first and last time that will ever happen."

"It's also funny," Dean said conversationally as he chomped on a piece of honeydew, which was only more evidence of his malevolence. No one actually liked honeydew, yet here he was, shoving it down his gullet as if he enjoyed it. "You said that after you kissed me at the bar."

"Yeah, and it never happened again." When he eyed me, my cheeks heated. "You started it this morning, and there was no kissing," I declared, with my finger up like that made it better. It did not, but I was grasping at straws here.

"Real nuanced argument there, counselor."

I rolled my eyes. "Shut up."

"Come on, babe." Gabe pulled Pavel up to standing. "We have to get on the road."

Pavel mumbled something that I didn't catch, and I stood when Dean did to offer each of his friends a hug, but as I sat back down, my cell phone buzzed in my purse. It was a text from my sister.

KENNEDY

Gas leak in the apt building

KENNEDY

Have to find another place to stay for a while

WHAT

Before I could finish typing out my second text message, my phone vibrated in my hand with an incoming call from the building manager, and I answered immediately. "Miguel, hey. What's wrong with the apartment?"

Dean turned sharp eyes on me, his brow furrowing in question, but I only shook my head, curling in on myself, my elbows on my knees, my free hand on my forehead.

"Hi, Taylor. Sorry to call with this emergency. Your sister told me you're at a wedding."

"I don't care. What's going on?"

"There was a break in the main gas line."

"Oh shit," I whispered, my mind immediately spinning at the possible outcomes for this. "Is anyone hurt?"

"No, everyone is fine. But the gas is turned off."

I rubbed at my temple. "What does that mean? Kennedy said we have to find a place to go?"

"Since the utilities are gas, that means no heat until we get it fixed."

Dean placed his hand on my shoulder, urging me to sit up. "What's wrong?" he asked, and I held my finger up.

"How long is that going to be?"

"Could be a day or two, could be a week or two. I don't want to give you any guarantees until I know more. The utility company is here now."

I didn't care that it sounded immature when I said, "Oh my god."

"I know," Miguel said. "I'm really sorry, but with old buildings like this, we have to be really careful, you know? If we make a mistake, it'll take much longer to fix."

"Yeah." I was full-on sulking now. "Well..." I swallowed thickly. "I guess we'll talk later?"

"Of course. I'll update everyone when I know more."

"Thanks, Miguel."

I hung up and ignored Dean's prodding and called my sister. "Hey, where are you?"

"I'm on my way to Jordan's."

I slumped back against my chair, my face up toward the ceiling. "Jordan's. Why are you going there?"

"I'm moving back in with him."

I breathed through my nose, mentally reminding myself to unlock my jaw. "You are? I didn't know you were back together."

"Maybe this gas leak in your apartment was kismet. Gave me the push to give him a second chance."

I rubbed at the spot below my jaw, finding the tender patch of skin where Dean had left a mark. "Is that what you want?"

She laughed. "Well, I don't want to stay in your freezing apartment building."

I squeezed my eyes shut, giving up on my attempt to relax my muscles, and instead sat upright. "I thought we would share a hotel room, but..." I sighed. "What about your job at the bar?"

She snorted. "I hated that place. I quit."

"Kennedy."

"What?"

My sister, the reason I had to start dyeing my hair already. "I wish you'd..."

Be more responsible, was what I wanted to say, but seeing as how I let my coworker pull my hair and finger-fuck me this morning, I didn't feel like I had much of a leg to stand on when it came to making good decisions.

"Text me later," I told her. "And let me know if you need anything."

"Yes, Mom," she droned then hung up with a quick, "Love you, Titi."

"Love you, Kenny."

When I flipped my cell phone to the table, Dean was on me immediately. "What the hell is going on?"

"My apartment building has a gas leak in the main line, so unless I want to freeze my ass off for the next week, I need to find other lodging. And my sister is apparently back with her ex-boyfriend and is on her way to the Poconos, even though she doesn't currently have a job."

After a few moments of him staring at me with a wrinkled brow, he stood up. "Okay, let's go."

"Go?"

"Yeah." He slid his arms into his coat then held mine out for me to do the same. "You'll need to get some things from your place, right?"

"I...uh..."

He pushed me toward the door, where his sister and newly minted brother-in-law were speaking to a few people. With his hand on my back, he explained, "We're cutting out early. Taylor has an issue at her apartment."

Laney turned concerned eyes on me. "Is everything okay?"

"Everything will be okay, but it's a gas leak."

"Oh, man." Ethan nudged his glasses up his nose. "Sorry about that."

Laney flung her arms around my neck. "I'm so glad you were able to celebrate with us."

"Thank you for inviting me," I said, and she pulled back from me, smiling.

"I'm sure we'll be seeing more of each other."

I didn't know how to respond to that, so I waited as Dean said his goodbyes to the happy couple and the rest of his family, before heading outside to his car.

On the way home, I looked up different hotel rates and had my thumb hovering over the *BOOK NOW* button for a Holiday Inn when we pulled up in front of my building. Two utility trucks were parked out front, a few men having a discussion on the sidewalk.

"Thanks for...everything," I said, stepping out of the car, but Dean shut off the ignition and opened his door as well. "What are you doing?"

"Helping you pack up your stuff."

I nearly choked on my next breath. "Why? For what?"

He glared at me like I couldn't pass a first-grade spelling test. "I figure you'll have multiple bags." He gestured to the door of the building. "Come on. I'd rather not stand out here and argue with you in thirty-degree weather."

"You're the one starting it," I grumbled and pulled out my keys.

Inside my apartment, he trailed me to my room, where he shook his head at the way I folded my clothes. "What now?"

"Didn't you watch Marie Kondo? You could fit in so much more if you folded them like this." He demonstrated how to fold up my pants into a tiny ball. "See?"

"Okay, I can take it from here. You can leave now."

"Novak, stop being such a rock right now."

"You stop being such a paper!" I tossed my balled-up underwear at him.

He caught it with a smirk and held it between his fingers. "Do you own anything that's not black?"

"You'll never find out."

He clucked his tongue at me but stuck the underwear in my bag and then added in everything else I tossed to him.

"Can you grab that pillow in the silk case from the bed?" I asked as I packed up even more of my toiletries than I had for my overnight with him. Going from one hotel to another was not what I had planned, and I really would have liked to do a load or two of laundry today. Yet here I was, about to unload my life into a Holiday Inn for at least a week.

Dean stuck my pillow under his arm and looped my backpack and duffel bag around his other arm. With a crossbody bag, my purse, and a garment bag with my work clothes in hand, I locked up once more. "This really fucking sucks. All I want to do is take a long shower, nap, and watch *Parent Trap*."

"It's a good thing you can do all those things."

I huffed, trudging back out into the cold toward my car. "Not in a hotel room. I'll be—"

"You're not going to a hotel room."

I unlocked my car and tossed my stuff in. "What are you talking about?" I swiveled my head back to my empty apartment building, while the guys started to work. "Where else would I go?"

"My house."

I barked out a laugh. "No."

"Yes."

"*No.*"

"You can follow me." Dean motherfucking Hargrove pivoted on his heel and marched right to his car, where he put *my* pillow, *my* duffel bag of clothes, and *my* backpack with my computer and charger in the back seat.

"I—no!" I reached around him for the back door, but he blocked my arm.

"Novak, stop arguing." He pushed on my shoulder. "Get in your car. You're coming with me to my house, where you can take a long shower, nap, and watch your stupid *Parent Trap* movie."

"First of all, *Parent Trap* is classic cinema, and secondly, I don't want to go to your house."

"So, you want to stay at a hotel? And since when is anything starring Lindsay Lohan classic cinema?"

I stepped up into his space, digging my car key into the middle of his chest until he winced. "Don't think you can white knight me just because you got me off this morning. I didn't ask you to do this, nor do I want you to."

He scowled at me. "This isn't about me getting you off, but do you want to say that a little louder? I don't think the guys in the back heard you."

I whipped my head around to spot one of the utility guys suddenly finding his cell phone very interesting. I growled a curse. "I hate you so much."

"I know. Now, get in your car. I'm not letting you—"

"Why? Tell me why you're doing this. Why are you insisting on taking care of me like I'm a child?"

"Because you need a place to stay, and I highly doubt you want to pay three hundred bucks a night to stay in a room with shitty sheets and more than likely semen on the walls, but hey..." He opened his back door. "You really want to? Fine. Go. But I don't want to hear shit from you this week that you're tired or don't feel well because you were forced to stay in a Motel 6 or wherever the hell you'll end up, when I have a perfectly suitable guest room." When I didn't reach for my bags again, he slammed the door shut, his nostrils flaring. "One of these days, you'll get it through your thick head that you don't have to do everything on your own."

"One of these days, maybe you'll learn to ask instead of steamrolling."

He crowded me, momentarily blocking out the gray sky behind him. "But you take direction from me so well, don't you? You like to fight, but you also *want* to give in."

Heat pooled low in my belly at his words, and I shoved him away, stalking away from him with as much dignity as I could muster. Because he was exactly right. I loved fighting with him, and I thought I loved giving in to him even more. Worse yet, I loved how he didn't give up on me, didn't take no for an answer when the rest of the world did.

Like the sex-crazed idiot I was, I tailed behind Dean's Toyota to his place off Sharpless Street. It was a brick townhouse with a small porch that appeared to have an original wood railing and arches under the roof. With the wicker chairs and American flag hanging, it was...quaint. Like something straight out of the 1900s. He opened the door for me, and I stepped into the living room.

As I explored the decorative sconces and touched the black leather chair, he explained, "I bought it a few years ago, and it was really run-down. Took me a long time, but I renovated everything myself."

"You did? How?"

With his hands in his pockets, he shrugged. "You can learn how to do almost anything from YouTube."

"Wow," I said, impressed. "Looks great."

"Thanks." He hung up my coat in the small hall closet. "You want the grand tour?" At my nod, he led me through the tiny dining room and into the galley kitchen, which had white cabinets and a marble countertop on either side. He pointed through the panes of the black-painted back door, which led to a small mudroom then out to the backyard. "Not much to look at out there, but I'll get around to it once it warms up."

Rounding back to the front of the house, we walked up the creaky steps to the second floor. "My room," he said, gesturing directly to the right of the staircase. Then to the first door on the left. "Office."

I poked my head into the room with gray walls, a big desk, bookcase with a few collections of hardbacks and some framed photos. Without asking permission, I crossed to pick up one of the pictures. It was of a bunch of boys—maybe seventeen or eighteen years old—in school uniforms, all of them with shaggy hair, untucked shirts, and big smiles. "These your friends?"

Coming up behind me, he wrapped his arm around my side to point to each of the boys. "That's Gabe, me, Patrick, Hank, and Ethan."

"You all look the same," I said then dragged my index finger over Patrick, the boy with bleach blonde hair hanging in his eyes. He was a few inches shorter than the rest, so his arms were up over his friends' shoulders. "You miss him this weekend?"

I felt Dean nod next to me.

"I figured those couple of shots you all took were for him."

"Yeah," he said, and a coil of melancholy unfurled in my stomach.

"It never gets easier, huh?" I set the picture back down. "Sometimes I wake up feeling...not quite right. Like I forgot something, but I go about my day, only to suddenly feel this wave and..." I inhaled deeply as I faced Dean with his hands tucked into his pockets, his head close to mine.

"And it hits you all over again," he finished for me.

I stared into his eyes that were lighter in this sun-soaked office, and sometimes I swore he could see right into me. See right through me, for the fraud that I was. I wasn't the tough, badass woman I portrayed. I was a sad little girl trying to keep everyone from noticing how hurt I was by mean-mugging the world into submission. But this one man never fell for it. Never let me forget I wasn't alone. Especially in this, in grief.

And the common thread between us was so real, I swear I could have pulled on it. Maybe I did without even realizing because he closed the inches between us, dropping his mouth to mine, his kiss unhurried, his lips soft and inviting. Too inviting.

When he teased his tongue along my lower lip, I jerked away from him. "We have to stop this."

He scrubbed his hands over his hair and face then propped them on his hips. "Why?"

"Because."

"Because isn't an argument."

"Because we don't like each other. Because we work

together. Because we're fighting for the same promotion. Because how many more reasons do you need?"

He dropped his hands to his sides with a gruff exhale. "What if..." He spun in a tight circle, fingers bunched into fists. "Fuck, I don't know, Taylor. I don't fucking know what's going on. It doesn't make any sense, but I want you. I don't know why, and I don't know when it started, but..."

He shrugged, resigned, and it was all so ridiculous to me, I had to laugh. "That's it? You said I have bad arguments, but you're the one admitting you don't even know why you want to do this." I lifted my arms, waving to the whole of his house. "It's bad enough I'm here and we did what we did this morning. Let's leave it at that. There is no way we can keep going without running headfirst into a dead end," I said, trying to convince myself more than him that this was an absolutely *horrible* idea. "In a few weeks, when I move in to my new office, you'll throw a fit, call me a bitch, and be pissed that you slept with me, and everything will be worse than it was before."

He crossed his arms over his chest, eyeing me in a way I knew he glowered at his opponents in a case. My palms turned clammy, and I instinctively took two steps back from him.

"Are you afraid to give in because you're afraid to get attached?" He took two steps forward.

I forced a laugh. "No."

"That's what it sounds like." He lifted one shoulder. "But I do no-strings-attached sex all the time." He cocked his head like the smug bastard he was. "I thought you did too, and I admitted I want you. I gave you an orgasm this morning. You know how good it would be between us."

I hadn't realized he'd backed me into the wall until I hit it, but he kept right on taunting me. "Nothing has to change between us. You'll still be a bitch, and we'll still fight over the same promotion, but we could at least get some stress relief in the meantime."

"No." I darted around him. "That's a terrible idea."

"Terrible because you can't do it."

I ignored him and picked up my duffel bag from the floor in the hall. "This my room?"

Not waiting for his answer, I flopped onto the bed, staring at the pale-blue walls. Dean leaned on the doorframe, his hands in his pockets, with a stupid smirk on his stupid face. "Bathroom's right there." He tipped his head back on an angle behind him. "Towels in the closet. Help yourself to whatever you want. Food's in the fridge if you're hungry." Then he lifted one pointed eyebrow. "Let me know if you need anything."

I flipped him my middle finger, and he laughed.

Fucking laughed.

I waited until I heard him trek back downstairs before whacking the bed with my pillow a few times to release my anger. Then I made myself at home in his bathroom, which was as well done as the rest of his home, with gleaming white tile, a big vanity, industrial-style lights, and even a hanging plant in the corner, right next to the self-standing shelf with baskets of soaps and Q-tips. He even had a candle that was half melted, like this dude actually used it.

I stepped into the shower with perfect pressure. Of fucking course.

The more I got to know him, the more I hated him.

I took my time shaving and exfoliating then helped myself to sniff his body wash and special beard shampoo. Just to annoy him, I moved all the bottles around. I wrapped a fluffy towel around myself and changed into leggings and a sweatshirt then hung up my clothes in the closet and checked on Kennedy through a few texts. After spending an inordinate amount of time organizing myself, I couldn't delay it any further and headed downstairs. Dean was in the kitchen, in the middle of placing a plate in the dishwasher.

"Finally," he said, closing the machine door. "I need to shower. I made myself a sandwich for dinner."

"You have the diet of a second grader."

He ignored that. "Plates are up there. Napkins over there. Clean up after yourself when you're done."

Then he brushed by me, and my jaw hit the floor. After his performance in the office, that was it? No pleading or persuading me to have sex with him?

I shouldn't have been surprised; this was what I wanted—for him to drop it—and yet as I opened up the bread, I recognized the pebbles that sat in the pit of my stomach as disappointment. I made myself a turkey sandwich, though I could have made it a triple-layer hoagie for all the cold cuts and cheese he had in his drawer. Not to mention the fifteen different types of mustard.

I ate at the round dining table and made sure to pick up every single crumb, lest the clean freak come after me. Then I grabbed the rest of my things from by the front door and made my way back upstairs. I heard Dean walking around. He spent some time in the office, and eventually, the sounds of the television floated up from the living room, but I didn't want to encroach any more into his territory.

Or face the increasingly harder to ignore desire that had been building since this morning. So instead, I gorged myself on Lindsay Lohan movies and turned in early. The bed was comfortable, and with my own pillow and pillowcase, I should have been able to sleep, but all I could concentrate on was the telltale creak of the staircase and then the soft footsteps in the hall. Yellow light filtered under the crack of my door, and I knew he was in the bathroom with the flush of the toilet and running water. The clink of his toothbrush on the sink. A cough. A yawn. Then the footsteps faded away toward his bedroom.

I rolled to my back, sighing up at the darkened room.

I closed my eyes again, but Dean's voice filled my mind, the ghost of his hands embedded themselves in my skin, and I kicked at the covers, suddenly too hot to be comfortable, even with the wind howling outside.

Reminded me of my roaring emotions.

You're soaked, aren't you?

So stubborn.

Suck.

I'll give it to you rough.

Without consciously thinking about it, I traced my fingertips over the mark Dean had left on my neck, along my collarbone where he'd scraped his teeth, over my breast, to my nipple, and plucked at it.

Nowhere near hard enough.

And I hated myself for it.

Hated that I wanted Dean Hargrove.

Settling my hands on my stomach, I focused on breathing in for four counts and out for four counts, imagining snow-capped mountains and babbling brooks. Green grass and early morning sunrises. Dean's hands on my waist and his mouth at my ear.

Look at yourself. Look at how you're breathing, you can barely stand it.

I knew the skin along my neck and cheeks would be pink, felt the heat between my legs, and I dipped my fingers beneath my underwear, stroking the warm skin. I was already wet, and my index finger glided over my clit, but as I stared unseeingly up at the ceiling, I imagined thicker fingers, rougher hands, and my touch just wasn't cutting it.

"Fuck me," I muttered, slipping my hand out of my underwear, wondering if Dean couldn't sleep either.

Then again, he probably slept like a baby. Sociopaths didn't feel shame about what they did.

But to be sure, I pushed myself up from the bed and quietly made my way down the hall, stopping briefly when I stepped on a loud plank. At the end of the hall, I positioned my ear against his door and listened.

"I know you're there, Novak."

Silently cursing myself, I placed my hand on the knob and turned.

When the door opened, a light next to his bed flicked on.

"You're awake," I said.

He sat up, the sheet pooling at his waist, revealing his bare chest. "So are you." Even in the dim glow, I could see how his gaze swept over me. Felt it on every inch of my skin, even through my sweatshirt and leggings. "Couldn't sleep?"

I refused to fidget under his inspection and lifted my chin higher. "No."

"Any particular reason?"

"Don't be such a jackass, Hargrove."

He stood up from the bed and faced me in only his boxer briefs. "Get on your knees and ask nicely, and maybe I won't be."

I snorted.

"Or be a brat and see where that gets you. Back to your bed, with your pussy still throbbing with need."

Ache spread from between my legs, my nipples hard against the cotton of my sweatshirt, my skin on fire now.

"You want it?" he asked with a raised brow. "Get on your knees and crawl to me."

CHAPTER TWENTY-THREE

Taylor

Sure, I liked a little pain with sex. I liked my hair pulled, a hand around my throat, but never in my life had I ever degraded myself by *crawling*. "You're delusional if you think I'm going to—"

"Taylor."

I froze. The way Dean rasped my name, I fell for it every time.

He shortened the distance between us by three steps, and now that my sight adjusted to the low light, I saw his cock straining in his underwear. He appeared wide awake, no hint of sleep on his face. He must have been as desperate as I was for a repeat. Both of us tossing and turning in bed.

Now I was here, obviously wanting him to touch me, ease the painful need burning through me, but was I really going to give in to him?

He smirked as if he could read my thoughts. Hear my mental debate out loud. "I bet you were down the hall, touching yourself. Running your hands over your body, but they weren't mine. Your fingers aren't the right size. They don't feel like mine. After knowing how I touch you, masturbating isn't cutting it, right?"

I refused to answer, though I felt myself giving in, my legs going weak.

"But I'll help you," he went on. "I'll give you what you need. My fingers, my tongue, my cock. I'll give it all to you. All you have to do is crawl to me."

I shook my head, unable to answer verbally when I was afraid of what I might confess. That I was losing not only the battle, but the whole damn war. I was nothing without my wall of anger, and he was breaking through my defenses, systematically tearing them down, brick by brick. If I didn't stop him, there would be no protection of my sad and broken heart. And if I let him have that, there would be absolutely nothing left of me.

"I'll take care of you, Taylor," he said, the fog of lust cleared between us for a moment. This wasn't an immediate promise, though I knew he would follow through with that, but he was speaking in the wider sense. He wasn't going to hurt me, and he'd protect me from anyone or anything else hurting me too.

I found myself lowering to the floor, the wood hard and cold under my knees and palms, and then Dean's eyes flared. He licked his lips, his chest expanding on a deep breath, and he readjusted his stance, spreading his feet wider. As much as I didn't want to acknowledge it, this position—this supposed degrading position—was powerful in that I could see how it affected him. See how badly he craved me, how his breath hitched as I crawled closer to him.

I kept my head up, gaze never leaving his, and with every inch of space I covered, the more the air between us crackled. Hunger blazed in his eyes and waves of heat wafted off him as I stopped in front of his feet. Without a word, he reached out his right hand to me, so agonizingly slowly, and I leaned toward him, dying for my thirst to be quenched. When his fingers finally touched my face, trailing over my cheekbone, I let out a breath, only for the next to be wrenched out of me when he fisted my hair while he wrapped his other hand around my throat.

"You're all tied up in knots, aren't you? You need me to loosen them for you."

I couldn't speak, not with his fingers tightening over my pulse points and my blood rushing in my ears. My nipples were hard, my skin tight. I did need him to loosen something in me. More than he'd already loosened my grip on sanity.

"I will," he said quietly. "I'll make you feel better. But first, you're going to use this sharp-tongued mouth for something other than cutting me down." He let go of my throat, and I sucked in oxygen, filling my lungs with air, my skin already hot and damp with perspiration. "Take my underwear off."

Without hesitation, I curled my fingers around the elastic, allowing the thick head of his cock to spring free, followed by the rest of his length until it stood straight out toward me. I inhaled his earthy scent, stared at the nest of hair surrounding him, and my mouth watered the longer he held me in place.

"No snarky comment?" he asked, voice laced with humor. "No threat to bite my balls off?"

"Then I wouldn't get what I want, would I?"

"Full of surprises tonight." He released my hair momentarily, only to gather as much of the short locks as he could, holding it in a tight ponytail, the pull on my scalp connected to a pull between my legs. "Show me how much you want it."

I tried to move, incline my head toward him, but his firm grip kept me in place. His answering smile was dangerous. "See how it feels? To be so desperate for something, to want it so bad, but you're held captive. That's how you make me feel."

Then he yanked, angling my head all the way back as he bent over me, his other hand gentle on my face. "I don't know what you've done to me. I don't understand it." His voice was pure smoke, his thumb a tender pressure at the corner of my mouth. "But I've never wanted someone as desperately as I want you." He nudged his thumb into my mouth, lazily dragging the tip over my tongue, teeth, and lower lip. "It makes no sense, how I've seen you every day for the past two years, but all of a sudden, I can't look away." He let go of my lip with a careless flip of his thumb and dragged the wet pad over my chin and down my throat, the soft touch at odds with the vicious clench of his other hand in my hair and the wildness in his eyes. In the darkness, they looked almost black, and his gaze seared every part of me it touched. Marking me with an invisible tattoo, etching his name across my skin. "I don't want to look away, Taylor. I don't want you to either."

Then without warning, he straightened and thrust his cock into my mouth. I gagged at the sudden invasion, but he only tilted my head the way he wanted and did it again. Even as my vision blurred, I kept my eyes on him. He didn't want me to look away. So I didn't.

We were unflinching. My gaze. His rough thrusts. The taste of him on my tongue. His tender fingers on my jaw, working to relax me even with his otherwise rough treatment. A juxtaposition, like our relationship. Love and hate.

"Touch me," he ordered, and I obeyed, wrapping my hands around his thighs, feeling the muscles clench under my palms.

"I'm going to fuck your mouth until I come, and after you drink down every drop, I'll lick up all the wetness I know you're dripping with. But I won't let you come until you beg for it. Until you're hoarse from screaming my name."

I was struggling to breathe, my jaw tight, my lips pinched and sore from his bruising treatment, but I nodded anyway. Because I was wet for him, from being used like this, from his delicious threats, his ragged voice.

His shoulders hiked up, his stomach tensing in front of me,

and I knew he was close, so I slid my left hand up the back of his thigh, kneading his balls for a few moments before teasing my fingers along the skin behind them. He trembled, his breathing harsh pants, and I pressed a little harder at the same time I curled my hand around the base of his length, taking control back from him. I worked my mouth over the tip, while keeping my finger moving over him in a steady rhythm, and I rotated my fist. It was wet and sloppy, and I was seconds away from bringing him to his knees.

"Oh fuck," he rasped, his spine curving in, his chin dropping toward his chest. "Oh fuck." His face scrunched, his eyes squeezed closed, and I felt everything in him coil tight before releasing. "Fucking hell, Taylor," he grunted, bowing over me as hot liquid spilled into my mouth. I couldn't swallow it fast enough, and it leaked out of the corner of my lips as he trembled with the aftershocks of his orgasm.

He unclenched his fingers from around my hair, his hand holding the back of my head reverently as he pulled away from me. He swept his other hand over my mouth and jaw, clearing away the remnants of his pleasure.

"My god," he murmured. "You must be the devil, that's the only rationale I can find."

I huffed, though I couldn't keep my lips from twitching with a smile.

"You liked that, did you?" he asked. "You ready for more?"

"As long as you can give it."

He lifted his brow at the challenge. "Stand up and strip."

I took my time, slowly rising, then dropped my sweatshirt to the floor. When I bent to pull off my leggings, he stuck his hand out. "Give them to me."

"Why?"

"Because." When I didn't move fast enough, he rolled his eyes. "Because I'm gonna fold them up and put them away," he deadpanned, then snapped his fingers like the impatient dick he was. "I'm gonna tie you up with them. What the fuck else do you think?"

"I don't know," I mumbled, unable to hang on to my irritation as my belly fluttered. I even felt my heartbeat deep in my core, my pussy quite literally throbbing. When I handed over my leggings, he gestured to my underwear. "Them too."

I slapped the thin cotton into his hands, and it was only then he offered me a satisfied smile, his eyes roving over me. "On the bed, witch."

"You know," I said in cool conversation, as if I didn't feel how slick I was as I crawled onto the mattress, "it's always the most insecure men who call strong women witches."

He clamped his hand down on my ankle, so I couldn't move up any farther, and I peeked over my shoulder at him. He tipped his head to the side, dragging his attention up from where it had been on my ass. "You're a witch because you've put some kind of spell on me with your evil ways." Then he yanked my ankle toward him, urging me to roll over and lie flat on the bed. He leaned over me as he pushed and prodded my body into the position he wanted, diagonal across his mattress, the comforter and sheet already thrown to the floor. "But I'm happy to prove how very much you enjoy my *security*."

"It's a good thing you have a dick big enough to back up your smack talk."

He hummed, stretching my arms up above my head. "Told you it was big."

"I wouldn't say big. Bigger than average, but not *big*."

He bit the side of my breast, and I gasped. "That's enough talking for you, I think," he said and stuffed my underwear into my mouth. Then he grinned, standing back to admire me. "Much better."

I kicked at him.

"Now, now. Be nice, Novak."

I cursed at him, but it came out all garbled, and he laughed as he continued his business of tying my hands together with my spandex leggings, cinched tight enough that I flinched when he tugged on it. With my arms straight and above my head, he used the other leg to tie me to the headboard, and when he finished his handwork, he sighed. "Perfect like this. Quiet and at my disposal." Then he strolled to the corner of the bed and pushed my legs apart. "Now, let's see about this needy little pussy."

Holding my thighs open, he wasn't gentle or sweet. He was *unrelenting*.

There was no warm-up.

No kisses to my calves or hips.

No massage of my muscles.

Just hard licks up my center, long sucks on my clit. He dug his fingertips into me when I tried to shift over an inch, and when I reflexively squeezed my legs together, he slapped my inner thigh.

I heaved out a high-pitched sound at the sting and lifted my head. He picked up his head only long enough to tell me, "Your skin looks pretty with my handprint on it," before putting his mouth back on me, this time adding his fingers.

Softening his tongue, he curled his fingers into me, using gentle, steady pressure until I felt the telltale draw toward the cliff. I whimpered around the godforsaken cotton still in my mouth, inching ever closer to my release, but then he pulled away from me, leaving me tiptoeing over the edge. I cried out, and he levered himself over me, his lips shiny. "What was that?"

I hate you, I tried to say.

He curled his hand around his ear. "Sorry, didn't quite catch that."

Fuck you, I mumbled around the now-wet cotton that was sticking to my tongue, and he snickered at my distorted words. Absently twisting one of my nipples between his wet fingers, he lay on the bed next to me. "You know," he started, scraping his beard over my shoulder, "I was thinking about Professor Landry the other day."

Professor Landry? I muffled and slammed my head back to the mattress as he droned on about one of our law school professors, all the while teasing my nipples, occasionally sucking on my throat. This son of a bitch was playing me like he'd play his guitar, strumming a chord here or there, nothing in particular. But I was as taut as a bowstring. He only needed to strum a little harder to let me go. Yet he never did.

"Do you remember that?" he asked, and I blinked at him, having stopped listening long ago, too focused on trying to orgasm even as he didn't help me.

"No? Don't remember that, huh?" He shrugged and moved between my legs again. "Oh well."

And he began all over again. Licking and sucking and stroking me, keeping me hovering at the edge of bliss without ever letting me go. I thrashed when he stared up at me, flicking at my clit with infuriatingly languid strokes, like he had all the time in the world. But I guess while he had me tied up like this, he did.

He could do what he wanted with me.

I hated him.

And loved it.

Once again, he sat up, but this time, he kept his fingers inside me while he gripped my measly A cup as if it were a DD and bit into my flesh like it was a juicy apple. I arched into him, and he granted me another sharp bite before laving his tongue over my nipple. I breathed harder through my nose, curling my legs up, and goose bumps dotted my skin as the pressure almost boiled over.

Only to lose it when he removed his fingers from me.

My eyes stung with unshed tears, the up-and-down too much, and I groaned in frustration. He ghosted his lips up my throat to my mouth and kissed the corner of it before removing my underwear. As soon as it was gone, I sneered at him. "You bastard."

He laughed into a kiss, and I bit his lip in retribution. He hissed in pain, though he didn't back away, only pinched my nipple hard enough that I shrieked, and he took my mouth, leaving no question as to who was really in charge. I had moments, but he was the one who'd brought me to the edge. He'd be the one to push me over.

"Please," I whispered as he placed openmouthed kisses down my throat. "Please, Dean. I need to come."

He lifted his head, eyes searching mine, seeking reassurance. So I gave it to him. "I need *you* to make me come. *Please.*"

That was it. He lowered himself enough to take one of my nipples in his mouth, while he pushed his fingers back inside me, immediately finding the spot to push me over the edge. Fire licked up my spine, and I let go with a shout. As he promised, it was his name on my lips.

I'd barely opened my eyes before he was moving over me, untying my hands and massaging feeling back into them. After a minute, when we were both quiet, reveling in what had just happened, he urged me up to my knees and planted himself in front of me, holding a condom between us.

"I want you to put it on," he said, and maybe it was because I was a little emotional from the physical roller coaster he'd had me on, but my heart burst open at the sincere reflection in his eyes. After what had happened with the last man I'd been with, this little offering of thoughtfulness tore me in two.

I shouldn't have been so grateful for it, but I supposed my bar for men was awfully low.

"Hey," he murmured, tenderly wrapping his hand around my jaw, "don't cry."

I hadn't realized I was, but he swiped the tear away then kissed the damp skin of my cheek.

I took the condom from him. "I'm sorry."

He nudged at the tip of my nose with his own. "Don't be sorry either."

I nodded and ripped open the foil, carefully pinching the tip to roll it down his hard length.

"On your hands and knees," he said, but there was no bite in his voice. Only aching gentleness.

Once in position, he slid his hand up my spine to my hair, but he didn't clasp it in his normal rough hold. Instead, he combed his fingers through it and draped himself over me to kiss the spot below my ear. The same place he'd left a mark this morning. "This is for asking so nicely."

He took his time pushing into me, and I worried about taking all of him, but I was so slick and pliant, he easily worked himself in. "You're so perfect," he told me. "Hot and wet and so, so perfect." He kissed my shoulder then straightened himself up, holding on to my waist as he rolled his hips, allowing me time to adjust to him. "You ready for me?"

I peered over my shoulder at him and licked my lips. That earned me a smile and a smack on my ass. Then he squeezed my hip, pulled out, and thrust back in, propelling all the air from my lungs. I had to widen my hands and knees to take his forceful movements. "Look at you. Jesus fuck, Taylor. Just look at you."

My toes curled as Dean hit a place so deep in me, my back bowed involuntarily. I tried to find my voice, tell him I felt so full I might erupt, tell him nothing had ever felt as good as him inside me, yet I couldn't do anything but whimper. It was too much, the penetrating pain and the rushing pleasure, and I closed my eyes, each breath its own staggering hill to climb as he drove into me over and over and over again.

"I'm... I'm gonna come," I finally got out between shudders.

"I know. I know." He draped himself over me again, one hand next to mine on the bed, the other holding my breast, not pinching or pulling, simply clutching me to him. "I'm coming with you."

And this time, I knew he meant it in the immediate sense, but I longed for it to be in a wider sense. That he would always come with me. Always take care of me. Always be with me.

After we found our ecstasy together, he rolled us over and deliberately didn't try to hide himself as he removed the condom and threw it in the trash before walking down the hall to the bathroom. I heard the sink run, and a moment later, he was back. I scooted by him with my clothes to use the toilet and put my sweatshirt and leggings back on, sans underwear.

As I stepped into the hall, I noticed Dean standing in his doorway, his underwear on, hand propped on the doorframe. "Where do you think you're going?"

"To bed."

"Yeah. So get in here."

I stilled, confused. "You want me to sleep in your bed?"

"Yeah. We did it last night. One of my best night's sleep in recent memory."

"That's because you drank so much."

He waved his hand at me. "Get in here, Novak." He didn't wait to see if I'd obey him. "Anyone ever tell you, the gaping like a fish thing is real unattractive?"

I got into bed beside him. "Anyone ever tell you, insulting someone you just had sex with is rude?"

He pulled the sheet and comforter back up to cover us. "Aw, did I hurt your feelings?"

"No, but I'm going to hurt you in a minute if you don't shut up and let me sleep."

"So violent. After I gave you three orgasms." He turned on his side, the weight of his arm settling over my middle.

"It was two," I corrected.

"Three, including the one from this morning."

I hummed and hunkered down. "Never thought you'd be the cuddling type."

"Never thought I'd enjoy cuddling a rock, but there's a first time for everything."

"Never thought I'd like being covered by you, but there's a first time for everything."

I felt him smile against my neck. "Paper beats rock every time."

"That's what you think."

CHAPTER TWENTY-FOUR

Dean

For the second morning in a row, I woke up with my arm around Taylor's waist, my face pressed against her shoulder, and my dick rubbing against her ass. Wasn't the worst way to greet the sunrise.

But it was still weird, and I wasn't quite sure what the new day would bring. More fighting or fucking. I wouldn't mind a bit of both.

As I shut off the alarm on my cell phone, she shot up, the hair at the back of her head like a bird's nest. I sniffed a laugh at her bleary-eyed blinking. The pillow crease across her cheek. The limp slap at my arm.

"Since I'm a gentleman, I'll offer you the shower first," I said, scooting up the mattress to rub a tired hand over my face and hair. We had been up well past midnight last night, and already, I could tell this Monday was going to be harsh. "I have a meeting scheduled with Raber anyway, so I'm not going to the office right away."

A shadow dimmed her eyes, and I knew she still had lingering resentment over being removed from the Mackenzie case, but I couldn't do anything about it. And I certainly wasn't going to pass up the opportunity to head it up. Sure, I'd fuck

Taylor into next week anytime she'd let me, but there was still no truce where the promotion was considered. No matter what was going on between us, I couldn't forget I had a job to do.

She turned to look at me, and when I thought she'd hit me with some feisty one-liner, she merely offered me a ghost of a smile and rubbed her cheek on her shoulder like she was shy. Except that couldn't be right. Taylor Novak was anything but shy.

"You all right?" I asked.

She curled her knees up, wrapping her arms around them, her lips pursed for a moment as she studied me. I didn't drop my gaze. This was the moment right here. It would decide if we'd move forward like nothing happened or continue this cat-and-mouse game.

"I suppose you'll try to convince me what we did was a terrible idea," I said.

"And I suppose you'll try to convince me what we did was an outlet for all our pent-up aggression," she countered.

Neither of us did either. Instead, she shifted closer to me, and I reached out to her mess of hair and combed my fingers through the tangled knots.

Problem was, this was a terrible idea. Having sex with my colleague. Really fucking great sex, but she was my work frenemy. That was a fact. And I didn't shit where I ate. That was rule number one. Yet, here I was, running my fingers through her hair, like *this* was a fact. An inevitable conclusion.

"I hear there's something called conditioner," I said, and she flicked my thigh.

"My hair's so fine, it always gets knotted at night. That's why I packed my silk pillow." Then she pointedly eyed my pillows with the regular old cotton pillowcases.

"You could've brought it in here." Followed by the rest of her stuff. A fact. An inevitable conclusion.

"I wasn't thinking," she said with a yawn.

I let my hand drift down her back, over her threadbare Temple University sweatshirt. I plucked at the hem and curled my fingers around the waistband of her leggings. "Fucked your brain to pieces, huh?"

"It was all right."

"All right?" I let the elastic snap back into place against her hip, and she swatted at me before unfolding herself to stand up.

"Anybody could do a job well once," she told me and padded down the hall. "It's the endurance of repeat performances that counts."

I watched her sashay away, my own smile growing. I'd had a lot of sex, multiple occasions to explore different kinks and desires, but last night had been different. Better. Perfect.

A fact.

An inevitable conclusion.

And now, I feared I wouldn't ever recover.

I had thought—hoped—after I got Taylor out of my system, that would be it. But I was fooling myself. I was in deep now. So deep, I was tempted to follow her into the bathroom, beg her to stay home from work and fuck me instead.

Like the snake in the Garden of Eden.

"Hey, so I was thinking..." I leaned against the doorframe of the bathroom while she brushed her teeth.

She rolled her eyes. "Please, put your dick away."

"We should call in sick today."

She rinsed her toothbrush and swallowed down some water. "You said you had a meeting this morning."

"I can reschedule."

She heaved out a sigh and pushed off the counter to turn on the shower. "You can reschedule if you want, but I'm going in. I actually work."

"We can work from home." I bent my fingers, using air quotes.

She ignored my suggestion and stripped off her sweatshirt, exposing her back to me. My tongue stuck to the roof of my mouth, so I couldn't argue any further, and she bent, pulling off her leggings.

Who would've thought her skinny ass would be so soft and squeezable? Not me. But now that I had firsthand knowledge, I wanted more. I stepped into the shower right behind her.

She squeaked out an indignant gasp. "What do you think you're doing?"

"Trying to convince you to stay home." I faced her away from the spray. "Hands on the wall."

I tugged on her hips, pulling them toward me, and slipped my hand between her legs. "You sore?"

"A little."

I gently rubbed my fingers over her flesh, parting her, finding her hot and wet. "You can't get enough either."

She didn't respond, but her moan was answer enough when I stroked two fingers inside her, then dragged them over her clit.

"I'll take it easy on you this morning." I had installed a waterfall showerhead, so she was mostly out of the spray, and while some of it did hit the back of my head, I wasn't going to be deterred. Even with water trickling over my face and into my eyes as I kneeled down.

I kept my left hand firmly on her hip while I massaged her clit with my right, two fingers steady and pulsing. Then I gently licked into her. Like I promised. It didn't take long until she was wiggling back against me.

"Needy girl," I rasped so low I didn't think she could hear me over the water, but she hung her head with an equally low laugh.

"Apparently."

"You sound shocked."

She tipped her head toward me, squinting through the fall of the water. "I am. I don't usually do repeats."

I squeezed her ass cheek, possessiveness winding through my chest that she was needy for me. This tough, brilliant, capable of bringing the world to its knees woman wanted *me*. Unable to help myself, I smacked the side of her ass then smoothed the sting with my palm. Her lips quirked to the side, and she arched her back, offering more of herself to me. All of her pink and glistening skin between her legs.

"You better hurry up," she said. "I need to get into the office."

I held her hips in a bruising grip and lifted my brow in silent direction. She knew what she had to do.

"Please."

I grinned. "Your wish is my command."

I lowered my mouth to her once again, working my tongue and fingers over her until she was panting so loud, her breaths echoed off the tiled walls. I straightened my arm to pinch her nipple as I trailed my tongue from her pussy to her ass, and she tensed.

"You want me to keep going?" With one peek over her shoulder at me, I had my answer, and I swirled my tongue around the taut ring of muscle at her backside while I stroked into her, circled the swollen bud of her clit. It didn't take long before she climaxed with a groan. That sound, that deliciously depraved sound, drove me out of my mind. It wound around my rib cage, set my skin ablaze, heated the back of my neck so even the warm water felt cool against my skin.

I wanted Taylor Novak more than I wanted anything else in my life. To please her. Make her mine. Earn one of her rare smiles. The last time I'd felt anything close to this all-encompassing hunger was in college, and that didn't end up well. Now, it was even more. Even worse.

And it scared the shit out of me. What I would do for her.

Once I stood up straight, she spun around, not hesitating to take my cock between her hands, grasping me hard, pulling and twisting her fingers as she stared at me. Her long eyelashes clumped together, and I held her face between my hands, stroking the drops of water from her cheeks as my own orgasm barreled toward me. Like my feelings for her. It was quick and unexpected but hit me so hard, I was momentarily blinded.

When my vision finally cleared, I found her grinning at me. "Tell me again who the needy one is."

"You have no idea, Novak." I wrapped my arms around her and kissed the crook of her neck, giving in to every stupid, happy, funny feeling I had about this and deciding to let it ride. "You have no idea."

———

I'd become obsessed. There was no other word for it. And I was convinced it really was because Taylor worked for the devil. We went to bed together, woke up together, worked together, worked *out* together, and yet I never tired of her.

We spent the whole week like that and didn't murder each other.

In fact, Taylor seemed to be enjoying this new weird obsession as much as me. We were still competitive in everything we did, but there was an underlying current that it didn't matter who won anymore. We weren't fighting against each other. Rather, with each other. We made each other better.

Which was why I was glad she had plans to go to Philly on Friday. I needed time to finish some paperwork, and she was a distraction. With her off having dinner with her grandmother, I had a few hours to myself.

Up in the office, I had my music loud enough to block out everything else, and I didn't hear her come into the house until she was standing right in the doorway. "Hey."

I lowered the volume. "Hey."

She stalked around my desk. "What are you working on?"

I answered with my eyes back on my computer. "The Mackenzie filing."

"Mmm. When's it due?"

"Tuesday."

She leaned over my shoulder, bringing her cinnamon-and-flower smell with her. Sparing a glance, I noted she wore my hoodie. And nothing else.

"How long have you been home?"

"Long enough to hear all of 'Free Bird.'"

"How was dinner?" I forced my attention back on my computer screen, but when she didn't answer, my gaze traveled back to her. "What's wrong?" She shrugged, and I turned in my chair, dropping my arm from the keyboard. She took advantage, nestling on my lap.

"What are you doing?" I lifted my hands up in the air as she made herself at home. I could feel the warmth of her bare thighs even through my sweatpants. Not to mention the heat of her pussy. I raised my eyes to the ceiling, biting my lip to keep from letting a moan escape the back of my throat.

"Just making sure you're doing it right," she said with a tip of her chin toward the screen.

"You're a pain in my ass, you know that?"

She huffed, silently gesturing to my computer, telling me to get back to work. In order to do that, I had to shift her closer to me to see around her shoulder. With my chest right up against her back and my hands on either side of her, I had her caged in while I typed on the keyboard.

But not even a minute later, her ass was wiggling in my lap.

"Novak," I warned.

"Hargrove," she grumbled. "I'm trying to get comfortable."

"Yeah? Maybe you should find a seat somewhere else. Or better yet, get out of my office. I'm almost done."

She wiggled again.

"Taylor. I need to concentrate."

With her bottom lip tucked innocently under her top teeth, she smiled. "Am I making it hard for you?"

I gave her a bland look. Because it was so very obvious she was making it *hard*.

I squeezed her thigh in warning and went back to concentrating on my screen.

"You used the wrong their." She pointed to my mistake. "T-h-e-i-r, not t-h-e-r-e."

"Will you shut the fuck up?"

She took a deep breath, the slight movement brushing her rib cage against my arms, lifting her breasts. I closed my eyes and tilted my neck to the side, cracking it.

"Are you going to get anyone to read this over before you submit it?"

I dropped my forehead to her shoulder and growled. "If you think you're going to steal that promotion out from under me by distracting me from work, you're sorely mistaken."

She hummed, turning so her lips brushed my temple when she said, "Are you sure about that?"

No. I absolutely was not fucking sure.

But I lifted my head and continued typing anyway. I didn't even know what I was writing.

The alphabet, I think. Maybe the words to Alanis Morissette's "Head Over Feet." Who the fuck knew. I didn't.

Because Taylor shifted, moving her legs on either side of my left thigh, arching her back slightly, so that hot center of hers ground down on me.

I banded my arm around her waist, keeping her from teasing me anymore. She exhaled audibly and sank back against me, practically begging for me to touch her. I could so easily slip my hand between her legs or up my sweatshirt.

I didn't. Instead, I wrote up a paragraph on going to mediation.

I think.

Taylor twisted in my lap, pressing her mouth to my neck, rasping out, "Are you done yet?"

And I lost it.

Absolutely lost it.

"Nowhere near done," I snapped, plowing my hand into her hair, gripping it hard to kiss her. She tasted like coffee, so it was no wonder she was wide awake at almost ten o'clock at night. And with how she clawed at me, wringing her arm around my neck and pushing at my sweats, I felt her frantic energy.

I scooted her back so that I could wrestle my pants down far enough to take out my cock and roll on the condom she produced. Wily minx, this was her plan all along. Her lips parted, her breath fanning over me, and I smiled at the hungry look in her eyes. Holding on to the base, I told her, "You want it so bad, you come and get it."

She placed her hands on my shoulders to steady herself, and both of us groaned as she sank onto me. I'd had her every which way, except like this, so close together with her in my lap. The leather of my chair creaked as I leaned back, and I dug my fingers into her ass, helping to take her weight as she struggled fitting all of me inside her.

"That's it," I rasped. "Go slow. There's no rush."

She breathed out through pursed lips as she took another inch of me. Sweet heaven. "Miguel called me," she said and rolled her hips, fully seated on top of me. "Oh god."

I thumbed her clit, and she dropped her head back to her shoulders, exposing her throat. I wrapped my hand around it. "What did he have to say?"

It took her a moment until she righted herself, moving over me, slow and seductive, even in my hoodie that covered her up. Nothing could hide her heat from me. The way she clenched around me. Her heartbeat under my fingers.

"He said…" She licked her lips, letting out a tiny moan. "He said the building will be ready next week."

"That why you're out of sorts?" I rested the back of my head against my chair, letting her drive. Maybe straight off a cliff, but as long as she took me with her, I was okay with that.

She nodded, hips undulating back and forth. I kept my thumb pressed to her clit, drawing her closer and closer to orgasm. "Mmhmm. Oh god." She squeezed her eyes shut, shaking her head back and forth. "Oh god. I feel so full, so…"

I squeezed my fingers on her throat, a tiny movement yet enough to bring her eyes back to mine. "You came back here, all worried that it would be our last time like this?" I gripped her thighs in my hands, standing up so I could drop her onto the edge of the desk. Like this, I was back in charge. She held on to my shoulders as I pulled out and thrust into her hard. "You want this to be our last time?"

She didn't answer.

"Tell me, Taylor." I drew all the way out again. "You want it to be the last time?"

"No," she whined, and I shoved back into her. She was so wet and I was so hard, the sounds we made every time we came together were obscene.

"Then it won't be our last time. You can have me whenever

you want me." I sucked on my favorite spot, right where her pulse fluttered beneath the thin skin of her throat. "You know I'm the only one who can satisfy you."

"You're so arrogant." Her laugh broke into a whimper, and with a few more thrusts, we were both sighing our release.

"Now." I clapped my hand on her thigh. "Get out of here and let me get back to work."

She slid off the desk as I removed the condom and cleaned myself up with a tissue. She watched from the doorway, and after throwing the trash away, I raised my eyebrows in question.

"It's Friday night, and you're here working," she said with the fakest smile I'd ever seen. "As the future partner of Novak & Novak, I'm already so proud of you."

I plopped back down in my chair. "You'll get that job over my dead body."

"Could be arranged, Hargrove." She pivoted on her heel, back to my bedroom. "Sleep with one eye open."

CHAPTER TWENTY-FIVE

Taylor

I was living in this in-between space where nothing made sense and everything I thought I knew was wrong. Because I used to sneer and avoid Dean Hargrove. Now I smiled, and we managed to take breaks at the same time.

"You sure you packed up everything?" he asked around a bite of one of the festive green-and-white St. Patrick's Day cookies Sandy had brought in.

"Mouth closed, Hargrove."

"That's not what you said last night, Novak."

I zipped my attention to the break room door to make sure no one else was around as my cheeks heated, and he chuckled.

"No witty comeback?"

I merely sipped my coffee because, no, I had no witty comeback after I'd sat on his face last night, riding him through two mind-numbing orgasms.

He closed the distance between us, his hand on the counter next to my hip. A place I'd so often found myself over this last week and a half, trapped under his gaze, immobilized by the pull between us. Even though Dean had said nothing would change between us, that *I could have him whenever I wanted him,*

I couldn't help but feel that my moving back home would be the end of what we had.

Just this morning, we'd packed up my car with all my bags, so at the end of the day, I'd drive to my apartment instead of to his house. It was silly to feel like we were breaking up when we weren't even in a relationship, and yet that was what it felt like. We were severing the tie kept us together.

I didn't want to go back to *before*, with the hatred and ire between us.

Then again, I didn't understand how we could build an *after* when nothing had actually changed. I was still Taylor Novak. He was still Dean Hargrove. And we were still colleagues in competition.

"Losing your edge," he murmured, dragging me out of my mental spiral.

But that was sort of what it felt like. The hard edges of me being sanded and rounded out. I was becoming more and more pliable under Dean's care. For so long, I had only known how to be sharp. I wasn't sure how else to protect myself.

So, it was a good thing we were going back to our separate corners. I'd have time to reevaluate what was going on. Sort through my feelings from a distance.

"You wish," I said and pushed past him. I didn't have to look over my shoulder to know he was staring at me. I felt it. That hot gaze on my back. The part of my body that he'd told me was his favorite. I didn't understand it, but who was I to argue when he'd opened up a jar of coconut oil to massage the muscles of my back before giving me multiple orgasms the other night.

Who would've thought Dean Hargrove was such an attentive and generous lover? Not me.

Out in the main space, I sat behind my desk, and a few minutes later, Dean reappeared with his own cup of coffee.

"Hey, Dean," Dominic said from his spot in the doorway of his office. "Just got off the phone with Chris Raber. He's really happy with the work you've been doing."

Dean nodded his appreciation then angled his chin in my direction, brows raised as if to say *See? I do good work.*

I knew that already and rolled my eyes. Arrogant prick.

When five o'clock rolled around, Dean and I were the last ones to shut down, the rest of the office already gone. He swiveled his chair to face me. "So."

"So."

"What are you going to do tonight?"

"Finally getting a good night's rest, that's for sure."

He blew out a skeptical breath. "Yeah. Okay."

I'd never admit that I'd become quite comfortable sleeping next to him.

"You going to color me something to hang on my fridge?" he asked with some faux paternal pride, and I threw a pen at him. He dodged it, laughing.

"Don't be gross."

"What's gross? Me wanting to hang up a picture you colored?"

"Yeah. You said it all creepy."

He crossed the few feet of space that separated our desks. "You going to miss me?"

"Not at all."

"Me neither." He stepped behind me. "Won't miss you taking too-long showers."

I stood, beginning to gather my stuff. "Didn't hear you complaining when you always interrupted them."

He hummed, his hand gliding up my thigh. "Won't miss you burning dinner."

I dropped my cell phone in my purse. "Like you have any room to talk. You think soup and sandwiches are gourmet."

His other hand fit against my neck, preventing me from moving any more. "Won't miss this mouth running twenty-four seven."

"Won't miss yours either."

"Liar," he said, and then his lips were on me. With my back against his chest, he smoothed his hands over my hips, hiking up my black skirt. I didn't often wear skirts, but I'd hastily thrown one in my bag when I'd packed up my stuff last week, unsure how long I'd be out of my home.

"I've had a hard time concentrating today," he rasped against my ear. "Ever since I saw you shimmy this tight skirt up your hips this morning, knowing you'd be strutting around in it all day today."

"Someone will see us." I tried to shove back against him, but he only pressed against me harder.

"We're the only ones here." He nipped at my earlobe. "Or was that a hopeful note in your voice. You want someone to see us. You want someone to see me fucking you over this desk. See how wild I am for you."

His breath was hot on my neck, and either we were experiencing an earthquake or I was trembling at his suggestion. Maybe it was what I wanted. Some kind of proof that what we had was real. Someone—anyone—to know we were...something.

But what was that something?

"What was that?" he murmured, leaning over, obliging me to bend, his groin right up against my ass so I could feel his hard belt buckle poke into me.

"No-nothing," I panted, his tongue licking at my throat.

He took my hands in his and pressed them into the desk. "You said, 'what was that something?'"

"Did I?" The sound of his zipper sent a chill down my spine.

"You're terrible at playing dumb." He curled his hand around my thong, pulling it to the side. "Because you're not dumb." He slid two fingers through my slick center, swirled around my clit, and pushed inside me. "So wet already, huh? So greedy." Then his mouth was back at my ear, his teeth scraping over the shell. "Tell me what you were thinking."

I hung my head. The feel of him crowded behind me as his fingers worked inside me drove all working order out of my brain. "I don't know."

"Yes, you do." His hand left me, only to be replaced by his cock notching at my entrance after he put on a condom. "Tell me what you want."

He pushed inside, and I released a breath, reflexively driving back against him. "I want more."

"Of course you do, greedy girl." His voice took on that deep growl I'd become so accustomed to. *Greedy* for.

If only I knew how to continue walking this line without leaving any damage in our wake.

"You know how often I've thought about bending you over a desk?" he husked, and I breathed out a laugh.

"As often as I did."

He pinched my thigh. "Fucking right, you did."

He and I, we were the same. He was wild for me. I was wild for him.

He pulled me up, holding me against him as he thrust into me from behind. "My greedy girl."

Goose bumps scored my skin at that label. *My.*

"Yours," I agreed, wrapping my hand around the back of his head, directing his mouth to my neck. He left openmouthed kisses down it, settling at the crook of my neck, where he bit into me. Like he was claiming me. With his other hand slipping between my legs to find my clit, I shook, hurtling toward release, but he didn't let up. Relentless as always.

When I orgasmed, my sigh was drowned out by his voice in my ear. "*Mine.*"

By the time I blinked back into reality, Dean's forehead rested on my shoulder, both of us breathing hard.

"Was it everything you'd hoped it would be?" I asked, turning to find him wadding up the condom in a bunch of tissues before throwing it away.

"What?" He pulled up his pants as I straightened my underwear and skirt. "Fucking you on the desk? Because I'll need more—"

"Uh..."

We both whipped around to the sound by the door. There was Seth motherfucking Blaine standing there with his metaphorical dick in his hand while Dean had his literal dick in his hand.

"I forgot my phone," Seth said, and I grabbed my coat, sprinting toward the door. I avoided eye contact with Seth as he walked in the opposite direction of me, heading toward his desk.

I could have thrown up, right there.

After Dean had put the idea in my head, it sounded good, having someone walk in on us, but not Seth.

"Taylor, wait." Dean's clomping steps thudded behind me, but I didn't stop. He caught up to me right outside the door. "Wait a sec."

"For what? Seth just caught us. I'm not going to stand there and be interrogated about it."

"Don't be so dramatic. He's not going to interrogate us."

I threw my hand out to the office building. "He could tell someone."

"He won't."

"How do you know?"

Dean folded his arms. "Because I'll talk to him."

I rolled my eyes. "Whatever. I don't trust him, and I don't like him knowing what's going on between you and me."

"While we're on the subject, what is going on between us?"

I puffed up my cheeks, shoving my hands into my pockets to keep warm. "I'm not sure."

He tugged at his earlobe. "But there is *something*?"

It was a long while before I was able to drag my gaze over to his and nod. His shoulders rose and fell on a deep inhale, a hint of a smile barely there and then gone again. He laid a swift kiss on my cheek. "Talk to you later."

I pivoted around at the movement behind Dean and high-tailed it to my car, though Seth's voice carried on the wind to me.

"Dude, what the fuck are you doing with her?"

I didn't hear Dean's low response, but the venom in Seth's question had my eyes stinging.

I slammed my car door shut and sped off, refusing to give in to the voice added to the chorus that had followed me my whole life. The one that told me to smile more, not to be so aggressive, to be nicer, to be smart, but not too smart, though as a woman, sometimes I'd never be smart enough. I knew what Seth thought of me. The same as a lot of men. And I feared whatever stupid fucking opinion he had of me would somehow affect what Dean thought of me.

And that was a hard pill to swallow.

Back at my apartment, I needed two trips to carry all my bags up, and I spent a few hours doing laundry and cleaning up. I hadn't expected a knock at my door and was even more surprised at Dean leaning against the doorway, freshly showered, according to his wet hair and the scent of his soap.

"What are you doing here?"

From behind him, he revealed a backpack. "Came for a sleepover."

I gestured him in then locked the door. "I thought you didn't like my pillows."

He let his backpack drop to the floor and eased his hands around my waist, kissing my neck. "But I do like you."

I wrapped my arms around his shoulders, burying my face against his throat. "What did Seth say?"

"Not much."

"Besides 'what the fuck are you doing with her?'"

He smoothed one hand up my spine to cup the back of my head, urging me to meet his eyes. "Why do you sound so offended?"

"Because I know what he thinks about me, and I know he's your friend."

"Friend is a generous term, and I don't give a shit what he thinks about you."

"He thinks I'm a bitch."

"You are a bitch." When I forced out an incredulous laugh, he smirked and pushed me up against the wall. "And you're mine." He sucked on my throat, palming my breast. "You're brilliant and beautiful and don't take shit from anybody, so I don't know why you're worried about what Seth Blaine has to say. You could eat him for breakfast. But..." He lifted his head, his eyes shifting between mine. "I told him in no uncertain terms before, and I reminded him again today, that if he has a problem with you, he has a problem with me."

"Aw." I leaned into him. "You going to defend my honor?"

He threw his head back, letting out one sarcastic chuckle. "No." He met my gaze and smacked the side of my ass. "But I would hold his arms while you kicked the shit out of him."

"That," I said, pulling him down the hall with a smile, "is even better."

CHAPTER TWENTY-SIX

Dean

Taylor and I spent the next week splitting time between her apartment and my house. It was shockingly easy to fall into this new life with her. Work was going great. The Mackenzie suit was coming to an end with mediation next week, which would be a major win for me, but also Novak & Novak at large, as long as I could get the settlement I'd promised Raber. Ever since Taylor and I had gotten together, it was as if everything else had become easier. Almost like finding that one piece of the puzzle made the rest of it all fit together.

"Do you want a glass of wine?" Taylor called from my kitchen.

"No, but could you grab me a beer?"

It was the first sunny and warm Saturday in all of March, and we'd spent the morning running. Or, rather, Taylor ran, while I limped along. She'd promised I'd be able to keep up with her soon. Though I doubted it. I had yet to experience the supposed endorphin high she did, and while I loved to watch her run in her skimpy tops and spandex, I knew I'd most likely have to find some other form of exercise to stay fit. Something she couldn't beat me in.

She sidled up next to me on the couch, handing me the

beer bottle, and when she set two coasters down on the table, I nodded my appreciation. "Old dogs can learn new tricks."

"Asshole," she muttered, kicking her heel into my knee.

I grabbed hold of her ankle and lifted her foot to kiss the bottom of it. "For the next trick, I'll teach you to be nice to me."

"You don't want me to be nice."

I pinched her big toe with bright-red nail polish on it. "You're right. I want you to be exactly as you are." Then I set her feet next to me on the couch and readjusted my guitar. "Any requests?"

She shook her head, and I let my gaze rove over her.

We had spent the afternoon lazing around. She'd gotten her period, so we'd watched a double feature of *The Parent Trap* —again—and my favorite movie, *The Wedding Singer*, which was the far superior choice. And then she had asked me to play the guitar for her.

So here we were, me unable to take my eyes off her as she snuggled back against a pillow in a long-sleeved T-shirt and baggy pants. Her face clear of makeup, a bit of hair pulled back into a tiny ponytail on the top of her head with a thick scrunchie, a tiny, contented smile on her face. Like there was no other place she'd rather be.

My chest burned, and I gulped down a few swigs of my beer, hoping it would quell the emotion trying to claw its way out of my throat. And there was only one song cycling around in my head to play for her. The one I had played from the cell phone the first night we'd put our weapons down. Even though it was written about moving on from a broken relationship, it spoke to me in a slightly different way. Taylor and I, we came from a broken place. But now, not even wild horses could drag me away.

I set down my beer and strummed a few chords to warm up. I didn't know a lot of songs by heart, but I had a pretty good number of classics memorized. Then with a glance Taylor's way, I closed my eyes and started to sing. It felt far too intimate to hold her gaze. Normally, I played in front of a crowd, and I wasn't used to being so close to someone while I basically serenaded them. While I poured my heart out to her.

It might have been Mick and Keith's song, but the significance, in this moment, was for us. My skin pricked at the back of my neck as I sang the chorus, and I forced myself to look at the woman who held my heart, challenged my soul. And if I wasn't mistaken, the tip of her nose was red, her eyes were misty.

I strummed on, and now that I'd dared to meet her dark stare, I couldn't turn away. Then again, that was the reason why I'd chosen this song. No matter what I did, no matter what she said, there would be nothing that could stop me from loving her.

My blood rushed through my veins at the revelation, and my palms went clammy. My grip on the pick was suddenly tremulous, and I focused on the strings to finish the song even as I trembled.

I avoided her warm gaze and leaned my guitar against the couch to rub my palms along my sweats.

"That was..." She sat up, placing her wine down on the table. "That was really beautiful."

"It was all right."

She curled her hand around my neck, urging me to face her, and when I did, my breath caught in my throat. It was overwhelming, the way I could see my entire future in her eyes. She lifted up onto her knees and settled herself on my lap, her hands on my shoulders, her face close to mine.

"Thank you for playing for me. For giving me some of Patrick's whisky. For letting me in."

I rounded my hands along her hips and ass, up to her back

and down again. I was still shaking, and she pressed her forehead to mine.

"Are you okay?" she asked.

"Yeah. I... It feels like...a lot."

"Eloquent." She smiled into a kiss, and I squeezed her waist.

"For a long time," I started, skimming the tip of my nose along hers, "I didn't think I could love anyone."

Taylor backed away a few inches, her eyes rapidly shifting between mine. I could feel her strain with nervous tension.

"I feel like I'm too broken for anyone to love me," I said, and the wrinkle between her eyebrows deepened as she shook her head.

"You're not broken." With one shoulder shrug, she cut through the dense wire around my heart and burrowed there. "Just a little bent. Like me."

"Think we could bend toward each other?"

She kissed me again, a soft, sweet brush of her lips over mine before sliding her tongue along mine. I held her close, one hand at her lower back, the other at the nape of her neck, while I tasted her. Like she was a flavor I'd never tried before.

Maybe she was.

I'd met Taylor Novak, the bitch.

I'd known Taylor Novak, the pain in my ass.

I'd become familiar with Taylor Novak, the gentle woman in need of assurance.

But this Taylor Novak, the one offering her heart to me, was new.

And I imbibed until I was punch-drunk.

I don't know at what point we ended up lying down, but I lifted up onto my elbow and brushed my fingers over her pink cheek then down to her throat, where I felt her pulse fluttering beneath my fingertips. The sign that she was alive and working her way into me with every breath.

I inhaled her exhales, and we stared at each other, our silent admission settling between us. But right as I opened my mouth to confess my love, her cell phone buzzed with a phone call. We both glanced to it and, on mutual agreement, decided to ignore it.

The buzzing continued.

"Lemme check who it is." She snagged it from the coffee table. "It's my sister." She brought it up to her ear. "Hey Ken, what—" She sent me a panicked look then stood up. "I can barely understand you."

I sat up, absently running my hands over my hair and beard as I watched Taylor rub her forehead. "Kennedy, you have to try to calm down. I can't understand what you're saying."

A few moments later, her eyes went wide, her jaw dropping. "He *what?*"

I hopped up, not liking that reaction.

"Where are you right now?" Taylor asked, pacing the length of the living room. "Are you safe?"

I stopped her on the next lap, my hands on her biceps. Her fury was palpable. Her eyes met mine as she told her sister, "I'm coming to get you. I'll take care of it. Keep the door locked, and if he tries to break through it, call the cops."

As soon as she hung up, we both spun in opposite directions, another silent yet mutual decision.

"You have the address?" I asked, pocketing my cell phone and keys.

"She's dropping me a pin," she said on her way upstairs. By the time she'd returned with socks and sneakers on, I had my coat on and offered hers to her. My nerves had me chomping away on gum.

"I'm driving," I told her, and she didn't argue. Merely ran out of the front door to my car.

I waited until we were on the highway headed north to Tannersville to ask what was going on. "What happened?"

She turned down the heat. Even though it was cold outside, I suspected she was hot from stress. She flipped her cell phone around in her palm, a constant action she'd been doing since we'd gotten in the car. "My sister and her boyfriend got in a fight. She was in the middle of taking her pills, and he smacked them out of her hand. When she bent down to pick them up, he shoved her back."

My fingers tightened around the steering wheel. "Is she hurt?"

"I don't think so, but I didn't get much out of her besides that."

We sat in silence, the robotic voice instructing me which route to take. It was while I slowed through the first toll that Taylor sighed. "I was home for winter break freshman year of college. Mom was out with one of her boyfriends or something. At this point, I don't remember, but what I do remember is the sound of the glass smashing."

I had no idea what she was talking about but reached over to lace my fingers with hers.

"Kennedy and I were going to have a movie musical marathon." She breathed out a watery sigh, though I couldn't see the emotion on her face in the dark of the car with only the occasional passing car. It was after nine o'clock, and this time of night, there weren't a whole lot of cars headed toward the Pocono Mountains.

Another minute passed, and Taylor went on, "She used to be a big theater nerd. She was in all her school productions, but then she had her first seizure, and she didn't want to do it anymore. She was afraid she'd have one onstage."

"Kennedy's epileptic?" I guessed.

Taylor rubbed her thumb over my knuckle. "She has juvenile myoclonic epilepsy. I found her that night in the kitchen, water everywhere and the glass smashed by her feet. There was blood, but I couldn't tell where it was coming from, and for one moment, one horrible moment, I thought she was dead."

With my own experience, I knew how terrified she must have been. "I'm sorry."

She sniffed. "She'd ended up cutting her arm on the glass, and besides a few bumps and bruises, once she came to with the EMTs, she was fine. I was with her in the ER and then through all the tests at the hospital. By the time my mother arrived, the doctor had pretty much already diagnosed her."

"That's why you're so protective of her." It wasn't a question, but she answered like it was.

"Yeah. I hated going back to school. I was worried about what would happen and came home almost every weekend. She had a really hard time in high school, rebelled a lot, like she didn't care whether she lived or died, and my mother never set any boundaries, probably hoping it would keep Kennedy with her. Make her want to stay."

When she sniffled again, I found a few tissues in the console and passed them to her.

"I worry about her all the time. I know she's a grown woman and has matured a lot, but she still doesn't make the best decisions."

"So, you've never met this boyfriend?"

"No." She thumped her head back against the seat. "All I know is that he's a ski instructor named Jordan."

"And that he's a piece of shit," I added.

"And he's a piece of shit," she repeated.

"When we get there, do not engage with him." She started

to argue, but I released her hand to curl mine around her neck. "You find your sister and get her out. I will take care of him. I don't want either one of you even speaking to him, do you understand?"

She didn't answer.

"I'm serious, Taylor. We have no idea what he's capable of."

"Okay," she agreed eventually, and I stroked my thumb along her jaw.

"We'll sort everything out. I'll make sure she's safe."

CHAPTER TWENTY-SEVEN

Taylor

In the midst of my chaotic thoughts, I couldn't believe that I had time to ogle Dean motherfucking Hargrove striding up to the little clapboard house. With his jaw working on his gum, hands in the pockets of his dark coat, and his legs eating up the sidewalk in black joggers, he looked like an avenging angel. I was two steps behind him when he banged the side of his fist on the door three times.

When I stepped up beside him, he eyed me. "Remember what I said."

I nodded, and he raised his fist again. The door opened after the second hit, and Dean lowered his hand from where he had it frozen in midair.

"Jordan?" Dean asked the tall and dark-haired man.

"Yeah. Who are you?"

"We're here to get Kennedy."

Jordan, who had a few inches on Dean, puffed up his chest, filling the doorway. "Go away."

"Not gonna do that without Kennedy, so let's not make a scene, hm? Step aside so we can collect her, and we'll be on our way."

"Who the fuck do you think you are, coming to my house like this?"

"I—"

Dean shot his hand out, keeping me from jumping in front of him to tell this motherfucker who the fuck *I* was. He scowled at me with a stiff shake of his head then turned back to Jordan as he pulled out his wallet. He held a business card between his index and middle fingers. "I am Miss Novak's attorney. Now, are you going to step aside, or are we going to have a problem?"

Jordan took the card, studying it as he shifted over, allowing us enough room to enter his house. Barely.

Dean stayed by Jordan, both of them glowering at each other, while I headed upstairs. "Kennedy?" I called, popping my head into different rooms. "Kenny?"

A door in the middle of the hall opened to reveal my sister, eyes swollen and cheeks red. She fell into my arms. "Titi!"

I rocked her side to side, running my hand over the back of her head. "Are you okay?"

"Mmhmm."

I held her at arm's length, a quick survey to make sure she was unharmed, and as far as I could tell, she was. "Come on. Let's get your stuff and go."

I tugged her out of the bathroom, noticing pills scattered along the floor behind her and in the hall.

"We weren't..." She panted, her eyes watering. "He isn't..."

I held her face between my hands. "We're going home. We can talk about it later. Get what you need." I ushered Kennedy to the door down the hall, where she started stuffing things into a bag, and I sought to try to pick up as many of her pills as possible. She took six every day, three in the morning and three at night. Missing even one could drop her body's defenses against an oncoming seizure. Screwing the cap back on the bottle, I stuck it in my pocket then clasped Kennedy's hand. "Let's go."

I tugged her down the hall, but she paused when we heard raised voices downstairs. "It's okay," I told her. "Dean is here. You don't need to be afraid."

She nodded absently, her eyes a little wild like she didn't know what to do, so I tucked her into my side.

"Kennedy, come on. Don't do this," Jordan said as soon as he spotted us on the stairs. He moved toward the steps, but Dean leaped into his way, and while he was careful to keep his hands to himself, he held them out, blocking Jordan from us. "Please, baby, don't leave. You know I love you."

I curled my arm tighter around Kennedy, pressing my other hand against the side of her head, over her ear. "It's all right," I told her. "I got you. It's going to be okay. We're going home now."

Dean didn't bother to turn our way, keeping his focus solely on the red-faced Jordan. Directly behind him, snow-boards hung on the wall, and I sped up, thinking about the damage one of those could do if someone wanted to wield it.

"Kennedy! Don't leave. You can't leave me!"

We were outside, tripping down the steps in our haste, but I shoved her into the back seat of the car, strapping her in because her hands shook so badly. Dean was hot on our heels, though he was still facing away from us, making sure Jordan didn't get anywhere near Kennedy. Once I had the back door closed behind us, Dean rounded the hood and jumped behind the wheel, locking all the doors. Jordan banged on Kennedy's window, crying about how much he loved her, how sorry he was. I didn't acknowledge him and kept my hand on Kennedy's head, making sure she didn't look at him either.

Dean sped away, tires squealing as Kennedy sobbed. He

met my gaze in the rearview mirror, our only communication a silent nod.

Once my sister calmed down, I handed her one of the bottles of water Dean had thought ahead to bring. Her hands still quaked, so I held it for her. "Little sips."

"I'm sorry," she said after wiping her face with a tissue.

"You have nothing to be sorry for."

"I do. I shouldn't have called you."

"Yes, you should have." I held her hand in mine. "You needed help, and there is no fault in asking for it."

I felt the awareness of Dean's gaze on me and met his stare in the mirror once again, this time his brow raised sardonically. Yes, I realized I didn't often take my own advice, and I rolled my eyes at him.

He smirked.

"What are we going to do about my car?" my sister asked, forcing my attention away from him.

"We'll take care of it another day. Don't worry about that." I wrapped my arm around Kennedy's shoulders. "We're going to go back to my apartment now, and we'll talk about everything tomorrow."

"Yes, Mom."

I playfully pinched her, and she laughed. As small as it was, it was a wonderful sound.

———

It had been after midnight when we had arrived at my apartment, so Dean dropped a quick kiss on my temple and headed on. Kennedy and I had slept in my bed, and by the time I woke up around nine, Dean had already returned my car and texted me a snotty message that read **Got it detailed for you. Try to keep it clean this time.**

He was the absolute worst.

Once Kennedy finally shuffled out into the kitchen, I had a plate of bacon and eggs waiting for her. I'd never been a great cook, except for breakfast food.

"Thanks," she mumbled, taking the plate to the living room, where she plopped down on the floor, setting the plate on the table in front of her.

I followed with a glass of water. "How do you feel?"

She shrugged, stuffing scrambled eggs into her mouth.

"Are you ready to talk about it?"

She held up a piece of bacon, extra crispy how she liked it. "There isn't..." She shook her head and tried again. "He didn't hit me, if that's what you're thinking."

"You said he hit your pills out of your hands."

She demonstrated with her own hands, using her right hand to slap her left wrist, the hand holding the bacon. "He didn't do it on purpose. They scattered when..."

"He did do that on purpose, Kennedy. It might not have been your face, but not far off."

She winced, setting the bacon back down.

"I'm sorry," I said quietly, not sure how hard to argue about it. She had to know the danger she'd been in, but I knew I also couldn't push her if she wasn't ready. Then again, she'd go back to that motherfucker over my dead body. "I'm not trying to scare you. I'm sure last night was terrifying enough for you."

She nodded and rubbed her fingers on a napkin.

"But you know this isn't your fault, right?"

"Well," she started, and I sank down to the floor next to her.

"*No*. It is not your fault."

"He only wanted me to talk to him. I was ignoring him because I was so mad at him," she explained, as if that gave him the right to yell and slap her wrist.

"That doesn't matter."

She met my eyes. "It's hard to know..." She licked her lips, and I offered her my water. She took it and swallowed down a few sips before continuing. "I love him, and I know he loves me, but sometimes he gets jealous and angry for no reason."

"That's his problem, not yours," I told her, my gut churning. I knew it was hard for people in abusive relationships to leave. During undergrad, I'd worked as a paralegal in the summers and helped on a case with a woman who was suing her ex-husband in a civil case for abuse. I'd seen the evidence firsthand, how it started with emotional abuse then escalated until he'd pushed her down a flight of stairs, nearly killing her.

That would not be Kennedy. I wouldn't let it happen.

"I know you think he loves you, but love shouldn't hurt. It shouldn't make you feel bad."

She eyed me suspiciously. "What do you know about love?"

Pulling my knees up to wrap my arm around them, I shrugged. "Not much." But I thought back to blue eyes and warm embraces, promises to take care of me. To always take care of me. I remembered heating pads and soup. I closed my eyes and recalled a strumming guitar and a gruff voice singing to me. It felt like weeks ago when it was just last night.

I peered at my sister. "I know love isn't perfect, but it should lift you up. Not tear you down."

Letting out a low breath, Kennedy sighed and dropped down to her side, placing her head in my lap. I combed my fingers through her hair. "I don't want to see you hurt, and I will always be here for you."

"I don't know what I'm supposed to do." I brushed a tear away from her cheek.

"Whatever you want. As long as it's not going back to him. Stay here with me and find a full-time job. Or go visit Mom, if you want. But please, don't go back to him. Don't even talk to him. Block his number and forget about him."

She sniffled, rubbing her cheek against my leggings, her tears wetting the material.

"I love you, Kenny."

"I love you too, Titi."

CHAPTER TWENTY-EIGHT

Taylor

When I called Dominic to let him know I was dealing with a family emergency and that I'd be working from home, he told me to take all the time I needed. I expected nothing less. Not because I was the founding partners' granddaughter, but because that was the culture of Novak & Novak. Family first. And as long as I got all my work done, he had no problem with me staying home.

Monday, Kennedy and I had a movie musical marathon, which consisted of Rodgers and Hammerstein classics. Dean, of course, checked in multiple times, and while he understood Kennedy and I needed sister time, he also told me he was antsy not being able to help. So, when I gave him the assignment of retrieving Kennedy's car from the Poconos, he didn't hesitate. I knew Kennedy would never be able to go there without seeing Jordan, and Dean was convinced I'd end up in jail.

"It's better this way," he said when he came to my place for a quick kiss and my sister's car keys. He told me Hank's toddler was having a hard time sleeping lately, so they were going for a drive and taking him along. I wasn't sure if that was the truth or not, but I accepted it and thanked him with the promise of sex whenever he wanted it.

Tuesday, Kennedy seemed to have more pep in her step until Jordan called, and we got into a huge argument over it. I shouldn't have lost my temper, but I wanted her to delete and block him from her phone and all social media. She said she "just couldn't do it." So that night, I stayed up late, listening for any signs of distress after she got off the phone with him. And even then, I tossed and turned from guilt over our fight, so around midnight, I gave up and called Dean to talk me down off the ledge. We stayed up until around two, when we were both too tired to stay on the phone anymore.

Wednesday, I could tell Kennedy was thinking about going to see Jordan, so I called in reinforcements, and Dean showed up midafternoon, bearing takeout and wine. The three of us talked and laughed, and while Dean and I hadn't made any kind of declarations to anyone, let alone ourselves, we didn't hide our relationship. We touched and kissed each other throughout the evening, and when it came time for him to leave, I asked him to stay. Kennedy didn't have a problem with it. In fact, she seemed to really like Dean and offered me a sly smile as she pretended to creep down the hall, a silent promise not to interrupt us. Though she had nothing to interrupt. We did nothing but cuddle and sleep all night long.

I didn't know why, but I always had a wonderful night's sleep when we were in the same bed together. It was truly one of the universe's great mysteries.

Thursday night, Kennedy and I headed back to Walt's to see the Anchormen play, and as usual, Laney was there, at the table up front.

"Oh my god! Hi!" She jumped up from her seat and hugged me. "How are you?"

"Good. How are you? You're so tan."

She grinned, still in post-wedded bliss, I assumed. "Might have been thirty-four degrees up here, but it was a balmy eighty in the Caribbean." Then she reached out for Kennedy. "So nice to see you again."

After we all sat, we chatted about the wedding, honeymoon, and the progress on the construction of Laney and Ethan's house. "Everything is an upcharge," she complained. "The fixtures, to have the walls painted a color beside beige, it's ridiculous."

"What's ridiculous?" Ethan asked, striding to our table with Dean at his side.

He smiled down at me as his sister explained, "How they're charging us for every little thing on the house."

Ethan nodded, his hands open like a book as he said to me, "We got a binder and flipped through, picking out what we wanted outside of their base plan. This one—" he pointed his thumb in Laney's direction "—chose the most expensive version of everything."

"Hey, it's not like it's a McDonald's and all the prices are listed next to the items. It was like going to a fancy French restaurant where you order without knowing what it is or how much it costs."

Dean muffled a laugh, and she shot out her fist in an attempt to punch him, but Ethan caught her hand.

"I told you," Dean said, "you could've had me for free labor if you'd bought an older house."

"Yeah, but this way, we're getting exactly what we want and need, and it's our forever home."

"You *need* four bedrooms?" Dean asked.

Ethan smiled adoringly at Laney. "Yeah. For all the babies we'll be making soon."

I could see the way Dean was fighting his instinct to roll his eyes since he hated any mention of sex and his sister in the same sentence, but then he turned his gaze on me, and I wondered what his future looked like. If he thought about it at all. If he thought about me in it.

Then he leaned down, brushing his lips over my ear. "Want some whisky?"

I tipped my chin up for a kiss. "A little sip."

With a squeeze of my neck, he headed toward the bar, and I tried to ignore the gawking stares of Ethan and Laney across from me.

"Oh, you guys didn't know?" Kennedy asked, index finger wagging between me and Dean's best friend and sister. "Yeah, those two are hot and heavy, aren't you?" she said with a scruff of my hair.

"Well," Ethan started, nodding, "I'm surprised and yet not."

"We knew he had a thing for you," Laney whispered, although not really because her voice carried like any other person normally spoke. I was learning that Laney's inside voice was equivalent to everyone else's outside voice.

"We just didn't expect him to be so..." Ethan circled his hand in the air. "Open about it."

I rolled my lips over my teeth, not sure what to say, so Kennedy filled in the silence for me. "I told her she had to fuck him to get it out of her system."

I elbowed her that time.

Ethan laughed. "Yeah. Hank said the same thing."

"Where is Hank?" I asked, craning my neck to search for the Hawaiian-shirt-wearing lead singer.

"Grayson's sick again," Ethan said.

Laney shook her head. "It's one thing after another with that poor kid."

"Yeah. Strep throat this time."

Laney, Kennedy, and I cringed.

"We told Hank that if he showed up tonight, we'd all kick his ass."

Laney nodded absently as she tapped on her phone. "What's their address again?"

"Why?"

She held her screen so Ethan could see it. "I'm sending them pizza for dinner. I'm sure they could use it. Probably exhausted or not feeling well themselves. Strep is so contagious."

"That's really sweet of you," I said.

Kennedy laughed next to me. "You'd never think of something like that."

I gave in to a smile. "Correct."

Ethan typed in the address on whatever app Laney was using to order dinner for the Laus as Dean strolled up with a glass of amber liquid in his hand.

"You singing tonight?" I asked, accepting the drink from him to sip the special whisky.

"Yep."

Ethan clapped him on the shoulder. "You'll be great."

"Let's hope. Or we won't be asked to come back next month."

I passed the glass back to Dean. "You'll do wonderful."

He let out a dubious sound then threw back the rest of the whisky and bent to kiss me on the lips.

"Good luck," I murmured against this mouth, and he inhaled, as if trying to swallow my words down. "Don't be worried."

He straightened, his fingers toying with the ends of my hair. "You know how I hate the spotlight."

I threw my head back to laugh, and he smirked before jogging up to the stage. He settled behind the mic in the center, looping his black-and-white electric guitar over his shoulder.

"Hey, everyone. We are the Anchormen, but no, I am not Hank, our usual singer. Not nearly as funny or good-looking."

I snorted because one of Hank's onstage lines was how handsome he was.

"We're going to start off easy," Dean went on, adjusting the stand that held an iPad, which I assumed displayed the music or lyrics to the songs. "If you know the words, it would help me out a lot if you sang along."

And then the Anchormen were off, playing the Police's "Every Little Thing She Does Is Magic," a band and fan favorite. Like Laney had said, they had songs on rotation, and I was sure because Dean was taking the lead tonight, they were playing the ones they knew the best. But he did great. Sometimes off-key, but no one cared, and I had a really fun time watching my...not-quite boyfriend but definitely not enemy singing and playing guitar.

When they finished, he hopped off the stage and beelined right to me. I stood to wrap my arms around his neck, kissing his cheek. "You did great."

"I need another drink," he said with a relieved-sounding laugh before he strutted to the bar for a beer. He returned with one for me and Kennedy as well. While I wasn't a huge fan of beer and barely drank mine, he and Kennedy got along like gangbusters, and they both drank another, even though everyone else in the band had left hours ago.

It was after midnight by the time I slid my hand along Dean's shoulders. He smiled at me, but I could tell he was tired. "I know what you're doing," I told him, and when he pretended he didn't know what I was talking about, I cupped his bristly jaw. "Thank you for taking care of me. Of my sister."

He slipped his arm around my waist and lifted me to his lap. "And I know what you're doing. Trying to seduce me with those bedroom eyes, but it won't work." His hand ventured down to the waistband of my jeans, where his fingers worked their way underneath. "I am not going home with you tonight. I have mediation tomorrow morning."

I stayed quiet but kissed his neck, and his fingers pressed into my skin.

"Devil woman." He pushed me off him and slapped my ass. "Come on. Let's go."

He paid the bill and held my hand, walking me to my car, where he kissed me soundly. "Talk to you tomorrow."

Kennedy, a bit tipsy, blew him a kiss. "Love you, Deanie."

"Love you too, Kenny."

She giggled and dropped into the passenger side. "I really like him," she said when I pulled out onto the road. "He's not at all the type of guy I thought you'd go for, but it's so clear that he's good for you." She folded her fingers together like she was praying. "Like, you just fit."

True. We just fit.

"So, I was thinking," she said after a while, her eyes closed, head back against the rest, "about going to Philly for a little. I was talking to Grace about staying with her for a bit."

"Yeah?" That piqued my interest because not only did I think it was a good idea to stay with our family, but because my sister wanted to do this of her own accord. She needed to get out of her own way. "I think that's a really good idea."

She opened her eyes and turned to me. "They said I could come whenever. I was hoping I could go tomorrow."

Our cousin Grace was Kennedy's age and lived with Uncle Kevin and Aunt Bea in Philadelphia, not too far from Nan's apartment. It was perfect.

"Sure. I'll take you whenever you want." Kennedy was fine driving on the highway, straight shots to her destination, but she didn't like to drive through cities like Philadelphia, where the streets were a maze and traffic was a mess.

At home, Kennedy packed up a few bags to last her at least two weeks, and then we slept in my bed again, with the plan to head out midmorning after rush hour.

We arrived at Uncle Kevin and Aunt Bea's brownstone in the Spring Garden district around noon. I loved their house, with original woodwork and details, which Aunt Bea maintained careful preservation of. She worked in high-end antiques, and their home was filled with them.

That was where my love of original architecture came from, growing up in Philadelphia, where you could literally walk through history. After my dad had died, and our mother had moved us across the state to a cookie-cutter suburb, where every house looked the same, I'd missed the cobblestones and brick, the arched windows and fireplaces older than me. So, I had always loved coming to visit not only my family, but the living history in the walls.

I'd bet Dean would love it too.

That thought had me both excited and terrified. I wanted to bring him here to meet my family. Officially. He'd already met them as an employee of Novak & Novak, but as my...not-quite boyfriend but definitely not enemy.

I supposed we'd have to have that conversation soon.

Kennedy and I spent a few hours catching up with Aunt Bea and Grace until our other cousin, Connor, showed up with his girlfriend, Shelby. Connor worked in finance now but had spent his undergrad working as a bartender, so he mixed me up a perfect martini. I was only two sips in when Uncle Kevin showed up with Nan, and she stole it right from my hands.

"Thief," I said with a laugh and a kiss to her cheek.

Uncle Kevin held his arms wide. "I love this, when we're all together."

"Oh, Dad," Grace whined, pinned in the middle when he gathered us all in for a big group hug.

We sat down for dinner, laughing and talking for a long time, and I was thankful to see Kennedy so happy, smiling and giggling with Grace.

"Can't I convince you to come back here?" Uncle Kevin asked, his drink raised toward me. "We could be doing this all the time."

I glanced to Nan on my left, but she only offered me a small smile.

"It's tempting, but..."

"I have an office with your name on it," Uncle Kevin said, and the offer was beyond tempting. But with the entire family's eyes on me, I felt my skin heat.

"I'd rather earn it on my own than have it handed to me."

Uncle Kevin nodded. We'd had that conversation before, when I had informed him I wanted to move branches two years ago. Sure, this was my family's law firm, but I still wanted to prove to not only myself but everyone else that I was there on my merit and not my name.

"Plus, I like West Chester," I added.

"Correction." Kennedy stuck her finger in the air. "She likes *someone* in West Chester."

Aunt Bea put her elbows on the table, practically foaming at the mouth. Nan tipped her head, and I didn't dare look her way again since she probably already knew.

"It's, uh, Dean...Hargrove."

Uncle Kevin slapped his hand on the table. "Dean Hargrove, the guy you've always complained about?"

Aunt Bea pointed at me with an olive from her martini. "The one you're always fighting with?"

My grandmother clucked a sound next to me.

"Oh no, Nan, not again," Connor groaned, sinking back against his chair and not so quietly saying to Shelby, "That's always the sound she makes before she tells us about how she and our grandfather fell in love by fighting all the time."

"Oh, shush." Aunt Bea swatted at him across the table. "It's a nice story."

But I was with Connor on this one. She was doing this to rub it in my face about how she was right and how she knew all along. "Your Nan knows," she said with a touch of her index finger to her temple. "Doesn't she?"

"My Nan also needs to stop speaking in the third person," I joked, and she pinched me before launching into her story.

We all patiently sat through the twenty-minute recitation of how she fell in love with her William.

"And now look at us all," Uncle Kevin said when she finished. "The Novak clan has had our ups and downs, but we're all here and thriving. Even if I can't convince Taylor to move home."

I shrugged, trying and failing to hide my smile.

"Stop it, Kevin," Aunt Bea said. "Leave her alone. She's in love."

My mouth parted as my breath left me in unsteady waves, the revelation almost knocking me over. But then my grandmother held my hand underneath the table, anchoring me.

"It's about time," she said quietly. "It's about time you found your soft spot to land."

CHAPTER TWENTY-NINE

Dean

"Hey, I thought I'd hear from you today," Taylor said once I answered my phone.

I rubbed at the back of my neck then stretched out along the couch in the living room. "Yeah, sorry."

I could hear the exhaustion in my voice. Taylor caught it too.

"What's wrong? Why do you sound like Eeyore?"

Holding my cell phone at my ear, I dropped my opposite forearm over my eyes, not particularly proud to relay the events of the day. "I overslept this morning."

"Overslept?"

The astonishment in her voice didn't make me feel any better.

"Yeah. I was late to the Mackenzie mediation."

"Oh shit," she said, so low it was barely a whisper.

"Yeah."

"What happened?"

I huffed, irritation flaring at having to recount this to her. I wasn't a perfectionist by any means, but I was serious about my work and my reputation. I didn't like disappointing anyone. And I especially didn't like feeling like a fool.

Which was exactly what had happened.

"I raced in there forty-five minutes late, and everyone was on their way out. They were all pissed. Raber, of course, chewed me out right there in front of them. It was beyond embarrassing." I sat up and trudged to my kitchen. I'd been like this all day, unable to settle down. I was up and down, back and forth all goddamn day. "I felt like a joke."

Taylor didn't say anything right away, and that only ratcheted up my anger. It wasn't her fault, and I had no one to blame but myself, and yet I needed someone—her—to calm me down.

"Dominic was furious with me, because, of course, Raber went back to him about it."

"Oh man, that really sucks," was all she said.

"It's my reputation, you know?"

"Yeah, but it was a mistake."

"A mistake during a really crucial time in one of the biggest cases of my life." I hung my head. "I shouldn't have stayed out so late last night."

"I'm sorry," Taylor said, and even though she had nothing to apologize for, I nodded anyway. "You didn't have to do that."

No, I didn't, but I wanted to. I wanted to be there for Taylor when I saw how hard of a time she was having with her sister. I wanted to take off some of her weight, show Kennedy a good time for a couple of hours, but in the end, I was so wrapped up in what was going on with Taylor, all I did was fuck things up for myself.

I realized with my fingers clenching around the lip of the kitchen counter that all week, I'd been slacking off. My intentions were good, sure, but the outcome was fucked.

With our reviews coming up soon, I couldn't forget that no matter what I felt for Taylor, I still wanted the promotion. I'd worked hard my entire life to get to this point; I couldn't give up now.

"Are you okay?" Taylor asked, and I pivoted to open the fridge and snag a beer.

"I'm not crying in a corner, if that's what you're asking."

"Sorry," she said defensively, "you don't have to snap at me. I was just asking. I know you're pissed, but this will pass."

"Will it?" I asked, tossing the cap into the sink. "Because it seems like I fucked up pretty well, and I'm sure Novak & Novak like their senior partners to be on time all the time."

"But it was one time, and your work speaks for itself. You've never had issues or complaints from any other clients. Everything will be fine. I promise."

Except she couldn't. Because we were both fighting for the same position, and my mistake gave her a leg up.

"Look, I'm gonna get going. I don't want to fight, and I'm in a bad mood, so that's pretty much where this will go."

"Right. Well, I was calling to let you know that I'm going to be in Philly for the weekend. I'll be back on Monday."

After swallowing down a gulp of beer, I set it on the table, sans coaster. Because that was how pissed off I was. Then I scrubbed my hand over my head. "All right."

"Text me…if you want."

"Mmhmm."

She let out a breath on her end. "I know you're upset now, but I hope we can talk when I get home."

"Sounds serious."

"It is."

I didn't like the tone of her voice, and my hackles rose in suspicion. Whether it was about us—whatever Taylor and I were—or our jobs, I had no idea, but I had a feeling I wouldn't like this "talk."

"I'll see you later, Novak."

"Bye...Dean."

———

I still wasn't in a much better mood by Monday morning. Taylor and I had texted a few times, but I couldn't seem to be able to center myself, which was pathetic. I was angry at the situation I'd unwittingly put myself in, and I felt myself falling down a hole that I was afraid I wouldn't be able to pull myself out of.

Even though it wasn't the same—*I* wasn't the same—I didn't want a repeat of what had happened with Patrick. I couldn't let myself get so wound up in a woman that I forgot about everything else. So, it was probably a good thing Taylor and I had spent the weekend apart after being together twenty-four seven for the last three weeks. Yet, it didn't feel right.

I was off and ornery, and Seth didn't help the situation.

"Yo," he said with a backhand to my shoulder, where I was leaning against the counter in the break room. "You'll never believe what I just fucking heard."

I rubbed my fingers against my eyes. "I don't have the patience today. Can you—"

"No, you want to know this. I was about to knock on Dominic's door, but it was open a little, and I heard him on the phone. They're going to offer the partnership to Taylor."

I set down my coffee mug and turned my full attention on him. "What?"

He nodded, waving his hand out toward the hall. "I don't know who he was talking to, but yeah. It's going to her, man. Can you believe it?"

I sank my forearms to the counter, running my hands over my hair as Seth jabbered on.

"She walks around here with her nose up in the air, like who the fuck does she think she is, you know? I mean, I know you have a thing with her, but not after this, right? You deserved that promotion. Not her."

My stomach roiled with guilt and disappointment. This had to be because of last week. One single mistake, and Taylor got the job. She was perfect all the time; I knew that. That was why I was always such an asshole to her, an attempt to crack her veneer. Yet I was the one who slipped up.

"Fuck me," I muttered then thumped the side of my fist on the counter, straightening up.

Seth gripped my shoulder. "It should've been you. I know it, you know it. They're only giving it to her because of her last name."

I shook my head. He hadn't heard what'd happened on Friday, and I didn't want to rehash it at this point.

"What are you going to do?" he asked me.

"I don't know."

"Certainly not continue fucking her." He snorted a laugh, and if there was ever someone I wanted to punch, it was him. "She's not worth it. Dude, if I were you, I'd tell them all to fuck off, starting with that bitch. You could get a job anywhere with all your experience."

I walked to the other side of the room, folding my arms over my chest so I didn't deck him.

"Hey, we'll go out this weekend. We'll find you someone new. Someone who isn't your boss and who won't snap your dick off."

"Just go away," I told him, my shoulders curving in, focus on the floor. I didn't want to talk to anyone, especially him and his incessant fucking misogynistic whining. "I'm not in the mood right now."

He started to maybe laugh, but it came out choked, and I

whipped my head up at the click-clack of heels on the linoleum.

"You have something you want to say to me?" Taylor asked Seth, her head tilted on an angle like she was ready to strike.

He glanced to me and then back to her before shaking his head and shuffling out.

"He's got no balls. He can talk a lot of shit behind my back but not to my face." She glared at me, eyes hard. "What about you? What do you have to say?"

Any trace of the Taylor I'd come to know these last few weeks was long gone. In her place was the Ice Queen. I'd already been feeling inside out, and standing here with her, in the little space where we so often fought and flirted, I didn't know if I should fall to my knees or wrap my hand around her throat.

"I guess congratulations," I said, my voice harsher than I intended.

"For what? Learning that no matter what you promised me, it wasn't true?"

"What?" I looked around to find any hints of what was going on. "What are you talking about?"

"You promised you'd defend me. That you'd take care of me."

I blinked my eyes wide. "Is that not what I've been doing?"

She jerked her thumb over her shoulder. "No. I heard everything he said, and you didn't do or say anything."

I dropped my chin toward my chest, tired and flustered and confused. In one weekend, I'd gone from being on top of the world to being buried under it.

"Taylor, I—"

"You let my colleague belittle me. He called me names, said I didn't deserve to be here. Insinuated that I've been coasting on my last name. When you, of all people, know that isn't true."

"I know. I know that," I started, holding my hands up. "I'm just a little stunned, okay? My head is..." I shook it and crossed the room in four steps to lean my hands on the counter. She stayed by the door, staring daggers at me. I felt each one.

"What, Hargrove? You're always running your mouth, but suddenly you're caught and have nothing to say?"

"Jesus, can you let up for once?" I reflexively reached for the packet of gum in my pocket. I unwrapped a piece and tossed it in my mouth before spinning around to face her. "You don't know everything that's going on from standing there for five minutes."

"Oh no? Then what else did I miss? Any big discussions of what kind of pussy you'd rather have. Maybe someone who is nicer. Someone who isn't such a bitch."

"Someone who doesn't fucking ride my ass all the time," I ground out. "Sorry I didn't jump in to defend you to a guy who literally means nothing to either one of us the *one time* you hear him talk shit."

"Do you know what it feels like to hear someone say those things about me and to then hear you stay silent? Not great, Dean!"

"I guess all the other times I have defended you don't matter. Guess I'm not good enough for you, is that it?"

She wrenched her head back. "No, that's not it."

"I have been bending over backward for you," I said, closing the distance between us.

She kept her chin up, eyes locked on mine. "I never asked you to."

"No, you never did. And I suppose it counts for nothing then either. Perfect Taylor Novak, up in her high tower."

"Don't turn this around on me." She stamped her foot, and

I almost laughed. She could be so childish when she wanted to be. "You were the one in here with Seth while he said that shit about me, and it hurt."

"Yeah, well, it hurts me to know nothing I ever do will ever be good enough for you. I wasted all that time, thinking we were something, but you can't even give me the benefit of the doubt."

"A waste?" she repeated, her eyes shifting over my shoulder. "Nice, Hargrove. Real nice."

"He said all that bullshit, but it's not like I care or believe it. And you don't either, so don't stand here and pretend to be all heartbroken about it. You're tougher than that," I said in defense of myself, but also to scratch the itch to poke and prod at her, like she was doing to me. After all this time, we'd retreated to our corners. Enemies once again. "He'd just told me you got the promotion, so excuse me for being a little emotional and not being able to snap right to it like you. Some of us have feelings to work through."

She huffed and met my gaze again, her eyes watery this time, all that emotion I accused her of not having floating right at the top. "Right." She sniffed. "Well, you'll be happy to learn the only person who offered me a promotion was my uncle. He said I have an office and title waiting for me in the Philly branch, if I want it. So that promotion you were so desperate for..." She swiped at a tear on her cheek, and I hated myself more than I hated anything else in that moment. "It's yours. You can have it." She blinked a few times, clearing her eyes to slide her mask of cold indifference back on her face. "I think I'll be moving back home with my family since there's clearly nothing here for me."

I was stunned into silence for the second time today as she spun on her high heel and strode out of the break room.

By the time I pulled myself together and translated the

meaning of her words, I jogged out to the main space, but Taylor was nowhere to be found, no evidence left behind that she was ever here. The woman I loved had effectively walked out on me and the chance at a life together.

And it was all my fault.

CHAPTER THIRTY

Taylor

SOME ASSHOLE

Where are you?

SOME ASSHOLE

We need to talk.

SOME ASSHOLE

I'm sorry.

SOME ASSHOLE

Taylor

SOME ASSHOLE

Answer me

SOME ASSHOLE

Come on

SOME ASSHOLE

This isn't how it's supposed to go.

SOME ASSHOLE

Stop being so fucking stubborn.

SOME ASSHOLE

Though if you stopped being stubborn, you wouldn't be the woman I loved anymore.

SOME ASSHOLE
Stay exactly the way you are.

It was that last text that had me calling my grandmother in tears. I'd been curled up on my couch, crying. Possibly more tears than I'd shed in my entire life.

"Start at the beginning," Nan said, and I explained everything that had happened between Dean and me, skipping out on the dirtier details, but making sure to let her know how I felt.

"It hurt so much because I'd started thinking of him as the one person who really knew me, who accepted me for who I was. So, to stand there listening as Seth said all those horrible things about me, verbalizing all the things I think about myself, I..." Sniffling, I tucked my hand into the arm of my sweatshirt and wiped my face with the cotton. "I wanted Dean to stand up for me."

"The world still resents a woman with a brain and a working mouth, and I understand why you're so hurt. It's because the people we love the most have the ability to hurt us the most. If it were anyone else, you probably wouldn't have cared as much, hm?"

I nodded to myself as she went on, "As a woman, we learn to let a lot of things roll off our backs, even when we shouldn't have to. Especially in this business that is sometimes so cutthroat."

"Yeah," I agreed, tucking my knees into my chest.

"You shouldn't need to defend yourself based on your gender or personality. Work, yes, but not anything else. And sometimes it gets to be too much, that you'd like someone else to take the load for a while and do the defending, instead of you all the time."

"Yes." I sniffed. "You get it."

"I do. I also get that what happened between you and Dean today can be worked out. I *know* he loves you, and you love him. You make each other better, like your grandfather and I."

"But won't it be weird when one of us does get the promotion?"

"Only if you let it be weird. A title is just that, a title. It's what you do in your day-to-day life that gives it meaning, and you and Dean will always support each other, right?"

That was what I had been hoping for. "Yes."

"So then, it doesn't matter who gets to say they're associate or partner or nothing at all. You two are the real partnership."

"What do I do?" I asked because I had no idea. It was as if all my brain cells had shriveled up from the liquid being leached out of my eyes.

Nan laughed. "Talking to him might be a good start."

"I just texted him," I said, having messaged him back **I'm at home** while I was on the phone with her.

She sighed. "You kids and your texting. Sometimes you need to actually use your mouths to speak."

"We do that all the time. That's what got us into this mess."

"And it's how you'll get out of it. Now, talk to him, and let me know how it goes."

"Okay. Bye, Nan. Thank you."

"Anytime. You know that. Love you."

After hanging up with her, I called Dean, like she said. But when he didn't answer, I tossed my phone on the couch, wondering if it was too late. If I was too fucking stubborn.

Then my exhaustion pulled me under, and I fell asleep right there on the couch.

CHAPTER THIRTY-ONE

Dean

BEELZEBUB

I'm at home.

DEAN

Answer your door.

I banged on her door again. I'd been standing there for five minutes, trying to get her to open up.

"Christ, woman," I shouted, and the door across the hall opened.

"Do you know what time it is?" a gray-haired woman, probably in her fifties, asked.

I did not give one single fuck what time it was. "Nope."

"It's nine, and people are trying to sleep. Clearly, she's not answering the door. You need to leave."

"Nope," I said again and banged yet again. "Taylor, it's me."

I had driven all over the map today, and I wasn't leaving this godforsaken doorstep until I at least saw her face. Her car was parked out front, so I knew she was home.

"Taylor! What are you doing? I—"

The door swung open, and there she was. The devil incarnate with wet hair and a towel wrapped under her arms.

"I've been out here for, like, ten minutes," I nearly roared.

"I was in the shower," she said as if I couldn't tell.

"You need to keep a leash on him," the woman behind me told Taylor.

She peeked over my shoulder at the neighbor. "Don't worry. I will." Then she pulled me inside and closed her door. "Why were you out there shouting like an asshole?"

"Because you weren't answering the door after you specifically told me you were home, and I wasn't leaving until I saw you."

"So you could get arrested?"

"If that's what it took." I shrugged. "Why didn't you leave a message when you called?"

Had it only been a few hours ago? Felt like a lifetime.

"Because I didn't know what to say, and I'd rather do it in person."

"Do what in person?" I asked, readying my arguments for when she cut the cord completely.

"Talk to you, you idiot."

"Don't call me an idiot," I said, following her down the hall to her room. "Not after all the shit you put me through today."

"*I* put *you* through?"

"Yeah." I leaned against her dresser as she picked up a small towel and dried her hair. "I'm busting my ass to make things better, and you're here luxuriating in a twenty-minute shower."

"I'm stressed!"

"You're stressed? I'm fucking stressed." I combed my fingers through my hair, making more of a mess of it, then plopped down on her bed. "All you had to do was leave a quick message or send a text to let me know where I stood, but no, you couldn't even do that. Forced me to drive to Philly to—"

"You went to Philly?" She froze, and her towel slipped to the floor, leaving her body gloriously naked in front of me.

"Yeah," I told her pussy. "I went to go kiss the ring."

"Eyes up, Hargrove."

"Then put some clothes on, Novak."

She slid into a pair of loose-fitting pants and a T-shirt. *My* T-shirt. I tugged her toward me by the drawstring on her waistband. "I talked to Barbara."

"As in Barbara, my grandmother?"

"Yes. Keep up." I hooked my hands around her thighs, guiding her to stand between my legs. "I told her my intentions for you."

She combed her fingers into my hair. It felt like it had been ages since she'd touched me. "Which are?"

"That I want to be with you. Wherever you are. In Philadelphia or here or wherever. You've got me on a leash, and I'm following your lead. I love you, Taylor."

She fought a smile. "Not so broken, then?"

I shook my head. "Just a little bent."

"Like me."

"Exactly like you."

She moved to kiss me, but I stopped her with a palm on her face, and she blindly whacked at me. I dodged her hands. "There's more. You're like a drunk badger." She landed a punch to my shoulder, and instead of trying to hold her off, I towed her to my lap and held her still with her back to my chest. "Be a good girl and stop fighting me, so you can hear the rest."

"There's more?"

I kissed the side of her neck. "Of course there's more. Before I drove all the way to Philly during afternoon rush hour to see your grandmother, I had a talk with Dominic. I told him about Seth, told him everything he said about you."

I felt her shrinking, as if anyone knowing would be embarrassing, but she had nothing to feel bad about. It was that other asshole. "He was little more than an intern anyway. Dominic fired him on the spot."

She gasped. "He didn't."

"He did." I slid my hand under her shirt, over the soft, taut skin of her stomach. "And I told him about us. I told him I loved you, and that you deserved the promotion, that I didn't want it."

Taylor spun in my hold. "No, Dean, why?"

"Because." I frowned at her. Wasn't it obvious? "I love you."

"Yeah, but I don't want you to give up."

"I'm not." I shrugged. "That was my whole thing this morning. When Seth told me what he'd overheard, that you were getting the promotion, I was disappointed and upset, but I was also really happy and proud of you. It was a lot to unpack for me, but I am sorry you had to bear the brunt of my emotional hiccup. I should have stuck up for you, but I was in my own head, and I'm sorry."

She pressed her forehead to mine, her cool fingers wrapping around my overheated neck. "I'm sorry I wasn't there when you were spiraling this weekend. I was wrapped up with my sister, and I didn't consider what you were going through."

I winced. "I think we both need some practice on setting boundaries."

She nodded, continuing, "And I shouldn't have jumped down your throat today. I'm sorry for not listening to you and losing my temper."

"You had every right to lose your temper."

"But not with you. I guess I'm more sensitive than I thought I was when it comes to you."

"Why?" I asked, though I already knew the answer. Felt it when we kissed.

"Because I love you, you idiot."

I grinned and wrapped my arms around her waist, forcing her knees on either side of my thighs, her chest up against mine.

"The thing is," I explained, "Seth misunderstood what he'd heard. Dominic was talking with your uncle about you possibly going back to the Philly office."

She hummed against my throat.

"Despite what Seth thought he heard, I still think you should be made partner. So after I spoke to Dominic, I drove over there to meet with your uncle. I asked him if he would be able to fit me in his branch, if you chose to move back."

"I can't believe you did all that," she said, her lips brushing along my Adam's apple before meeting my gaze.

"And in one afternoon. I think I earned myself at least one blow job, minimum."

She sniffed a laugh, and I kissed her smiling mouth.

"So, to recap, we have the blessing of Dominic, your uncle, and your grandmother. Now, it's up to you where you want to work."

She squinted one eye, toggling her head back and forth, mumbling, "Choices, choices."

"I do have one caveat." I squeezed her waist so I had her full attention. "If you do decide to stay here, you need to move in with me. I sleep like shit without you in my bed."

"Maybe we should write up a contract."

"We could do that." I lay on the mattress with her in my arms. "One more soul to take back to your master."

She didn't resist when I rolled over and extended her arms up above her head. She arched one eyebrow. "He'll be so proud."

I lifted the hem of my shirt she wore and kissed her breast-bone. "Drag me to hell. I don't care."

Her back arched, and I took advantage by sliding my hand along her spine and ass, taking her pants off so she was bare to me once again. I stared at the soft pink skin of her pussy, brushed my palm over the thin strip of dark hair above it. "But first, I want your answer." Her eyes met mine down the length of her body, and I sank on my knees to the floor, placing her legs over my shoulders. "Are we staying here or moving?"

"Staying," she answered immediately, and I released a breath against her, eliciting a shiver.

I licked my tongue up the length of her. God, I'd missed this. Missed her. And we hadn't even been separated. Not literally anyway. Guess I really would have to make a deal with the devil to make sure this woman was mine for all of eternity. She was my heaven and my hell.

And that was exactly what she tasted like. Everything good in this world, and everything I'd give up for her.

I had her crying out in a matter of minutes and barely had my pants down my legs before she was grabbing for me.

"Slow down," I told her. "Let me get the condom on."

"Hurry up," she whined sweetly.

"I'm trying my best here."

"Not good enough, Hargrove."

With the rubber on, I leveled myself over her, gripping the back of her neck with my right hand, holding myself up with my left. "I dare you to say that again, Novak."

She opened her mouth to no doubt lob some other grenade at me, but I smothered it with my lips, thrusting my tongue into her at the same time as my cock. Home sweet home.

She let out a soft sound, and I licked at her lips, circling my hips the way she liked, our clothes rustling against each other.

Both of us so greedy for each other, we didn't attempt nor care to finish the job of stripping down.

She raked her nails over my back all the same, and I sucked in a sharp breath. "I love you so fucking much. Don't ever forget it." I punctuated my statement with a hard thrust, making her gasp. "I'll do this every damn day if I have to until you remember."

"Such a hardship," she said on a moan as her inner walls clenched around me.

"Touch your clit." When she followed my orders, I smiled in satisfaction. "That's it. You feel so good. This greedy pussy needs to come, huh? Gonna come for me?"

She nodded, her mouth open, lips glistening from a swipe of her tongue.

"Let me see it. Let me see how bad you need it." I sucked on my favorite spot, and she was falling off the cliff, dragging me down with her, both of us heaving out breaths and desperate sounds.

Taylor wrapped her legs around my waist, her arms around my neck, and I felt her heart beating against my chest, her pulse against my mouth. "I love you," she rasped against my temple. "Even if your handwriting and grammar leave something to be desired."

I tumbled off her and onto my back, turning my head to meet her gaze. "Anyone ever tell you, you really know how to ruin a moment?"

She grinned, her eyes bright, cheeks flushed, hair a mess. She was the most beautiful demon I'd ever seen. And I most definitely took a bite of the forbidden apple.

It was fucking delicious.

Epilogue

TAYLOR

We were back at the place where it all began, Perkins. It was a gray and cold morning in February, almost a year to the day we'd originally met here. But this time, we were celebrating.

"Why do you sound so far away?" Nan asked through my speaker.

I turned up the heat another degree. "Because I'm in my car, trying to stay warm. Waiting on Dean. Again."

"Some things never change, do they?"

"If that man ever arrived anywhere on time, I think I'd pass out from shock."

Nan laughed. "Well, you are still coming up this weekend for dinner, right?"

"Yeah. We'll be there."

"Joseph will be there too."

"Joseph from upstairs? Look at you, Miss Thing," I teased.

"Oh, stop, or I'll uninvite you."

"You wouldn't," I said.

"I would, indeed. Though Dean could still come."

"Traitor."

"Love you!" she sang then hung up, and I rolled my eyes. That was when I spotted him.

The son of a bitch was unfolding from his car like some kind of commercial in his tweed pea coat as he combed his hand over his hair then stuck both hands in his pockets, walking with enough confidence to knock a camel on its ass.

I hopped out of my car. "You're late, Hargrove."

He showed me his phone screen. Ten o'clock on the dot. "No, I'm not." His jaw worked as he smacked his gum, and I curled my lip. "What's that face for?"

"You."

"What's new?" With his hand on my back, he escorted me into the restaurant and up to the hostess at the small podium. She led us to a table in the back, where we ordered a pot of coffee.

"It's like déjà vu," I said, crossing my legs under the table so the toe of my shoe cracked him in the shin.

"Ah shit," he hissed.

"Sorry."

"Yeah, you look real sorry," he said, leaning over the table, lowering his voice. "You're gonna get it later."

I raised one eyebrow, my skin heating at the threat. "Oh yeah?"

He nodded, taking his time as his gaze drifted over my face. "My order finally came in."

My thighs automatically tensed, my belly fluttering. Weeks ago, he had ordered special under-the-bed restraints as a birthday present to himself, but they'd been on back order. Until now, apparently.

"Let's see how long that smug look lasts when you're begging me to fuck you."

I tried my best not to appear as excited as I was, but from his growing smirk, I knew I was failing.

Then he reached across the table and rubbed his thumb

over my bottom lip. "I think we'll start with this mouth of yours. What do you think?"

"I think you need to stop talking about this in public since our clients will be here any minute." And as if I'd summoned them, Ariel, Kelly, and Julissa strolled in.

As soon as she spotted us, Ariel threw her arms up, squealing. I stood from my seat and accepted her hug. "Congratulations!"

"We did it," she said, holding me at arm's length.

"*You* did it." I looked to Kelly and Julissa behind her. "You all did it."

After I greeted each woman with a hug, Dean followed suit then gestured for them to sit. This time around, everyone ordered breakfast.

"So, how does it feel?" Dean asked after the server left. We had reached a settlement last week, with Ron paying out a good chunk of change. It was a win for the women of Sunset Lounge, but also for everyone working in their industry. Management was on the hook, and our winning case could and would be cited by future dancers in need of help in an unsafe work environment.

This was one of the most important cases of my career to date, and I'd won it with Dean at my side. Both of us partners in the accomplishment.

"I feel really proud," Kelly said.

"I feel safe," Julissa added.

Ariel smiled, her bright-red hair curling around her shoulders. "It feels like a future."

"Yeah?" I folded my hands on the table. "What are your plans?"

"I'm going to open up my own club. I'm going to take back control."

Dean lifted his coffee cup. "Hear, hear."

We all clinked our mugs together, and while every day with Dean felt like a really good day, this one was a *very* good day. We worked and lived together, and we had swiftly learned to find a balance of what Taylor Novak and Dean Hargrove were like at work, and what Taylor and Dean were like at home. We made sure to leave our work at the office and kept precious hold of our time away from each other. Because while I loved Dean more than anything in the world, I couldn't stand to be around him every minute of the day. Same for him. So he kept up his poker nights, gigs with the band, and I discovered a coloring club—it was amazing what you could find on the internet—where we got together every so often to chat and eat snacks while sharing markers and books to relieve stress.

I was visiting my family more often, and Kennedy was back living in West Chester. Everything was perfect.

Who would've thought I'd find my happily ever after with Dean motherfucking Hargrove? Not me.

When we finished breakfast, we hugged the girls goodbye and made our way to the parking lot, where Dean crowded me back against my car.

"Let's fuck off the rest of the day and go home."

I huffed. "Maybe you can, but I can't. I have things to do."

"No, you don't. I checked your schedule. You have nothing."

"I have emails to write."

He slipped his hand under my coat and leaned in to kiss my throat. "Fuck your emails."

"And we have the deposition next week."

He flicked at my earlobe with his tongue. "Forget working ahead and fuck me instead."

"You have a persuasive argument, but..."

He gripped my waist, his beard scratching along my cheek, and spoke his next words into my mouth. "Tell you what,

Novak. If you're not home in half an hour, when you do get home, I'm going to strip you down, tie you up, and leave you there, naked and aching, for the rest of the night."

"Don't threaten me with a good time."

He coasted his hand down my hip, across my thigh, and between my legs, where he cupped my pussy like he owned it. "That's not a threat. It's a promise." He squeezed me once, a gentle warning, then opened my car door and nudged me inside. "See you soon, Novak."

I turned the ignition over and rolled down my window to smile sweetly up at him. "Suck my dick, Hargrove."

He merely tossed his head back and laughed.

God, I loved him, that son of a bitch.

Acknowledgments

Indie publishing is a wild ride. Thank you, reader, for coming along with me.

I wouldn't be able to put out these books if not for the encouragement of my friends, especially Ellis Leigh and Brighton Walsh, and the help of my editors, Libby and Lisa. I'd especially like to thank my street team for helping me spread the work about my books. I'm forever grateful.

If you'd like more information about me, you can find it at: https://sophieandrewsauthor.com.

Sophie Andrews is a contemporary romance author who writes steamy books that will leave you smiling. As a millennial, she's obsessed with boybands, late 90s rom-coms, and will always be team Pacey. When she's not writing, she's most likely trying to wrangle her children or drinking red wine. Or both at the same time.

Also by Sophie Andrews

Tangled Series

Tangled Up

Tangled Want

Tanged Hearts

Tangled Beginning

Tangled Expectations

Tangled Chances

Tangled Ambition